THE PIPER'S PROMISE

Alex Breck

SEILACHAN
FORT

Published by Seilachan Fort

Copyright © Alex Breck 2017

www.alexbreckbooks.com

ISBN: 978-0-9933887-2-9

For Denise and for a promise made

"The woods are lovely, dark and deep.
But I have promises to keep,
and miles to go before I sleep"
Robert Frost

Chapter 1

The killer gripped more tightly around her neck, to afford greater leverage. He felt vaguely ridiculous, guessing that he must look like an amateur actor from across town at Kabuki-za. It's true what they say, he thought ruefully. A dead weight for some strange reason is far more awkward to lift or manoeuvre. For normal people, a part of the problem might have to do with their respect for the fact that this piece of inanimate flesh had once been a living soul, perhaps someone they had been well acquainted with or even in love with.

He'd not yet experienced true romantic love, not even with this girl. She had been beautiful and vibrant but she'd never have made an appropriate life partner or anything resembling that. A Westerner, she'd none of the innate class of his own race. She'd never have made the grade as a geisha. Too sloppy. Too loose. And right now, even after she'd breathed her last tortured gasp, her sweat soaked body seemed determined to fight him every inch of the way across this teak laminated floor. Her long-limbed and lissom frame had flopped grotesquely like some bizarre doll each time he'd clumsily altered his posture to lift her, becoming increasingly more cumbersome and heavy with every minute. Until he'd decided to simply blank out the fact that she'd ever been a human being or even his lover of seven weeks. Once he'd crossed that line, then he could just haul her across the apartment floor by the neck as you would pull the lead of a recalcitrant dog.

The killer considered her lifeless corpse. He had liked her and felt genuine sadness that she had died. Died by his hand; both hands to be precise. He liked to be precise. He liked to live by certain standards, an exacting set of rules that seemed to be out of fashion with the modern world. He wished that Japan could go back to the old ways, to a more traditional era, a time of respect and honour. There had been no honour with this girl. Although he felt sorry that she was dead, he knew there would be plenty others willing to take her place, disposable toys for his pleasure and entertainment. To him, they were not real. The real world that he inhabited allowed him little time for his recreational pastimes. There would be some who might argue that his world owed much of its power and influence to the unreal facade it portrayed to others but to him, it would only ever be work. He glanced at his watch. The real world called upon him right now. He grunted in annoyance and dropped the girl by the French windows, the back of her head clunking loudly on the hard floor. Within five minutes he had entered the elevator, freshly showered and changed, and any last vestiges of the girl's scent had vanished like cigarette smoke in the breeze.

Chapter 2

Looking considerably more confident than he felt, Thaddeus Le Grange tossed back his luxuriant mane of jet black hair and stuck his jaw out. He dropped the girl's delicately boned hand and punched the air. 'Taxi! Yay! We got one look!' He saw the red light turn green as the car slowed to a halt and he stepped out into the busy traffic. It seemed even in the fashionable Ginza district people liked to get an early start.

In Thad's case, however, it had been more of a late finish and he thanked his international parentage as not for the first time, his Amerasian complexion worked miracles to camouflage the worst effects of another debauched Tokyo night. *This is my kinda town*, he thought and exchanged brave smiles with his beautiful but vaguely ill-looking taxi companion. It wasn't so bad for her; she would soon be safely tucked up in bed, whereas he was headed for a full morning on the catwalk. Their evening had begun what felt like days before at an exclusive fashion party at Hinode Pier on the futuristic Jicoo Floating Bar where they'd danced their way around Tokyo Bay. Then he remembered being enveloped in the warm embrace of the Womb over in Shibuya but then things had become a little hazy after that. He ducked his head and folded his six foot three frame into the taxi nearly taking his eye out on the horns of the cutest devil he'd ever seen.

'You're always laughing Thad! What's so funny now?' The girl pretended to scowl at him, but there were few women or men who could resist his twinkling eyes and infectious grin. He pointed at her head.

'The wig? Oh! Yes, I totally forgot I stole this!'

Nea pulled at her auburn bob for a moment and the wig slipped off to reveal the shorter fuzz of her naturally ice-blonde hair. All of a sudden her deathly pale pallor became transformed into the haughty luminescent beauty of the classic Scandinavian. Although Nea detested being labelled as such. *I am Finnish* she would declare proudly. Enmeshed in the tangle of fake hair was a flashing red devil horn, purloined, if Thad remembered correctly, from a handsome bare-chested matador.

The girl often reminded him of his old pal Ridge Walker, whom he'd not seen for a year or two now and to whose daughter Thad was godfather. Ridge and he had survived some incredible and dangerous adventures all around the world, but everywhere they went, Ridge would get unreasonably annoyed when people assumed he was English. 'Fuck off!' he would say. 'I'm not English, *or* British. I'm a Scot, and bloody proud of it!' Thad hadn't heard from him in ages, despite texting him a couple of times over the last few months since he landed this dream modelling job in Tokyo. They'd both been devastated by the death of their hero, David Bowie, and a long night of tequila-fuelled singing of songs had been scheduled as soon as they could get together. But that had been more than a year ago. He'd repeatedly invited Ridge over at his expense, as the only thing wrong with this exciting and chaotic town was the fact that Ridge wasn't there. If anyone liked to party it was his mad Scottish pal and he couldn't wait to see him belt out an old classic like *Starman* in one of Tokyo's famous karaoke bars. He smiled as he decided that even this washed-out fellow passenger would look positively ruddy next to the pasty-faced party-mad Scot.

Thad lowered his head to look out at the frantic neon melee and saw that he mustn't be far from the studio. His contract ran out in only a few weeks and then perhaps he could stop off in Scotland on his way back to the States. He'd still never been there and now Ridge and Orla had a baby son, Alexander. He'd always threatened to wear an authentic Scottish kilt and so maybe he could ask Ridge to arrange that for him. The taxi braked sharply and Thad caught the girl gently as her slight frame became momentarily airborne and they embraced clumsily before he jumped out into the warm and airless Tokyo morning.

Standing a full head above the other pedestrians, he waved goodbye to Nea who he figured would be asleep on the back seat within minutes. He liked her a lot, but she hadn't even hit her twenties yet and he'd felt more like a big brother to her rather than a lover. He hadn't been short of lovers of either gender since arriving in Tokyo, but there would be times like last night where he just liked to hang out with a friend. They both knew they made an unusual couple, his tall, broad frame and dark features and Nea being blonde and petite like a Tinkerbelle to his black Gulliver.

Unlike most other models, Thad had a healthy appetite for food as well as for parties and so he took a swift turn back onto the street as he felt his stomach complaining. He needed some real food to keep him going, not a few calorie-counted canapés. He had a half-day modelling shoot, followed by a gruelling two-hour martial arts class before he could next sit down again.

Chapter 3

It was the damn birds that had wakened him up as per usual, but now in an unbeatable double-act, the insistent sunlight seeped through his eyelids to ensure there would be little point in trying to get back to sleep. Ridge inched a hand across the mattress to find the rest of the bed empty and cold. Orla must be up with the baby. He sat up bleary eyed and cocked his head to one side so as to listen better, having recently discovered he had become deaf in one ear, courtesy of an exploding grenade a couple of years previously. *Ah, there she is,* he smiled as the sounds of a soft Irish voice sang gently up to him through the small cottage. Little Alex hadn't been sleeping so well and the pair of them had been taking turns to see to him at night. But the night was a commodity in ever diminishing supply here on their beautiful Scottish island. Already past Easter, the sun rose earlier every day and despite being perpetually dog-tired and occasionally tetchy, Ridge knew that the advancing seasons suited him just fine. They'd had an awful few months and their wee gurgling baby had been a godsend for the entire family.

He jumped out of bed and stretched, bumping his hands on the low bedroom ceiling as he continued to do almost every morning, despite their having moved into their new home almost a year ago. He dropped back onto the wooden floor and lay prone for a brief moment, the tip of his nose gently pressing into the thin gap between two floorboards. He admired the fine handiwork of his freshly sanded and varnished masterpiece as he always did at this stage of his day. It's more a case of procrastination as opposed to pride he thought, before squeezing the muscles of his strong back and pushing upwards. Seventy-five push-ups later he rolled over onto his back, light-headed and wheezing but satisfied. The elusive hundred would soon be in the bag. Thaddeus would be proud of him these days he decided.

Throwing his boxer shorts in the basket he bounded downstairs to find Orla gently crooning to their little son in the cosy kitchen. He felt her eyes examine him up and down then waited for her to shriek like she always did.

'Jaysus! Will you put some clothes on!

What'll the neighbours say?

And just tell me *exactly* when you're after fixing up those bleedin' blinds?

Ridge laughed and almost managed to avoid her well-aimed hand before feeling the stinging rebuke across his right buttock. She would always be faster than him and no matter how much stronger he'd become over the last year, he knew Orla would always beat him in a fight.

But he hoped her fighting days were over. They'd battled hard together and at times he hadn't even known if they had been on the same side. Ridge allowed the freezing shower to play across his shoulders for a second longer than the previous morning before turning the dial and relaxing his body under the welcoming stream of hot water. Despite being chased halfway across the world by a murderous cabal of gangsters, government agents, terrorists and assassins, they had prevailed against the odds. Hidden away in a drawer somewhere in this cottage, they even had medals from the President of the United States in appreciation of their bravery.

Yet the spectre of almost certain death that they thought they'd successfully out-run had finally tracked them down to the supposed sanctuary of this sleepy island. After everything they'd been through and all the precautions they'd taken, it had slyly side-stepped them altogether, sniffing out an easier prey. Ridge switched off the shower and shivered, not just from the icy draught he felt across his skin. It had only been a handful of weeks since Ridge had dropped a handful of earth on his father's coffin. They'd had no warning. His old man had been struck down by a massive heart attack which killed him just as surely as a bullet out of the blue sky on a bright morning just like today.

Chapter 4

Nea stared out unseeing across the Tokyo skyline. A constantly changing technological miasma she'd once laughingly described as a 'retro-futurist aquarium.' Tonight it felt as alien as the CGI manipulations of some dystopian sci-fi movie, complete with its own unique brand of vicious monster. She'd stopped laughing. Shocked at how easily she'd been caught completely off guard, she wondered if she would ever laugh again.

Despite living in a capital city all her young life and having travelled through many of the world's most famous cities, she'd never encountered any issues regarding her personal safety. The low crime rate in Helsinki, like most of Finland, had been much publicized for years and five thousand miles away in Tokyo she'd often forgotten to double-lock her apartment door to Thad's great annoyance.

But it had been this misjudged feeling of safety in Tokyo that had prompted her to take her first longer term modelling contract in the first place. Previously, she'd be in and out of jobs and always on the move, making brief but valued trips back home to her parent's house in Toolonlahti Bay where she'd famously been 'discovered' serving tables in one of the outdoor cafes as a schoolgirl.

Living here in the Japanese capital, despite the seemingly endless sprawl of the vast city, hadn't felt as challenging to Nea as say Los Angeles or even Paris. Helsinki and Tokyo both shared a reputation for being high tech and ridiculously expensive and while she'd have to accept this as fact she'd also tell people that back in Helsinki, you can see the forests from almost anywhere in the city and apart from her home city she'd never found another with parks to match Tokyo. Nor for honesty either; it had been only a few weeks ago that a tiny Japanese man had chased furiously after her as she jogged through Koganei Park after inadvertently dropping her apartment key.

So it had come as a horrific awakening yesterday afternoon when that revolting beast punched her in the face. She'd been working out in the apartment and her music had been deafening, one of the typical Finnish Metal bands, *Apocalyptica* or *Insomnium* she couldn't remember exactly, it had all happened so fast. Nea had dropped her damp trainers to air near the door and had just peeled off her vest when she felt rather than heard the door banging. Of course, in the television detective dramas, they always seemed to be able to tell when a murder victim had known their intruder and in her case, they'd have been right. She'd squinted through the spy-hole and been surprised and bewildered to see her boss standing there looking annoyed. Without thinking, she unlocked the door, not worrying for a second about her state of undress as he'd seen her nearly naked a hundred times before.

11

The next thing she had been aware of had been this huge fist filling her vision and she'd not had a second to react. The physical force of the blow had been enough to send her flying backwards across the room and she clattered onto a small glass table, shattering it into a thousand pieces and launching a mug of water through her flat screen television.

Without a word being spoken, he'd dragged her across the glass splintered floor into her bedroom and violated her repeatedly and without sympathy, treating her worse than an animal. Then afterwards, as she cowered sobbing under a blood-soaked sheet, he simply said that she belonged to him now and if she breathed a word of this to anyone he'd slice off her head before throwing her body in a dumpster. Nea felt herself flinch as he swung his arms mimicking the sword action of a Samurai. He demanded her passport and mobile phone before leaving her curled up in a tight ball on the floor, her back pressed up hard against the corner walls of the room.

She'd lain for hours, drifting in and out of consciousness, trying to pretend it had all been a bad dream. But then the pain would stab into her and she'd come to with the awful realisation that she'd been raped by a powerful and influential man who now had her in his power. Nea hadn't considered for a second he'd want to subject her to any further assaults, thinking he'd made his appalling conquest and that would be it. If she could withstand this horror, then she might survive.

But it had been early evening, under the protective cover of darkness, before she could summon the strength to stagger, shivering and disorientated, back through the open-plan living area towards the bathroom. There in the reflected neon glow from the building opposite she saw something alien and violent. A hot wave of nausea coursed through her body and the acid contents of her stomach gushed out of her, burning her throat, before splashing noisily over her bare feet. This couldn't be over. There on her sofa sat a thick wad of bank notes and a new iPhone. He had taken ownership of her.

And so now hours later she was still sitting hunched up on the leather chair just staring at the phone in the twilight, her eyes unblinking, waiting for it to ring like you'd watch for a rattlesnake to strike. She'd not even switched a light on. After soaking her bruised body in a long bath until the water had gone cold and then applying every lotion and potion she possessed, the hot tears rolled down her face once more as she found fresh blood on her pristine bathrobe, realising she'd gashed her feet on the broken glass. Wanting to tell someone, but with her family so far away, Nea felt she'd been severed from the world she'd known and for the first time in her young life, completely and utterly lost.

Chapter 5

Ridge switched on his mobile for the customary message checking, as he did every morning. His IT consultancy work had taken a definite back seat since they'd moved into the cottage and then with all the changes in the family, both positive and not so, he'd not given it the time it deserved. Thankfully, there were no new messages of any note requiring his attention today. He powered it off and chucked it back onto the Dutch dresser in the kitchen and got back to the real business of the day. Building his *Castle Strong* as Orla would facetiously term his attempts at home improvements.

But the one thing they both agreed on wholeheartedly and often without even having to discuss it had been their need for the utmost security. They would never ever be caught off guard again.

They'd shown Orla's brother Colm when he'd been over from Chile for the funeral. It had been wonderful for Orla to see him and Juanita again, but bittersweet for Ridge, not only because of the sombre reason for the occasion but also the fact that it inevitably dredged up unhappy and mixed up emotions. Previous to this visit, the last time they'd met, Colm had put a bullet through the forehead of a young woman who Ridge had been extremely fond of. Colm's mysterious world of espionage and shadow play had come too close for comfort in the foothills of the Himalayas and Ridge had pledged to his wife that never again would it be allowed to compromise the safety of his family. So much so that he initially tried to put off his brother-in-law from making the Scottish trip, but he'd been over-ruled by Orla. Ridge might have survived all manner of life-threatening situations, but he'd long accepted that Orla remained a battle he'd never win.

And the visit had been a bridge building exercise too. Colm and Juanita graciously accepted their positions of godparents and Colm had given them crucially important advice on their 'home improvements.'

Their quaint little cottage appeared to be just like the majority of dwellings on the tiny island of Sorsay on the West Coast. Built for practicality rather than comfort and set slightly into the lee of the small rise that ran along the eastern coast of the island, the cottage still had its original stone walls which were almost three feet thick. The windows were so small that on anything but the sunniest of days you were required to switch on an electric light. The houses were intended for eating and sleeping, a place where you'd take a brief respite from the labours of the farm or the fishing. People weren't expected to want to sit and do nothing in them as most of the residents now did.

People weren't expected to want steel doors disguised as original wooden doors either. The pair of them would try and laugh off the unusually heavy weight of the doors with jokes about Ridge fitting the hinges back to front and how they required constant lubrication just as he did and so forth. The triple deadlocks were harder to dismiss, but here the blame could be laid firmly at the door of the greedy 'English' insurance companies. Orla had achieved a little success from her two novels and her advance for book three had swiftly been converted into a full height extension at the back of the house complete with a massive roof window which, along with the removal of the original rear wall meant the majority of the cottage became basked in glorious sunlight even on days where the light seemed minimal. Their daughter Isla, now almost two years old, would look up and laugh at the white clouds scudding past on windier days. Only a beyond-classified pay grade security operative would have spotted that the gorgeous tinted glass had the capability of stopping a 0.50 calibre round courtesy of its aluminium oxynitride layer, a US-led military development for which the commercial side had been spearheaded by a company owned by Thad's dad. They had a nickname for him - *the man who can* - as he'd used his powerful military connections to pull them out of the fire more than once literally saving their lives.

Each room in the cottage had a hidden electronic safe containing a loaded 9mm pistol and a stun grenade and protected by a security code known only by Orla and Ridge. The single bathroom had been fitted out to Orla's exacting specification and provided the safest refuge on the entire island. The floor, ceiling and walls had been reinforced with plate steel and the room had been designed as both their panic room and their HQ if the cottage were to be attacked. A full armoury of weapons had been stashed under the floor along with portable power packs, infrared goggles and the latest communication devices including a 20-metre band HF radio transmitter.

Because their cottage had been a ruin prior to their purchase and a former playground for Ridge and his brother as children, it hadn't formed part of a terrace as had been common practice in days gone by where the islanders worked and socialised together. Nor was the plot encumbered by any outbuildings or other attached buildings as these had simply rotted away over the years. This had allowed the couple to build a bespoke 'garage/workshop' which hid a much larger underground store of weapons and survival equipment in a bomb-proof basement. Equipped with water filtration devices and enough food to keep them going for a month it had become the 21st Century equivalent of a nuclear fall-out shelter. Even their entirely innocuous wooden bike shed, barely large enough for three or four mountain bikes, but perfectly sized for two people caught in the open had reinforced walls and a concealed gun.

Their final security device would be arriving in a couple of months once it had been born. They were going to be the proud owners of what they expected to be the best impersonation of a hound from hell, based on their knowledge of the parents who were both a mixture of Alsatian and black Labrador and despite being as gentle as kittens, had the outward demeanour of very large black wolves.

With each new modification, which had to be carried out by contractors from the mainland to protect both Ridge and Orla and the rest of the islanders, the couple would tell themselves that they had become one step safer in the event of an attack. When at times, they'd question their sanity for the epic scale of the work, they'd remember their friend Ed back in Guatemala who had saved their lives. His reward for helping them had been to endure the knowledge that his wife had been tortured before being incinerated in her own home. Driven half mad with guilt, their grief-stricken friend had sacrificed himself shortly afterwards, dying in a ferocious volley of bullets to give Ridge the few seconds he needed to survive.

As the spring sunshine spread its warming fingers across the garden, Ridge flexed his sore shoulder and thought back to that hellish time when he'd thought Orla had died and he'd reconciled himself to the prospect of joining her. The bullet which had torn through the bones and muscles of his left shoulder still caused him pain at times, especially when he did anything physical like this. He tossed the pickaxe to the ground and surveyed the results of his efforts. It would have been so much easier if he'd thought about doing this when the specialist contractors had still been on-site with their amazing wee hydraulic digger. Still, a lot had happened in the last few weeks. With his dad's death and his grieving mum on her own, there would be one or other of them over at his parent's house a lot more than they'd planned for, especially Orla with the uplifting addition of the two children. So they'd had to factor in a safe communication link between the two houses which meant an underground cable of well over 300 metres masquerading as a telephone panic alarm for the elderly in case of a fall. Ridge had received a little help from a couple of lads, but only until the fishing season had started in earnest and so he'd spent the last ten days wielding a pickaxe, his new best friend.

He wiped his brow with the back of his arm and shielded his eyes from the sun. He shouted up towards the open door of the cottage.

'Orla love! That's me done at last.

What d'ye think?'

He could just make out a thick head of red hair briefly poking around the door and the unmistakable sound of his son's wailing.

'Sure, it's a bit squinty is it not?'

Chapter 6

Kazuo checked the street as he always did. Nothing suspicious or unusual. It had been a sensible idea to rent this apartment. He'd taken it under a false name of course, as he'd done with half a dozen other small apartments. He rented the others out to his foreign staff and to models or photographers who planned to stay for more than a few weeks. It had always been notoriously difficult for foreign visitors, he called them *gaijin*, to source affordable accommodation and many of his people had baulked at the prices especially when they saw the minute size of most standard apartments.

But this particular apartment had always been for a different purpose. It had been the most expensive and remained the only one he had in the Ginza district so it would be conveniently close to his studios. But looks can be deceptive and in his business, he knew this better than most. Outwardly the apartment appeared elegant, sophisticated and exclusive. But for those unfortunate souls that had ever seen inside, then it would be better described as an exquisite dungeon or more recently a more appropriate title might be Death Row as his aggressive side had become the master of his pathological madness and he found himself killing the girls almost as soon as he'd devoured them sexually. He knew he'd gone mad. He also understood the relationship between sex and power and he'd a fairly good notion of what had tripped his sanity switch in his younger days. So he didn't need a psychiatrist. What he required was a cure, a reset button. Something he planned to address in the very near future.

He choked as the door opened, but he soon found that this had been more of an anticipated response rather than one based on actuality. His Shotokan training should have steeled him against such an error and he made a mental note to punish himself for such weakness that evening in the *dojo*. Yes, the place needed a thorough airing, but the putrid stench of rotting flesh had not yet found enough oxygen to begin its cruel chemistry. He often found the scent of death to be vaguely intoxicating provided the corpse hadn't been exposed to the elements nor had decomposed to too great an extent. This sweet bouquet reminded him of certain fruits, perhaps apples or even cherries. Yes, these dead girls, beautiful in life, had become like cherry blossoms in the afterlife, a fitting tribute paid by the outlandish *gaijin* towards the traditions of his Japan of old.

The girl lay where she'd been dropped, shielded from any unwarranted attention by the sun-blind. He threw open the French windows and took in a lungful of air. Never the most satisfying of cities from this point of view, he consented to take a few minutes until the air in the apartment levelled out to match the warm mugginess of its surroundings.

There had been a bath in the apartment before he'd had it remodelled and replaced by a shower and wet room several years ago. The contractors being too lazy to remove it had simply dragged it onto the balcony, 'out of sight, out of mind' being their obvious train of thought. But in a flash of inspiration, he'd decided to utilize it as a makeshift grave. He'd several bags of sand originally intended for a decorative Zen garden style feature for the apartment and now with the two extra bags brought up today he should have just about enough to cover the girl's body.

Rigor had set in now and this made lifting the body easier, but then he'd the awkwardness of bending the reluctant limbs into a suitable position to fit the small bath. He poured the bags over her grey body, astonished at just how simple it could be to erase a human life. Still slightly short of material he raided his apartment and found various powders, salts and luckily a ten-kilo bag of tiny stones which he'd intended to use for drainage in some large cactus pots.

It was convenient that she'd died here, he thought, devoid of even the smallest feelings of remorse. It saved him the long car journey to the forest like he'd normally have to do and he felt sure that her body would soon waste away under the sand, leaving a tiny skeleton which he could dispose of in a year or two. The next job on his list would be the relocation of another girl but this special one still lived and he'd not remotely exhausted his feelings for her yet. He had been incandescent with rage to discover her quickly formed friendships outside the studio. He should have anticipated this when she'd first arrived by the way she instantly and wholly captured his attention and he knew it would be an unnecessary complication in terms of his grand plans.

But then it hit him! He felt his heart rate accelerating as he absent-mindedly prodded at a belligerent hand refusing to accept its sandy resting place. He now knew the exact method he would employ to crystallise the hatred he felt into one final and eloquent statement that would give true significance to his life's work. It would be a perfect and precise plan that would make his father proud! She would have to be eliminated far earlier than he'd have liked, but it would be fitting that her death served his noble purpose. The connection to him could be an issue and he knew it would have to be severed. But not yet. First, he needed to take care of some finer details, like a general bringing together his powerful and precise battle plans.

*

Nea sat staring blankly at the broken television as if she expected it to suddenly come on like one of the many times she'd soldiered on after several cracked screen iPad misadventures that

23

littered her early teenage years. She'd not left the apartment since the attack, maybe two days ago, or was it three? Thad had called asking why she'd not returned any of his messages and she'd had to lie about losing her phone. He'd offered to buy her a new one and come up with it, but she'd fobbed him off with more lies about feeling under the weather since their wild escapade and that she'd hook up with him at the weekend instead.

The studio had been fed further lies and the upshot had been she hadn't been required to move from this chair. She had slept there most of the daytime and then sat wakeful and vigilant most of the night time, unable to face her bedroom, the sheets still bloodied and awry.

The bank notes lay where she'd dropped them along with the phone. Nea had prayed that it wouldn't ever ring and she'd woken from one ghastly nightmare after the next imagining it going off. She tried to guess what it would sound like and soon it had assumed the properties of some demon from the underworld. The fact that it had remained mute had become an increasingly positive development. Maybe he'd had a heart attack at the wheel of his car? Been run down? He might have been murdered by a vengeful boyfriend as she doubted that she would have been the first girl to be raped by him. The callously efficient and calculated manner of his attack suggested otherwise.

He must have entered the apartment without a sound and just like that, he stood towering over her, the sweat glistening across his forehead.

'We go out. Why you no dressed?'

He grabbed her roughly and she braced herself for a blow that never came. He forced her to stand in front of him while he inspected her face carefully. Then he undid her bathrobe and pulled it open, his eyes greedily scanning her nude body.

'Take off!' He barked. Nea had no option and feeling like a vulnerable little mouse she stood trembling in her nakedness. He grabbed her shoulder and propelled her towards the only bedroom. 'Get clothes and plan for trip, seven days. Hurry now, not time to lose!'

Nea stumbled through into the other room and hastily dressed, paying little or no heed to what she was putting on and realising that she felt relieved to be leaving this place despite the probable danger she still faced. His car had been in the underground car park that she'd never once used and within minutes they were out in the frantic traffic. It felt like she lived in an entirely separate world now and she watched the busy pedestrians weave in and out in what resembled a perfectly choreographed display of a modern civilized society. But now she saw through the facade. She knew how fucked up it had become. As the car picked up speed for a brief moment she thought about opening the door and taking her chances with the traffic. But the door had been centrally locked and so she laid her face against the glass and stared blindly out, her tears running down the window like rain.

She'd been in a trance for what must have only been a short time, but now they were back in another underground car park except this one had better lighting and more space. She dared to hope they were at the airport and he had decided to do the decent thing and return her to her parents. Or was he getting rid of his trash? Kazuo had jumped out and retrieved her suitcase before opening her door and carefully helping her out. Taken aback by his apparent gentleness she glanced around and saw the battery of cameras situated all over the brightly lit subterranean chamber. Of course! He knew how to play for the camera; after all, he ran a successful studio didn't he?

The spacious elevator sped them upwards quietly and efficiently then the door opened into a beautifully furnished apartment. Verging on the kitsch for Nea's clean and simple Scandinavian taste she took in the large Oriental lions and the sophisticated water feature before she felt his hand grasp her less gently this time and they were again in another smaller elevator. Seconds later they were outside. Not in the airport but for a tiny wonderful second she thought they were as a gigantic airliner thundered across the sky seeming so close that she could have reached up and touched it.

'This is your new home!

No escape from modern world, but still very beautiful, yes?'

Kazuo glared angrily at the sky before smiling and spreading his arm generously, obviously proud of his penthouse apartment and at the same time completely oblivious to her feelings. She glanced anxiously at the closest edge of the building, no more than ten metres away and contemplated just running off and ending this nightmare. But he could read faces even if he couldn't feel any sympathy with what was behind them. He must have seen this internal battle and he grasped her arm and pulled her closer.

'You no come up here without me. Good for you to get sunshine and fresh air.

And only if you good girl, get me?

If you bad, then I can make you scream and nobody gonna hear you up here.

You can watch me golf. You wanna try?'

He dragged her over to a raised block of vivid green fake grass and hauled a golf iron out of a bag, brandishing it at her. Nea shook her head and instead stared at the enormous sail of black nylon netting set up to catch his golf balls. Again she thought about jumping. She shivered as an image of her dead naked body came to her, luminous white and wrapped up like a fish in that net. She stared back at him as she felt the head of the golf club tracing the curves of her trembling body and she knew then that he could kill her in a second without the slightest remorse. Any thoughts that she'd see her parents ever again vanished as that leering smile spread across his sweating face. She knew what would come next.

Chapter 7

'Motherfucker!' Thad yelled and threw his mobile hard into the enormous bean bag that dominated the centre of his sparsely furnished yet stylishly minimal apartment. He wanted to punch something so bad that it made him shake. The irony of it all hadn't been lost on him and that had only contributed to his anger. He knew he'd get all the opportunities he'd ever need to release his pent-up fury later that night at his karate class. He forced himself to sit down heavily unintentionally causing his mobile to become airborne once more. He'd need to conserve as much energy as possible as this wouldn't just be his usual karate session, which was usually tough enough anyway, but tonight he'd be undertaking his 2nd Dan Black Belt grading. And foolishly, the man he'd just been shouting at down the phone just happened to be his Sensei.

He'd always known that there might come a time when the cosy relationship between Kazuo Shimura being his boss of sorts at the Tokyo studio and also his karate Sensei could become a problem. Thad had studied various forms of martial arts and he knew how good he could be in a real life or death fight. But one of the persistent issues from living a peripatetic lifestyle like his was the difficulty in finding decent classes to attend and maintaining his training and grading records. Consequently, most of his martial arts skills had become rusty at best and at worst totally forgotten. So when he discovered that one of the principal partners of the model studio also ran an English-speaking martial arts school which specialized in teaching *gaijin* students, he'd been delighted and it had been a major factor in his decision to base himself in Tokyo for a while.

But now he had a major confrontation on his hands as the man didn't seem to be taking his concerns regarding Nea seriously enough and had expressly forbidden him from contacting the authorities.

His grading would begin in four hours time, so Thad slid off the bean bag onto the wooden floor and pulled himself up into the lotus position, no mean feat for a man of his size. He closed his eyes and took a deep breath. He seriously needed to calm the fuck down. He would empty his mind for an hour and then if that hadn't worked he would practice *kata*. As he felt his pulse return to its normal fifty beats per minute he remembered his enigmatic fighting companion Colm who could hang upside down by his legs and slow his heart rate almost to a standstill. He still couldn't believe he could be related to that fierce lassie Orla, the crazy wife of his best pal Ridge Walker.

Three hours later, Thad walked into the modern karate HQ feeling calmer and with purpose. He'd arrived early for two reasons. Firstly, it was considered good etiquette to attend a class in time to help clean the *dojo*, particularly if you happened to be an ignorant *gaijin* and even more so when you were about to undertake a grading for the grade of *Nidan*. But he'd also hoped to be able to speak to Sensei Shimura face to face about Nea and to work out why she'd apparently vanished off the face of the earth. It had only been a matter of days but it had been weird that she'd not replied to his messages nor been on social media. She'd mentioned ordering a new mobile phone so perhaps she just hadn't had time to set it up. Perhaps she'd been posted on an urgent modelling assignment down in Kyoto or there'd be some other innocuous explanation.

He'd already decided that if he didn't like the answers he got this evening his next port of call would be his father. Pop knew this part of the world as well as anyone and he'd be able to advise Thad on the fastest way to cut through any bureaucratic complications and get to the truth. He threw down his sports bag and rolled his shoulders easing out the tension that would only slow him down when he got upstairs. Then he smiled. What did he have to worry about anyways? Apart from having a super-power dad at his disposal, he was a US Marine and he didn't plan on allowing anyone to get in his way.

*

Shit! He struggled to catch his breath. *So much for the plan.* The grading had been going on for over three hours now and still, Sensei showed no

31

signs of bringing the marathon trial to a close. What felt like a lifetime ago, Thad had attempted to talk with Kazuo but each time the man had rebutted him, not even giving him the benefit of eye contact. He'd then begun the karate pre-grading class by publicly ridiculing him for a greasy spot on a mirror which Thad had naively owned up to having polished only minutes earlier. Foolishly allowing his anger to overcome his common sense, Thad had responded with a flippant comment for which he'd been awarded a heel-kick to the solar plexus which brought him to his knees and literally gasping for air.

The actual grading had been tough, but nothing more than he'd been expecting and in line with his training and diligent practice. Apart from Sensei Kazuo, he had been marked by three other 5th or 6th Dan masters from the HQ club who had barely acknowledged him with more than a nod but who'd been scribbling furiously every time he glanced over. He'd been made to fight each of the other students twice, whereas the others had only had to fight once, but he'd anticipated some form of further retribution and being much taller than most of the others he hadn't been put under too much pressure. The much more formal kata segment of the grading had gone well, he thought, and he locked his eyes onto those of his Sensei, eagerly waiting for the first indication that the grading had been completed satisfactorily.

Kazuo glared over at him and then Thad saw him slowly scan the large hall as if appraising each and every nervous student. Thad saw his eyes grow smaller and his hands come up as if to clap. At last! He felt the tension flow from his aching body, closing his eyes and bowing as he heard the sound he'd been praying for. Standing back up again, he made to move off amongst the sudden hubbub of excited students. But then he saw Kazuo pointing angrily at him.

'Not you! You stay. *Nidan* grading not over.

Kata very good, very good. But *kata* not everything.

Karate is life and death. You must fight as if life depends on it!'

Thad flinched as Kazuo clapped his hands twice and as the echo reverberated around the hushed hall, Thad allowed himself a quick glance over his shoulder towards the door. Just then a tall Japanese man bowed and entered the dojo. Behind him came another guy, taller than anyone he'd ever seen in Tokyo. Soon a lengthy procession of long-limbed black belts trooped in and the rest of the students erupted into chaos.

'Silence!'

Thad stared in horror. He recognised the emblems each guy had on his black karate *gi*. They were all senior black belts from the infamous Takushuko University *kumite* team. He'd only heard people talk about these guys under their breath as if it would bring bad luck down on them if anyone were to overhear. Possibly for good reason. These guys lived to fight. Takushuko had provided the team that regularly won the All-Japan tournament and whose reputation for extreme violence had been legendary for many years.

The men lined up behind each other facing Thad like some bizarre bus queue. He guessed with no small degree of relief that the first guy, although possibly six feet tall, couldn't have been more than a teenager. He knew exactly what Kazuo had got in mind. Thad would have to fight each of these men in turn. Just as he'd become tired then the bout would halt for a second or two, then he'd have to fight the next fresh fighter in the line. He guessed that the fighters were lined up in order of competence and then on looking more carefully, he saw that they were arranged in height order too. Thad counted. He saw twelve grim faces. *A dirty dozen*, he thought, that's no problem. I've fought more men than that before and they'd been armed.

Thad listened as best he could with his heart beating hard as Kazuo barked instructions to the first youth. Even with his limited Japanese, it sounded as if he'd have to fight each of them for three minutes. *Holy fuck*. That meant thirty-six minutes in total. He heard the clap again and took a deep breath.

'*Hajime*!' Kazuo screamed for the first opponent to begin the fight.

The boy launched his attack and his arm shot out like a black missile – stronger and faster than Thad had expected. He managed to block it safely enough, but the power of his punch worried him. He'd just started to prepare for a second attack when he felt the blow hit him hard. He stepped back and saw the other man shake his head in disgust. Thad knew in an instant the terrible mistake he'd made. These guys hated for you to step backwards. They considered it dishonourable and he'd only made the guy even more determined. The next few attacks were savage and ferocious, leaving Thad barely able to defend himself never mind counter attack.

But he survived his first bout and now he knew the severity of the challenge he faced. The next guy would be faster and stronger. And the next one after that. He would need to bring out every ounce of his strength and determination to prevail here tonight. He thought back to that mouth of hell that he'd escaped from with Ridge. The pair of them shot to pieces and him with his blood splattered body spread-eagled across the body of a car as it smashed through a garage door. Compared to that, this was child's play!

Fortified by that thought he managed to fight his way through the increasingly larger opponents and he found to his relief that some of them were slower because of their greater bulk. By the time he'd fought half of the men Thad had travelled beyond normal fatigue and he almost felt disconnected from his body at times. The black-clad students seemed to have noticed this and he imagined seeing a slight hesitancy or even fear cross their faces at times. Could nothing stop this crazy looking *gaijin*?

But then exhaustion began to take its toll on him. If he moved forwards in time to block attacks, then the blocks were too weak to be effective and if they sometimes forced him to step backwards then his blocks became too slow. Either way, he knew he had begun to struggle and there remained two fighters yet to tackle.

Even in his depleted state, Thad could see something different about these two. Their faces were contorted into a snarling hatred and the first one made no efforts to pull his punches. Full contact was not permitted in traditional karate in the way you'd see it with MMA or cage-fighting and the idea was supposed to be that you punched or kicked with full force but used your training and experience to stop just short of breaking bones. Painful but not lethal. But this guy wanted to kill him. Thad felt it as he blocked and countered as hard as he could, fighting fire with fire. It happened as he blocked upwards towards his right ear in an attempt to stop his head being taken off. He heard a loud snap. The entire hall must have heard it. He'd broken something in his hand!

Kazuo shouted and Thad's opponent immediately stopped and the pair of them bowed.

Thad couldn't miss the sly smile on his opponent's face. A junior black belt scampered out of the hall.

'You have one minute to attend to injury before last fight.' Thad glared at his Sensei in utter disbelief and then across to where the panel had been sitting. But they had all left the room and he'd no idea how long ago.

He took as long as he could to have his hand strapped up but in a moment of inspiration, he asked the confused young man to strap up the wrong wrist. This was a US Marine they were dealing with and he had the measure of their plan. All he had to do was keep standing for three more minutes and he'd have proved them wrong and then he could get back to the main task of finding out what had happened to Nea.

'Hurry now! Last fight.' Kazuo smiled and seemed unduly pleased with himself.

When Thad studied his final opponent, he suddenly saw why. The guy had literally no neck and his face had probably been run into a brick wall more than once. Yet despite fatigue and now pain wracking his body, Thad felt freer than he had for a long time. He knew it was the adrenaline rush. He would have a 'golden period' in which he might just stand a chance of beating these guys before the pain would become too great. But right then, it felt exhilarating, almost like being high on cocaine or tequila. Lyrics from his favourite Bowie songs came unbidden into his mind as if the great man watched over him Jedi-style.

If you want it, boys, get it here thing.

Huge overblown orchestral versions washed over him, wrapping him in a protective blanket of sound.

With you by my side, it should be fine.

But the voice didn't sound right, it seemed sadder than it should have done. Thad shook his head and pulled himself back into the here and now. He could do this.

He stepped up to his position and pointed theatrically at his face. 'Just watch the face big guy, watch the face!' No-neck smiled, which didn't improve his looks one iota, his few remaining teeth giving his mouth the look of an abandoned graveyard.

Kazuo shouted to start and a split second later Thad felt himself kicked hard in the chest and then become airborne. He picked himself up and began to counterattack hard. As he'd guessed would happen, the guy focused all his punches on Thad's strapped right arm. Thad couldn't restrain himself from grinning as he forced the man to punch the uninjured arm thrusting it in his face as if to say 'is that all you got buddy..?' The downside of this meant that his unstrapped and broken arm couldn't be used in any serious attacks so Thad leant forwards for the briefest of moments in order to swing backwards and wrap his foot around the guy's head. But it had been a mistake. Before he could alter his stance he knew he'd put himself in real danger. The last thing he saw was a huge foot across his field of vision and then his head burst in an explosion of light and sound.

Chapter 8

Thad awoke to the sound of a drum, a marching drum. For one glorious moment, he thought he must still be in the Marines. *Semper fi*. Always faithful. They'd come back for him, their fallen comrade. Then he opened his eyes, very slightly but then shut them just as fast. His head swam. Still feeling delirious from what he thought must be the fight, he lay still and tried to process his tangled thoughts. The drumming continued, a solitary snare beating out a slow count and in the background, he could still hear the gender-bending Jedi singing to him. *Having so much fun with the poisonous people, spreading rumours and lies and stories they'd made up.* Songs and memories had become woven together and he couldn't distinguish one from the other. Something serious had happened, of that he was positive. But what?

He tried to move and pushed down with a hand, the wrong hand as luck would have it and a current of pain wracked his body. He screwed up his face in agony and that was when the pain in his head kicked in. Thad opened his eyes in shock as if a bucket of ice water had been dumped over him. He wrestled himself up into a sitting position and tried to work out what had happened. The small room was bathed in a warm light, not too bright but still efficiently illuminated and somehow familiar. He knew it had to be a hospital but they'd made a tremendous job on the ambience front. His left arm had a plaster cast on it from the elbow all the way to the end of his fingers. He lifted up his good hand, shocked to see it heavily bandaged. With just the tips of his fingers protruding, he cautiously explored the contours of first his head and then his face. Not the face! Not having the full use of his hands didn't help matters but it sure didn't feel like his face. His nose must've been damaged as it seemed to be covered in surgical gauze and his face felt twice its normal width. Satisfied that his skull seemed intact, he breathed out and decided he hadn't died, this wasn't heaven and that he'd survive this, whatever had happened to him. He guessed his nose must have absorbed the worst of the impact from that vicious *mawashi-geri* kick.

He saw a button next to his bedside cabinet and so he pressed it. Within seconds the door to his room silently opened and a nurse appeared, smiling brightly and seeming to know him. He found out he'd been taken to a private hospital; one of the benefits of a wealthy father and a top-flight career in the modelling industry.

He had to ask. The face?

The nurse smiled as if she'd been expecting the question.

'Your nose will be fine!

You have little more than a hair-line fracture and our top Orthopaedic consultant has told me to reassure you there will be no lasting damage and certainly nothing that would be noticeable from your career point of view.

However you will have to put up with what will be a nasty concussion and you do have a seriously hurt left hand. The scaphoid bone is badly broken, the one just at the base of your thumb and because it's close to your wrist it will take longer to heal. I am sorry.'

'Can I have my phone?' Thad had some serious calls to make, assuming he could get his fingers to work. At least he hadn't broken his right hand. The bandages had been for superficial cuts and bruises to his knuckles. The puzzled nurse had said they had noticed teeth marks on the wounds.

*

Later the same day and way across town, another man busied with his hands. He'd covered up his face with an anti-pollution mask partially to help combat the smell but also to hide his identity despite the fact it had been dark for several hours. He wouldn't be taking any chances from now on. He'd made one mistake and he didn't like that at all.

He couldn't afford to have any more visits from the *Keishichō*, the Tokyo Metropolitan Police Department. He'd been lucky they had come to the studios and he'd been able to talk to them privately. Kazuo had been impressed with the civility and honour shown to him by the police Inspector. The man had obviously come under duress and he admitted to being acutely embarrassed to be turning up unannounced and troubling an honest businessman during what must be a busy day.

Kazuo explained the hysterical personality of the bisexual playboy *gaijin* and the two men exchanged knowing looks and discussed the sad turn of events that had brought about the influx of so many foreigners to Japan. It turned out that the policeman had studied at Takushuko University and had himself been a fervent admirer of the budo arts. Kazuo promised to send the man two tickets for the final of next month's All-Japan karate tournament and to speak harshly with the young student who'd overstepped the mark the previous day. Kazuo sensed the man had wanted to broach another subject and so he decided that attack would be the best form of defence.

'The *gaijin* would still be in shock I imagine.

I'm surprised he didn't start raving about a girlfriend of his who presumably ended their relationship a week ago. One of my most in-demand models, she had come to me asking for an overseas posting just to be as far away from him as possible.

Right now she is in Rio de Janeiro doing an Olympics-related contact. Don't you agree Inspector, it will be such an honour for Japan to host the next games? I could call her for you but it will still be early over there.'

The Inspector shifted uncomfortably in his chair before springing to his feet and bowing deeply.

'*Kazuo-san*, that will not be necessary. I will not trouble you again. Goodbye.'

Kazuo knew he'd been fortunate. How that meddling idiot had managed to talk an Inspector into making the time to investigate such a trifling matter had shocked and surprised him. He liked order and routine in his normal life and he'd not expected that to happen.

But then it became obvious why the Inspector had been forced to come. As always, it would be the overbearing influence of the Americans. Even today, so many years after the terrible events of 1945, the United States still wielded a rod of iron over them. Financially and militarily the Japanese would always have to bow to their ignorant masters. Far better and more honourable, Kazuo often thought, that the entire Japanese race had died in the hot winds of the atomic bombs.

He thought of his father, Hiroshi, a broken man wandering in the forest, their family business having been destroyed by an onslaught of indiscriminate and relentless nightly bombing raids in which his own parents had been consumed, perishing amongst the burnt out remains of their violin factory. At least Kazuo's grandfather had been spared the national ignominy of surrender which had slowly but steadfastly suffocated the life out of his young son and driven him to insanity. Hiroshi had never been found despite many searches. Kazuo knew parts of that enormous dark wood better than most and he fully accepted that it had been whilst searching for his lost father that his own soundness of judgement had been lost. The stress of those depressing weekends traipsing through the endless silence like a nightmare you can never wake up from had stretched his powers of reason like an elastic band. Then one day his once lucid mind had been forced to stretch too far and had snapped. Avoidable but totally irreversible.

Now he'd become consumed by his need for revenge. The unfortunate girls he'd ravaged and killed were just a symptom of his madness, a way to momentarily sate his unquenchable rage. He would have his father's honour restored. Those who had disrespected the traditions of Japan would have to pay and it would be down to him and him alone to see this done.

Now it would be his turn to make some calls.

Chapter 9

Ridge rubbed his eyes and checked his watch. Still dark outside but there seemed little point in trying to get back to sleep. The pair of them had been up half of the night with Alex, and Orla must have taken him down to the warmth of the kitchen. He decided to go make them both a mug of tea and then see about sorting out some small trees for the new ornamental defence he'd planned for the more exposed left-hand side of the garden. Beech had been his preferred option as it would grow reasonably fast and even although it was a deciduous plant he knew from his research elsewhere that a strong beech hedge would retain its leaves throughout the winter having become a dry rustling gold colour by then. All the better for disguising the barbed-wire fence he'd be growing the hedge through.

'Mornin' love' he muttered as he stumbled into the kitchen and slammed the kettle under the cold tap. Orla rocked manically on her favourite chair, the little boy wrapped up in a blanket in her lap.

'Don't you be "morning" me, ye eedjit.

Left that phone on again last night, so you did. I'd just got him down and then it goes off, jumping about on the dresser there like some demented sex toy!'

'Sorry angel! I keep forgetting to put the bloody thing off.'

Ridge could see his wife laughing despite herself. She'd obviously been savouring that comment for hours and he placed his hands lightly on her shoulders and rubbed his face in her thick red hair. Then he put two mugs of tea onto the heavy wooden table and went to pick up his mobile. He'd upgraded it a few weeks ago although he didn't see the point as he hardly used the thing. So now he was habitually pressing the wrong buttons at night and often it stayed on when he'd thought he'd powered it down. The upshot was on the odd occasion when he'd wanted to use it, the battery would be as spent as the teenage winner of a weekend wanking competition.

He stared at it now. Still defiantly holding a charge. And ten messages from Thaddeus. Plus one phone message. Interesting.

'It's been Thad.

You'd think with all the globe-trotting he does he'd realise the time difference! He's probably just gloating that he's found another rare Japanese Bowie LP.'

Orla growled like a sleepy mountain lion. 'Well seeing as he's bleedin' well called you so many times d'ye not think you could at least call him back?' But Ridge already had the mobile up to his good ear and he waited for the voicemail to come through. Orla watched him with only a half interest until she saw his eyes go wide and his mouth gape open in a credible impersonation of a whale at dinner.

*

Two hours before Ridge had put the kettle on, another man had just received the shock of his life and he hadn't been smiling either. Almost six thousand miles to the east of Sorsay and eight hours ahead, it had been late morning when Thaddeus had received some unwelcome visitors. He'd been feeling a lot better and the swelling in his face had reduced considerably. The bandages had been removed from his right hand and so he could use his phone more easily although he'd been having problems getting hold of people. Feeling incredibly guilty for his poor communication skills of late he wondered if his mobile contacts were even up to date.

He had just been anticipating getting out of the hospital when he heard a commotion out in the corridor. Normally a haven of peace and serenity, the raucous voices and banging of hospital gurneys alarmed Thad and he'd felt his body stretch and then set hard, his natural instincts preparing him for battle. Instead, everything went deathly quiet again and just as he'd relaxed back down into his comfortable pillows for a last nap, the door opened.

The stream of uniformed policemen would have been comical to see on a YouTube video but Thad wasn't laughing. At least seven Japanese officers filed in and then their chief. The Inspector didn't waste any time and without anything more than a brief introduction he reached over and cuffed Thad's right hand to his bed's metal guard rail. Staring at the floor and speaking entirely in Japanese, the man told Thad that he was now under arrest and from what Thad could understand he had been accused of murder. Feeling like he had awoken into some Kafka-esque nightmare, Thad began mouthing his protest.

A doctor came into the room looking more harassed than anyone else. An African-American woman, she raised an open hand in front of the policemen and forced them to stand back.

'I am this man's doctor and I forbid you from removing him from this room until I get written authorisation from your commanding officer. He may remain here under restraint and with your officers at the door but under no circumstances can I allow you to take him from my protective care.'

She turned around ignoring the policemen and put a hand on Thad's arm.

'Son that's the best I can do for you. You're being accused of murder and I hope to heck you know a good Japanese defence attorney.'

*

Orla looked aghast as her husband dropped the phone onto the kitchen table and sank into a chair, his mouth moving but nothing intelligible coming out of it.

'It's Thad' he eventually said, his voice a monotone.

'I'm after guessing *that* part! What's going on?'

'You're not going to believe it, love – he's in hospital but he's been accused of murder!

Here, listen for yourself!'

Ridge passed her the phone while he tried to come to terms with what it had just told him. Orla put it on speaker and played the message back.

'Ridge, I hope this is your correct number, man... I'm in deep shit over here! They're accusing me of fuckin' murder, man and they're taking me from the hospital in a few hours. Oh yeah, I got beat up bad in a karate match... Ridge, there's somethin' weird going down here, my Sensei is also my boss at the studio and my friend has gone missing and I think the motherfucker's got something to do with it...gut instinct right? I think I'm being framed for her murder. I can't get hold of Pop and I think they're gonna take my phone. Get him will ya? Tell him what's happened... and Colm too, anyone man...Just don't ignore this, will you? I need some help here. It's no fuckin' joke man, I'm in serious goddamn trouble.'

The two of them just stared at each other. Orange fingers of light inched their way across the wooden table as they played and replayed the message. Ridge gently took Orla's hand and then gestured his head towards the walk-in larder. 'I'm going to need the box...'

Ridge and Orla had survived some tough times over the last few years and a huge part of their reason for living in such a remote and tranquil environment had been their visceral response to the maelstrom of death and destruction which had nearly consumed them. They'd both been guilty of some gross errors of judgement but they had also performed acts of incredible courage and initiative. Their love for each other had been tested to limits most couples would be unable to comprehend and yet they'd emerged from their nightmare with an unbreakable bond forged from adversity.

Then less than two years ago, Ridge had plunged them back into danger and this time it had included their baby daughter who had almost been born in a Black Ops helicopter gunship whilst it was under attack from ground to air missiles.

So they had both sworn an oath to each other that they would never ever allow themselves to get embroiled in any further international escapades and Orla had even gone so far as destroying their passports. Two young children and a Scottish island would be just enough adventure as far as she was concerned.

One of the many consequences of their past exploits remained the strong possibility that there could be various groups of multifarious malcontents who would happily see the pair of them skinned alive. Not just them either.

Orla had an older brother, now living quietly in South America, whose C.V. made the pair of them look like angels. Colm had lived a shadowy double life for many years and had infiltrated terrorist cells in Ireland, evaded duplicitous governmental agencies both in the UK and the States and somehow cultivated a reputation around the globe as the last man you'd ever want to bump into on a dark night.

Colm had been the prime mover in the daring rescue of Ridge's friend Juanita from the clutches of a hitherto untouchable Central American drug cartel followed by their almost complete annihilation. Again, it had been Colm who'd rescued Ridge and Orla from their fire-fight in Northern Pakistan but at a terrible cost. Feared by evil men and even more delinquent governments, Colm had been known by various *nom des guerres* as *The Piper* and *The Phantom*. Even today, in his alleged retirement, Orla was forbidden to contact her brother unless via a protocol devised by him, the exact format of which remained hidden in encrypted files in a locked steel box buried underneath a case of fine Chilean Cabernet Sauvignon. His argument had been sound. He'd been a professional spy and the pair of them had just been enthusiastic amateurs. If someone wanted to find Colm, their best bet would be through his family. In return, Colm had promised his wee sister that he'd never willingly involve Ridge or herself in any further international incidents.

But Colm wasn't the only powerful ally who Ridge now needed to contact. Thad's dad had to be awarded equal credit for saving them all in Central America and Pakistan. Born to Hawaiian and Japanese parents and brought up amidst the dust and wreckage of Pearl Harbour, Tadashi Kamaka made a killing from war and he'd been responsible for the building of most of the US military bases in Vietnam and later around the world. He possessed a vast wealth and possibly more political friends and military contacts than even the US Commander in Chief.

Thad had a sister in D.C. who worked for Tadashi and so Ridge felt confident he'd be able to get hold of him fairly easily once the American continent had woken up for the day. Quite how he would word the telephone conversation he'd not worked out just yet.

Five hours later the sun had tried its best to warm the occupants of the little cottage kitchen. Orla had taken Isla and her wee brother over to Ridge's mum for a while but now they were all back and Ridge sat in the same chair with his forehead on the table. Tears continued to flow down Orla's red cheeks. They'd thrashed out all the arguments, for and against. Orla had dredged up the various moments when she'd thought he had died and then he'd responded in kind. They played emotional ping-pong for hours while all the time he tried unsuccessfully to make contact with anyone of any use outside their peaceful sanctuary. The first time Ridge had entered the lion's den he'd been powered by the twin engines of guilt and grief. The second time he'd allowed monetary gains to influence him. He'd never do that again.

But now they were seriously talking about him leaving once more. He couldn't go immediately as they'd destroyed their passports. Ridge could have kicked himself for acquiescing to Orla on that one. Their passports hadn't even been in their real names and for the 'official' world of the state, they had been forced to construct a complete set of false identities because of their past adventures including the staging of their own funerals. Ridge now seriously doubted if they could even get 'lost' passport replacements for these fabrications. But he had to try.

This time would be different he promised, feeling like an adulterous husband or a relapsed addict. This time he would not be going into battle. No-one would be trying to kill him. He would just be performing the duties of a good friend, being there when he was needed. He knew he couldn't provide any practical help whatsoever and he fervently hoped that these charges would be dropped before he even arrived in Japan, ridiculous as they were.

He'd been unable to get hold of Colm. Their complicated method of communication involved coded messages, bouncing between servers all around the world. After being eventually decrypted, innocuous comments would be posted in secret Facebook special interest groups. It could never be a speedy process but still, Ridge's frustration had become unbearable. He stared at the laptop, willing a message to appear on the *Organic Wine For You* page. If Colm had received Ridge's messages then this would be where the final message should be posted and also in a code that would be easily understood. Colm had reluctantly agreed that all concluding messages should use the format of Bowie lyrics or song references at both Ridge and Thad's insistence seeing as all three of them were party to this system.

But there had been nothing for hours. Orla had gone all throaty and her beautiful eyes flashed defiantly in one last attempt to dissuade him from his plan.

'But Ridge you just don't *know* who might be involved!' she said.

'Orla love, do you seriously think Thaddeus is after killing some girl?'

'Of course he didn't. So what's going on? That's all I'm saying...

What if it's some kinda trap? What if-'

Ridge stood up and began to pace up and down the kitchen, scared at what he knew he would have to say and hating himself for saying it.

'I HAVE to go love! Thad's no murderer. But you know how he can be. He's a daft laddie at times and he's probably not done himself any favours by shagging the wrong person at the wrong time, that's all!

He came for me remember? We might not be sitting here with these two beautiful kiddies if it hadn't been for that big poof!

One week that's all. One week. Just until they sort out this screw-up or, at the very worst, until he's bailed and we can all come back here, okay?'

Orla nodded. She went upstairs and came down with a small brown envelope. 'Here, you'd better be having this then.' She passed it over to him, looking directly into his eyes.

'I hid them in my fancy knicker drawer! Figured they'd be safe enough in there seeing as it's been a long time since I've been after needing any.'

Ridge blushed as he opened the envelope to find their two passports undamaged.

He sighed with relief. 'Well, just you look for yourself what happened *last time* you opened that drawer!'

Ridge nodded his head over at baby Alex and winked. This time it was Orla who blushed. He knew she wouldn't sleep the whole time he was away and only minutes later he felt his guts tighten as he pressed the 'Pay Now' button for the flight booking. He closed the screen and flicked back through his various bogus Facebook accounts to see if Colm had finally got back to him. There'd have to be a whole new set of messages now of course.

Ridge blinked. There it was - right in front of his eyes. Orla saw his face and sat back down beside him, her green eyes shining with emotion. 'What's it after saying?'

'Let me see... it's on the organic wine page and it's using the right avatar which means it's going to be the one that counts - the final message. See? There it is!

Drink to the men who protect you and I.'

'What's that hon? Sure it'll be somethin' to do with the police won't it?'

'No I somehow doubt that my love, it's also a lyric on *Station To Station.* So-'

'You're such a geek!' Orla laughed despite the bizarre situation. 'What else is my eedjit brother saying then?'

'It says, 'The vineyard is mad busy – *I guess there's always a change in the weather.* My vintage wine choice for you has to be number five. Number five for sure.'

Ridge darted over to his vast collection of CD's and grabbed the Bowie album *Station To Station.* He stared up at his wife in horror and all frivolity left her face in an instant.

'Well! What's it mean then?'

Ridge swallowed.

'He's quoted another piece of a lyric from a different song from the same album. Then he's confirmed it with the track number of the song on the album, track five.'

'And?'

'Track five on *Station To Station* is called *Stay*. He wants me to stay here!'

Chapter 10

It had only been when he'd finally been able to contact Orla from the sanctuary of his hotel room that an exhausted Ridge had appreciated the enormity of his task. It seemed like a lifetime ago when he'd gazed out of his window in sleepy amazement as the jet swept down over the city of Tokyo, sparkling in the early morning sunshine. He'd been to some huge cities before but the sheer vastness of this unending urban sprawl had overwhelmed him. He'd had to give himself a good slap for the ridiculous notion that he could simply fly into a foreign city with a population almost seven times that of his entire country and somehow find and free his friend despite not being able to speak or read a single word of Japanese.

A lot had happened over the last few days and Ridge had thought he'd prepared for the expedition fairly thoroughly until his plane touched the tarmac at Narita. After all, this wasn't the first time he'd undertaken a rescue mission, was it? And at least this time there were no guns involved. Orla had reluctantly agreed to let him go with the firm proviso that he'd call every day and come home at the soonest opportunity. They'd not received any further communications from Colm and Ridge had persuaded his wife that her brother had probably made a mistake with his last message, him not being a proper David Bowie fan. He'd still only had the briefest of communications from Thaddeus, who'd now been removed from the hospital and had been incarcerated in a local prefecture prison after his formal indictment for murder. They hadn't expected things to have gone that far and even as Ridge had been heading down to Glasgow airport, he'd half expected a call telling him that it had all been a cruel mistake and Thad had been freed.

The US Embassy had been helpful up to a point and Ridge had been almost on first name terms with some of the staff as he'd tried to work out what the hell had been happening. Japanese prisons do not allow family or friends to communicate with prisoners and so Ridge had had to rely on the Embassy a lot. They'd provided a duty attorney who'd performed all the expected duties and escorted Thad to prison. He'd been refused bail at that point which Ridge had been told was standard policy for foreigners although Ridge had been striving to contact Thad's dad to get that changed.

It had been obvious at first that Thad had definitely been accorded a greater amount of co-operation and service due to his father's overseas reputation but, as no-one seemed to be able to contact the man, this goodwill had gradually evaporated. To the US Embassy, it appeared as if Tadashi Kamaka had simply washed his hands of anything to do with his son. Neither of Thad's sisters had any idea of his whereabouts either and so Ridge had been awarded the twin tasks of securing the release of his big friend and locating his missing father. None of this would be helped by the fact that Ridge had adopted a false identity for his Embassy-related activities. Not that his passport had been entirely bona fide either of course.

The plan for tomorrow would be to visit the Embassy over towards the west from his hotel and try to convince them he had been appointed as a lawyer by the family back home in the States so he could get permission to actually visit Thaddeus. He'd brought a suit along with him but it hadn't survived the trip too well particularly his several 'lost' hours in the city since leaving the airport. Luckily, his hotel had proved to be an oasis of Western normality and he'd arranged for his bogus lawyer outfit to be dry-cleaned and his shirts ironed overnight. Ridge had offered a silent prayer of thanks to Tim Berners-Lee for his invention of the internet as he'd staggered into the cool ambience of the Hotel Monterrey in the Ginza district. At £150 a night, it could only be a fleeting acquaintance but he doubted if he could have summoned the strength to find a better hotel from the street. To say he'd not exactly mastered this intoxicatingly confusing city just yet had to be the understatement of the year.

Despite being a seasoned traveller and used to 'winging' his way around, the spectacular lack of English from the locals combined with his complete inability to communicate back to them had resulted in total confusion at his every turn. Ridge decided he had probably covered around five times the distance he should have on the complicated subway system and unless the British pound had taken yet another tanking since he'd left then he'd also been royally shafted at the airport currency exchange. That had annoyed him and mostly because he knew how stupid he'd been. Backpacker Rule Number One – don't get money changed anywhere near an airport. He'd find out which travel pass to buy once he reached the Embassy and where to get some cheaper cash before he bankrupted himself. Leaving the tranquillity of a Scottish island to travel to London then Tokyo was never going to be an easy adjustment, he knew that, but still the bewildering events of the last few hours had left Ridge wondering if he could still cut it.

In many ways, he had found London a more jarring experience despite the obvious lack of language difficulties. Compared to the homogenous Tokyo, he'd been struck as always by the incredible cultural melting pot that London had become and, straight off the plane from Scotland, it had seemed every bit as foreign as the garish metropolis he now found himself in. But so far here in Tokyo, he'd not seen any six foot tall Rastafarians, gangs of pierced and tattooed teens or troops of women covered from head to toe in black. There hadn't been anyone sleeping in draughty doorways outside the airport or poor souls with obvious mental health issues pestering travellers as they queued for cash machines.

The streets in Tokyo, despite being as incredibly crowded as he'd been expecting, were far quieter and more relaxing than even back in Glasgow. He'd been amazed at the orderly way people always seemed to walk on the left of the pavement and so very few of them had been talking. The custom of wearing surgical masks had been far more prevalent than he'd been led to believe and so the overall result had been a weirdly robotic somnambulistic feeling about the streets. Alongside the perpetual thrum of traffic, people were certainly busy and they all walked fast and with purpose yet they hardly interacted with one another and with half their faces covered that only left their blank and uninterested eyes to indicate any human emotion.

But they'd certainly noticed Ridge. He felt as if he had become the main attraction in a technological goldfish bowl. Wherever he looked he would be faced with a wall of concrete, flickering neon and nodding faces. It couldn't have been more different from his wee island. There, the bowl had been turned upside-down and it felt as if Sorsay must have been perched on the highest point with the very best views and the biggest, emptiest and most panoramic skies. But he'd suffered continual embarrassment at almost every point in his confused journey over the last few hours. Each time he'd stopped to peer at his Tokyo street map with his new reading glasses balanced on the end of his nose, checking if it was actually upside-down or not, someone would stop and gesticulate enthusiastically then take his arm to point him in the direction they thought he might be after. He'd quickly learned to say thank you in Japanese but he feared that many of the unfortunate denizens of the city were now a lot more familiar with the more prosaic of Scottish expressions, words like *fuck's sake...* Now safely in his room, he had a hotel flyer carefully folded into his wallet so as to wave at people the next time he got lost. *But that would be tomorrow*, he decided. He'd had enough adventure for one island Scot and for now he'd be quite content to watch the city go by out of his hotel window while he rehearsed his plans for the next day.

Ten minutes later, Ridge knew he'd become too tired to sleep and his jangling brain would only respond to one thing. He needed a drink. Gathering up the last of the family inheritance, he made his way down to the hotel bar to give the bar staff some serious coaching in the art of whisky appreciation.

Chapter 11

The young lawyer checked himself in the mirror for the last time having lost the battle to tame his wild hair, an inevitable consequence of falling asleep on the hard chair by his hotel window. Swallowing nervously he grabbed his briefcase and made for the elevator. Even now Ridge could taste the sour alcohol on his breath and he vowed to do the old toothpaste on the finger trick before he met with the US Embassy staff. Thad had given him a shopping list of emergency items to bring including his favourite Arm & Hammer toothpaste. Eschewing a sweaty breakfast for the cool relief of morning air he strode towards the subway station trying to look more business-like than he felt.

He only had to take the Ginza line a few stops west and jump out at Tameike. Thad had instructed him to pop into the American Center Building and pick up some basic essentials which bizarrely included a woollen v-neck jersey from the Dunlop golf shop which he'd been promised would be right next door. Then he'd only have a two-minute walk to the Embassy.

*

The Marine Private scrutinised him carefully up and down with a measured coolness and Ridge felt every crease of his ill-fitting suit. He wiped his mouth nervously wondering if he'd left a streak of toothpaste across his face like some demented Joker. Once he'd been swept and questioned, his appointment and false identity both confirmed, they led him into a stuffy interview room where he fidgeted for what seemed like hours. He prayed fervently that whoever came to speak to him wouldn't be the same woman he'd struck up a loose friendship with over several panicked 'phone calls before he'd left Scotland. His throat felt as dry as the desiccated little beetles and flies that lay scattered across the window ledge, the apparent losers of some ancient insect battle. He toyed with the idea of putting on a pretend Gerald Butler accent like the character from that film where he's guarding the White House. Then the door burst open and Ridge instantly relaxed. The guy couldn't have been more than twenty-five and he had an open smile and a shirt only marginally whiter than his own.

'So! Mr... Findlay? You're the *special* legal consultant, is that correct?

Great to meet you sir.

Let's get out of here, shall we?

What the heck, right?'

Ridge had formulated a sequence of carefully worded responses to what he'd anticipated being asked about and the unlikely possibility of his client being a murderer had been top of his list. But as the aide ushered him out of the building to a waiting car,

Ridge discovered it had been another topic altogether that they guy had been on about.

'A freaking golf jersey... that's cool, that's really cool.'

Ridge used the brief journey to pump the guy for as much information as he could get about the overall opinion of the American Embassy and the chances of getting Thad released. It was obvious that Thad's military record, the parts that weren't classified, made him a hero with anyone stationed there and then, of course, Tadashi Kamaka had been a household name for decades. The guy spoke in a reverent hush as he explained how *the actual Ambassador herself* had altered her schedule to make the time to go and see Thad. Ridge tried to appear casual as he asked if they'd established contact with Mr Kamaka but it seemed that no-one had found him yet.

Originally Ridge had been told he'd be allowed to talk to Thad without the Embassy staff being present, but when he eventually filed into the long room his heart sank when a tall Japanese prison officer fell into step beside him and proceeded to sit only a couple of feet away. The drab room had several large tables along its length, each one bisected by a large glass screen with no possibility of physical contact between the prisoners and visitors. Ridge felt a wave of sadness wash over him as he saw he wouldn't be able to give his big friend a customary hug. He'd had an inkling of the emotional roller-coaster the next few minutes might involve but stupidly, he'd not factored that into his lawyer-client act. Faced with the sudden realisation that he'd come hopelessly unprepared for what was going to happen he steeled himself. He'd be in trouble the second he saw him and then just at that moment he knew he'd been right.

Thad had lost his usual bouncing stride and he looked awful. Ridge fought to hold back the tears as his big friend enveloped the plastic chair and thumped his elbows onto the desk, his right hand pressed white against the glass. They both glared across at the prison official and he held up his hands as if expecting trouble. 'I am language-qualified officer. But only to monitor.' He smiled at Ridge, obviously sensing some relationship between these two men. 'Not to listen... But you only have five minute time, so!' He waved his hand at them and then gazed down at his immaculate shoes as if he'd just noticed an unauthorised blemish.

Thad's ashen face had fallen in on itself since they'd last met. His broken nose had almost healed but the swelling made it seem too big for his face. Ridge had never ever seen Thad with a five-day growth but even through the stubble, he could see a face that had aged years. Normally a muscular and energetic man Thad had lost a lot of weight and his eyes had that haunted look of someone who has seen too much.

Ridge forced a smile and locked his eyes to those of his best friend.

'Okay then! So you got me to come to Tokyo! Enough of the drama, eh!'

Thad smiled thinly but Ridge could see the pain in his eyes. 'Thanks, amigo, appreciate it man.' The glass had been drilled with small holes and Ridge found he could hear quite naturally. He leant forward so his face could be as close to Thad's as possible and lowered his voice to a whisper.

'Tell me everything, Thad. Speak as fast as you like and I'll take notes.

What happened, what do you want me to do and how are we going to get you out of here?'

So Thad poured it all out. Some of it made sense but at times it was impossible to copy down, more like a stream of consciousness and Ridge felt his forearm cramping all too soon with the unaccustomed activity. He had to stop Thad every time there was a Japanese name and ask him to spell it and as the clock ticked onwards Ridge could see the weary frustration in Thad's face. Wishing he could write shorthand like his accomplished wife, he resorted to writing every other word and even making up words so as to remember better. He'd convert it to long form as soon as he left the room before the chaotic city squeezed his memory banks clean.

The main 'takeaway' points he didn't need a pen for. Thad had nothing to do with the killing of the girl and so there had to be some official set-up. His missing father worried Thad more than anything else although he doubted there could be any connection. But what he needed Ridge to do above anything else was to get hold of Colm again as soon as possible. Ridge hadn't taken offence from this. They both knew that if anyone could find out where Thad's dad had gone it would be Colm.

As far as Thad's immediate predicament had been concerned, Ridge had been surprised but relieved to find that his friend didn't think it would be a long-term issue. He gave Ridge details on a man called Kazuo Shimura who ran the modelling studio and told him to focus on him.

'If the motherfucker's clean then we *do* have a problem.'

But his real lawyer had told him that. There had been DNA evidence on the girl's body and all over the apartment where her body had been discovered in a bath of sand. The apartment had been owned by the studio but rented in Thad's name. But why would Thad have been renting two separate apartments in a city as expensive as Tokyo? And they'd find no evidence of any rental payments which again presupposed one extremely generous employer. Thad had been given a firm assurance that given time to investigate this thoroughly, they were confident he'd walk away from the case a free man.

'But unless we can get bail arranged, I'll be stuck here in this goddamned hole until the case is heard and that won't be until next year!'

Chapter 12

Almost forty-eight hours after waving a sad goodbye to his best friend, Ridge needed to unload some of his mounting anger and frustration. He'd not been allowed back to see Thad yesterday, not that he'd anything particularly positive to report. He'd enrolled as a gaijin student at Kazuo's karate school and the first class would be this evening. He couldn't see what he'd gain by going there but it seemed the best way to get close to the guy without raising any suspicion. Ridge knew he was clutching at straws but maybe the guy would be more relaxed and although he'd be unlikely to let his physical guard down he might reveal something useful. In a way, he relished the thought of being able to blow off some steam and right now anything that kept him away from whisky had to be a good idea.

He'd been back down to the hotel bar last night having proved to be quite a hit the previous evening. They'd provided him with a map of Scotland and so he'd drawn out where all the best whisky distilleries were located and then pointed the relevant bottles out behind the neon-lit bar. He explained about the importance of the peat for the 'Islay' malts and the history behind the craft of whisky on islands such as his own. But then he'd got himself so drunk that he couldn't even find his way back to his own room with or without a map.

So now, as the tourist map swam in front of his eyes, he downed his third cup of black coffee and waited in the plush hotel reception for his booked taxi. He'd plumped for a trip to Mount Fuji, somewhere he'd always fancied and a chance to stretch his legs and get some fresh air.

The trip took a couple of hours most of which Ridge spent fitfully sleeping much to his eternal shame but then he *did* feel a whole lot better by the time he arrived. Having climbed many mountains in his youth he and his older brother had often talked about Mount Fuji, but Ridge realised that the iconic pictures of the majestic snow-topped mountain were not what he would be looking at today. The mountain had been hidden by fog on his arrival and just like with many famous Scottish hills, you'd be hard pushed to know they were there unless someone told you. Despite being four times higher than Ben Nevis back home he discovered that there would be no snow in evidence until the late autumn and feeling weary from the effects of his hangover, he plumped for a gentle but relaxingly informative tourist tour. He'd chosen the safe and pedestrian alternative to striding off on his own because he'd not wanted too much drama for a pleasant change but on looking back at the later events of the day he wondered if it somehow had all been part of a bigger plan.

He certainly could never have foreseen *this* place he thought only an hour later. It had been one of the scenic boards that had initially attracted his attention, pulling him inwards. On the board, he saw a massive area of greenery in the foothills of the mountain and a name written in English which rang a bell back in the mists of his travel memories. Aokigahara Forest. He remembered years ago, back in San Francisco, talking with Huw about the place. At that time, Huw had just read in the San Francisco Chronicle that the Golden Gate Bridge had been awarded the unfortunate sobriquet of being the number one suicide venue on the planet. This Aokigahara Forest had been number two.

Ridge had no idea what had possessed him to want to investigate further and now standing alone on a fire-trail, he could hardly remember having made his way down. He'd left the main road only minutes before having had a bizarre interlude with a man outside a cheap cafe. At first he thought the guy was only trying to hustle him into the place but then he worked out that the man actually wanted him to leave, not stay. Polite and deferential just as everyone else had been towards him since he arrived in Japan, the man nevertheless remained resolutely in Ridge's path. Then Ridge twigged. *He's trying to stop me going into the forest because he thinks I'm going to top myself.* So he pulled out his wallet and showed the guy photos of Orla and the kids. He put on his best joke smile and proceeded to laugh manically until the man eventually bowed having accepted this overly-happy idiot must just be another morbid rubber-necker come to gawp at the forest.

But that had been such a very short time ago, Ridge attempted to reason with himself. He'd strayed off the main path deliberately, his curiosity piqued by the incident just back there. A rope had been strung across the narrow track he'd now found himself on. Hanging from the rope had been a square metal sign, rusted around the edges. It showed a red box with a diagonal slash through it. Ridge didn't need to understand any Japanese to know that it said KEEP OUT. So naturally, he'd stepped over the rope and found himself in a different world within minutes.

He had walked, run and cycled many miles through forests back home in Scotland but none had made him feel like this. If asked, he'd probably have said that he normally liked the peaceful sanctuary and solitude that you often found in a forest. Orla, on the other hand, would always prefer to be out in the bustling warm sunlight of a beach promenade rather than the damp cold of a densely packed wood. 'But this place is something altogether different,' he heard himself saying. He wondered if maybe it was because he already knew this forest had some kind of reputation for the macabre that he thought he could feel some other-worldly presence there. The mushrooms pushing up through the mossy remains of fallen branches were more vividly coloured than any he'd seen in Scotland and everywhere he turned there would be giant webs spun between the trees. So far he'd not spotted any giant spiders to go with them. In fact he'd not seen or heard any wildlife whatsoever since turning off the main drag. Instead just total smothering silence.

Ridge couldn't shake the feeling that he didn't belong there. Yet he also felt compelled to venture further inwards. He couldn't see too far ahead as the trees were so thick the sun struggled to penetrate anywhere near the ground. He heard a faint sound that reminded him of being on the shore, back on Sorsay. Welcoming at first in the eerie quiet, it rapidly built into an angry roar as an icy blast of wind enveloped and buffeted him like the crashing of an invisible wave. Then it was gone. Ridge shivered, not just because of the cold air. He decided to attempt to walk a little faster and to limit himself to half an hour. He checked the time on his phone and saw that there would be no use relying on it for anything other than telling the time as cell reception was zero. Well, that's more like home, he thought, feeling oddly comforted by that.

It was impossible to move fast and Ridge grew colder rather than warmer and he had to concentrate hard on his footing so as not to trip. Like all country walks everywhere, however, he found this physical challenge freed up his mind to think about other things. Unbidden as usual, memories of his older brother Gavin flooded into his head. He often thought of Gav when out walking alone and that probably accounted for him not walking much on his own any more. The cold mists of Ben Cruachan wound their way around his feet, trying to make him fall as they had all those years ago when he failed to save his brother's life, left him lying stricken on that gravelled scree. His broken ankle still hurt him to this day more than any other injury he'd ever sustained even after all his running tears and strains and more than one bullet wound. Of course his rational mind told him he couldn't have done anything to save his foolish brother who'd made the fatal error that day of experimenting with drugs during a dangerous mountain ascent while being in sole charge of his very young brother. Ridge couldn't have tried any harder, having run miles down a mountain track on his badly broken ankle and eventually passing out with the pain of his exertion.

But he found it onerous to think rationally in this place. He sat down against a tree and felt the tears running hot down his cold face. He surveyed his surroundings and wondered how bad it would have to be before he would choose to end his life in a place like this. Hauntingly beautiful though it was, he knew he still had a life full of beauty and promise waiting for him back home. The ghosts of the Suicide Forest would not find another soul mate in him.

Then he saw the thin ribbons of tape and string that stretched away from the lower slopes deeper into the forest. He'd noticed a few small ribbon badges, twisted and pinned onto trees like upturned hearts, but never given them much thought. Presumably they were way-markers so people could find their way back out of the woods, assuming they wanted to leave. Maybe that's what these ribbons are for, he wondered. Could they be for people who'd not yet reconciled themselves to actually committing suicide or maybe they just wanted people to be able to find their bodies more easily? Ridge remembered Huw telling him that there could still be hundreds of bodies decomposing in the woods due to the difficulty of traversing the darkest parts of the forest.

He felt as if he was being pulled by invisible forces as he hauled himself back onto his feet and decided to follow one of these ribbons to see what he'd find at the other end. If nothing else, he reasoned, all he would have to do to find his way back would be to retrace his ribbon journey. He'd not been walking for too long when he found to his horror that he'd inadvertently pulled some of the ribbons off the trees they'd been pinned onto, and so he'd probably not be able to find the exact same way back down into the light. He found that some of the ribbons were actually rope and vowed to continue but only to follow one of these stronger rope trails which would hopefully prove more robust. He began to see little wooden phone boxes periodically, a last ditch attempt by the authorities to reach out to the anguished and alone. He recalled Huw reading from the newspaper about the Suicide Forest having unusually high deposits of iron ore which rendered compasses and GPS systems inoperable. So here when you were on your own you really were on your own. That's precisely how he started to feel, like the last man on earth.

The light continued to weaken and the only sounds Ridge could hear were the muffled cracking of branches underfoot and that spooky wind that he sometimes confused with his own breathing. He tried to think of the swirls of cold air as spirited lovers, dancing their lively courtships, cavorting and blithely freed forever from the earthly constraints that might have sent them to wander anguished into the dark forest alone.   Thinking he had maybe envisioned this paradise too well, he now he began imagining he heard real people and that he was being watched.

Then he thought he saw someone. A dark haired girl perhaps? He could hardly see between the narrow gaps in the trees but he could have sworn it was a small girl in an old-fashioned sailor suit. He crashed through the lower hanging branches scratching his face in the process. There he saw what he'd foolishly taken for the girl. A hideous bald-headed child's doll with permanently astonished blue eyes like marbles fringed by enormous black glued-on eyelashes. Then he saw what was next to it and he recoiled in horror. A bizarre Disney-type doll nailed to a tree. Upside down with rusted nails driven through the torso, hands and feet. It made Ridge think of an inverted crucifixion. Minnie Mouse on the Cross. He shivered. He despised all that American schmaltz but at the same time, he felt his entire way of life personally attacked by this barbarous depiction. To him, it had to be the sick manifestation of a curse on the Western nations, especially the States. This doll's sacrifice showed utter contempt for the modern world and he wondered if the person who did this had gone further into the forest to end their own life.

He knew now that the forest winds were only the tortured souls of those who'd perished and they existed only as ghostly spirit sirens, enticing ever more unfortunate people to swell their growing numbers by drowning in the Sea of Trees. As he continued to push deeper into the forest he came upon more and more litter and debris. He twice found an abandoned tent and each time held his breath until he could determine that there were no deceased occupants. Maybe the campers had seen sense and gone home? Ridge tried to reason that if they'd had enough time and presence of mind to pitch a tent then they were probably undecided and in no hurry to take the final step. He found several copies of a small pamphlet, some of which were very waterlogged and tattered. On closer investigation he worked out it had to be some kind of suicide 'guide' and he threw the paper to the ground as if he could catch something from it. Just after that, he found a tiny nylon rope noose close to a completely decomposed paperback which crumbled as he tried to prise open the cover.

Properly freaked out by this time Ridge checked his watch and jumped. He'd been in the forest for hours. Or was it years? He glanced wildly around him and decided just to head straight back downwards away from the darkest part of the woods. But he knew he hadn't been climbing all the time so that meant he couldn't rely on gradient alone as a means of finding his way back. He glanced several times to the left and right and each way seemed eerily familiar.

He was lost!

Fighting the temptation to charge madly through the increasingly dark undergrowth he steeled himself to stay calm and take one course of action for ten minutes by which time he reckoned he should have been able to cover half a mile and if he felt he hadn't got any closer to the road then he'd retrace his steps for exactly ten minutes and then try an alternative route. That way he couldn't get any more lost nor waste too much valuable time. That's when he came upon a length of thicker rope and using it to pull himself along he began to make quicker progress. The terrain rose and fell intermittently making it impossible for Ridge to work out if he was on the right route or not. He thought of Orla and the little children and cursed his stupidity for once again putting himself in such a ridiculous situation. Then he shook himself and told the entire forest that he, Richard Walker, would walk out of this little patch of trees very soon and within a few hours he'd be back in the safety of his exorbitantly priced hotel bar.

That would have been about the time he found a friend. A friend more lost than him admittedly and one who'd never feel the warmth of sunlight ever again. It had been the trainers that first alerted Ridge. Even in the gloom, the fluorescent yellow reflected unexpected colour through the undergrowth and Ridge stood shocked. It had been some time since he'd seen anything as gruesome as the scene before him. A complete skeleton lay in a perfect anatomical position. Fully dressed in what must have been some type of hideous shell suit from a bleak period of recent history, the poor unfortunate soul had obviously hung himself. Just above the remains swung a thin nylon noose like the one he'd found earlier. Ridge guessed the body must have decomposed to the extent that the head slipped through the rope and so the body landed underneath. The bones had been picked clean and were it not for the fashion faux-pas it would have been difficult to say whether the body had lain for one or one hundred years. Ridge saw with revulsion that the white nylon sports socks still clung to the grey ankle bone like they had been made for the task.

Lying there in the damp and murky undergrowth, it didn't seem like a heroic way to die. Ridge couldn't see the glory or the romance there. He found it deeply saddening not to be able even to work out if the body had once belonged to a man or a woman. The flesh of the person, the part that had distinguished them from the 7 billion other souls on the planet had been subsumed by nature. *The way of all flesh*, he heard himself mutter. He turned and ran.

Bouncing off trees, tripping and falling, he didn't care. He just had to get out of there before he became lost forever. What had seemed fantasy and fable had now become all too fucking real and he knew that as long as he moved fast he'd get to the end eventually. *As long as you don't break an ankle again*, a voice inside his head kept whispering. But he shouted back at himself, *so what if I fall and break a bone? I've done that before, I can do that again!*

The light started to brighten a little and he instinctively knew he must be heading in the right direction. He slowed down and all of a sudden he could hear birdsong again and the rushing of water and at that moment he thought they were the most beautiful sounds on earth. He stopped and leant over, the air rasping in and out of his lungs and he held onto his knees and tried not to be sick. The relief that he'd soon be out of the forest was incredible and he even started to imagine he could hear people, like men singing with a rich deep mournful bass. Deciding it had to be the forest winds he shook his head as it hit him it must be the underlying thrum of traffic which you become so inured to in any modern city. But as he straightened up, the sound stopped in mid-flow and Ridge stood still, staring directly ahead, instinctively aware he'd been spotted.

He saw a smallish man and a taller thin girl in a bright woollen hat. She seemed to be looking down at her feet and hadn't yet been aware of his presence but he saw the man grimace at him and urge the girl onwards. The two men exchanged stares for all of a second and just for a moment Ridge thought they were about to change direction and turn towards him but then the man waved in an amiable manner and strode off. Still struggling to breathe, never mind talk, Ridge waved wildly back just so glad to see living humans again after his ordeal. Wondering what they had been doing in the forest, he imagined there would be lots of families spending fruitless hours searching for lost loved ones.

Ridge walked for another twenty minutes or so further but this didn't worry him as he found the paths widening and the trees thinning almost with every step. He found a clump of half a dozen different bouquets of cut flowers, still fresh and lovingly wrapped in pristine cellophane or brown paper at the foot of a large tree. He knew instantly what the flowers signified. That's the biggest problem with suicide, he thought. You never really die alone, no matter how lonely you might be feeling at the time. There will be other's left behind, people who loved you, who missed you. Surely no-one is totally alone.

He smiled as he saw the main road ahead and felt his phone vibrate back to life again.

Chapter 13

'Jesus Christ!'

Ridge turned to the shocked barber.

'You've made me look like fuckin' Renton from *Trainspotting*!'

Seeing that the young man hadn't understood the cultural reference any more than he'd been able to comprehend Ridge's garbled hair-cutting instructions, there seemed little point in making any more of a fuss. Ridge already felt like a complete bastard and so he forced a huge smile and fished out some cash to stuff awkwardly into the bewildered barber's small hand.

Later, after he'd had time to shower and prepare for the next ordeal of the day, Ridge decided it might not be such a bad coiffure as he'd first thought. True, it had to be the shortest haircut he'd ever had but at least he'd not need to let a brush worry it for a while. Back home on Sorsay, he and his pals had called a haircut of this severity a 'Malkie,' and both he and his brother had often begged their father to let loose with the cutthroat razor and give them the same haircut as all the other wee boys on the island. But his mother had thought it to be too rough or 'common' as she'd say, and she'd persevered with a pair of professional barber's scissors for many years and eventually got reasonably good, so much so that there'd be a queue out the kitchen door most Saturday mornings. It wasn't until years later when he'd moved away to University that Ridge would be amused discover that in the rest of Scotland the word 'Malkie' meant to headbutt someone. His poor mother would be horrified if she ever found out that her son had once applied this very technique to end a life, albeit by accident.

He wondered if he still had it in him. To kill or be killed. He examined the face in the hotel room mirror again but couldn't quite take himself seriously yet. He laughed and thanked his lucky stars that his beautiful wife hadn't been accompanying him on this trip as he reckoned his life would be seriously in jeopardy if she copped a look at his head. Ridge checked his watch and decided to chance it with a Skype connection and maybe give Orla a wee laugh at the same time. She couldn't wallop him from all the way over there after all.

*

He found himself still chuckling about the call three hours later as he sat in the changing rooms of the international karate school listening to the other, mostly American, students talking about how terrible the Japanese were at almost everything. He'd discovered most of them seemed to be employed in the digital media arts arena and he quickly shelved any ideas of getting to know the other students. He knew he'd have a real problem bullshitting them about being a landscape photographer which had been his original hastily-devised plan. They seemed to inhabit an illusory world of dreamlike images and conceptual artifice where technology allowed them to push back the boundaries of artistic invention and he honestly didn't have a clue what they were talking about most of the time. It reminded him of when sometimes Orla would talk to him about her writing buddies and a parallel universe of 'grammar Nazis' and 'sock puppets' and she'd see his eyes glaze over after only a few minutes. He pulled on his shitty-looking jogging bottoms and reckoned he'd have been far better off pretending to be a landscape gardener.

The actual karate session proved less embarrassing than he'd expected and he'd been able to hide at the back for most of the hour-long class. He'd actually enjoyed the warm-up element until he realised just how exhausted his forest adventure had left him. The instructor had been American and the atmosphere had been relaxed and friendly. They partnered him up with another beginner, a wide-mouthed American girl called Kim who was every bit as uncoordinated as himself but seemed to be having a lot more fun than anyone else. When the head teacher arrived, the Sensei, Ridge felt an instantaneous frisson of excitement ripple through the rows of students. They were treating this guy like some kind of rock-star! Knowing that he probably wouldn't be returning meant that Ridge hadn't invested a great deal of intellectual or emotional capital into the venture. He'd earlier decided the best course of action would be to keep his head down and go through the motions before extricating himself from the situation as soon as he could.

That had been the plan, for what it was worth. But then he saw the man's face. The guy might as well have floored Ridge with one of the amazing looking kicks he'd started showing off with. The effect on Ridge would have been broadly similar. He knew that face somehow but it didn't make any sense.

Certainly not from the tiny photographs in the karate club brochure, he'd have struggled to recognise his own father from those grainy pictures. So where then? He'd only been in Japan for a matter of days and if pressed he'd have admitted that in this homogenous society, he would be utterly hopeless as a witness at a police line-out.

Then a cold shiver ran up his back as the memories of his afternoon adventure wrapped their tendrils around his throat. He knew it in a second. Kazuo had been the guy in the forest! Ridge immediately ducked as low as possible and for the rest of the twenty minutes or so he did his level best to avoid eye contact, while at the same time he struggled to remember every last detail of the man he'd seen pushing a girl into the dark of the forest.

Knowing nothing about the art of karate and with only a flimsy understanding of the traditions and honour of the martial arts meant that Ridge couldn't quite work out if the guy was a sadistic narcissist or just a tough teacher but his overall impression was that the man loved himself and had no particular affection for his students. He reduced Kim to tears and seemed to get great satisfaction from humiliating as many of the front row of students as possible.

Ridge peered over a shoulder in front, staring at the teacher's eyes. There was something eerily familiar about them, as if he'd met the guy more than once and not just in passing either. Had they met before he even came to Japan? Having had personal experience of powerful international intrigues in the past he struggled to weigh up the possibility of this man being connected to either Colm's shady past or some involvement with Central American drug cartels or even the Irish paramilitaries. Could the situation with Thaddeus have been staged to draw Colm out of hiding? It seemed totally implausible. Even in his heightened state of anxiety, he couldn't see why there would be any connection between Colm and this little dictator of a man.

But the longer Ridge thought about the events in the forest, the more he became convinced that Kazuo had been the man he'd seen. What had he been up to? He had to be the person behind Thad's wrongful arrest and the murder of the young girl. He tried to picture that fleeting glimpse between the trees. The girl walking with him in the forest had been unusually tall. Tall like a catwalk model? The report that Ridge had seen indicated that the murdered girl had been involved in the modelling world but Ridge had no idea if there had been any connection with Kazuo. Thad's fears about the dead girl being his Scandinavian friend had proved unfounded although her whereabouts had yet to be ascertained.

The US Embassy had confirmed that Thad's allegations had been taken seriously and dutifully followed up and he knew the police had actually interviewed the guy but had found no case to answer. He scrutinized the man's face at every opportunity, searching for any clues about his personality. To the uninitiated, you'd think it would be obvious just from looking at someone whether they had the capability to commit acts of violence. But Ridge had met many interesting characters over the last few years that had passed muster yet proved to be deadly as cornered rattlesnakes. Not every murderer looked like the evil bastards you'd see on police mug-shots on the evening news bulletins. No, he couldn't see anything conclusive either way although he definitely showed all the hallmark signs of what Ridge's father used to call 'little man syndrome.'

Terrified that the man would recognise him from earlier in the woods, Ridge continued to keep a low profile until the class finished and he filed out amongst a large group of relieved students. Kim had waved over towards him and much as he would have enjoyed a few beers with a friendly girl right then, he knew he had to get out the door fast, before there would be any after class mingling. And he'd obviously have to make this his last class, so he politely nodded his way through an earnest conversation about the relative merits of various 'green screens' before darting down the stairs and out into the muggy Tokyo night. He didn't even bother picking up his sweat-soaked training clothes.

But as he stood patiently on the opposite side of the street and admired his scummy reflection in a bus stop advertisement he smiled broadly and gave thanks for his inspired idea to have his head shorn. Even his own wife had hardly recognised him.

Chapter 14

The man shifted awkwardly in his less than comfortable seat. He groaned, but then laughed inwardly at the thought of a previous flight he'd once made in somewhat more unpleasant circumstances if that were possible. At least this time there would be no bodies hiding in the wheel wells. He certainly wasn't used to flying anything less than business class these days, but it had been a very long time since he'd been the proud owner of his own airline. Those had been heady days and thinking back, perhaps he had been a little full of himself. Perhaps his youthful arrogance and self-assuredness had been part of the toxic cocktail of circumstance that had led to this very moment. A Japanese version of karma come back to bite him on what felt distinctly like his bruised ass.

He tried to look out of the small window next to him but the black sky refused to divulge any of her secrets. The only clue to his imminent arrival at Yokota air base had been a steady dipping towards the nose of the massive US 5th Air Force 374th Airlift Wing C-130 Hercules. It had been a while since he'd been to Japan and despite the serious nature of his beyond-classified visit, he couldn't help being interested in seeing how the infrastructure of the base had changed since he'd helped revamp it in the 1960's. He guessed it would be a little like himself, creaking around the edges and going soft in the middle. The 5th Air had been born in the very same year as himself and he of all people knew that things had changed a lot since those days. Nowadays personality politics trumped sound judgement and he worried that national security concerns, despite the rhetoric, had been pushed into the background in favour of 'trade deals' and co-operation which rarely benefitted the United States.

He couldn't argue with the fact that people called him a maverick dinosaur in today's politically correct climate. Back in his prime, when a man wanted to do something he just went ahead and did it. And he'd become extremely successful because of that 'can-do' attitude and the fact that several US President's still had his telephone number attested to his perceived value amongst those who actually made things happen. Anyways, the last time he checked, the dinosaurs had ruled the planet for a hundred million freakin' years; he'd like to see the human race beat that.

But he knew he wouldn't be around for a whole lot longer. He felt that more strongly than ever as the mighty engines of the cumbersome plane roared and she gradually banked around and sank down to meet the lights of the runway with the majestic sight of Tokyo all around them. Tadashi Kamaka had arranged to arrive in the middle of the night for a very good reason; he didn't want anyone to know he had arrived in Japan. Not even young Thaddeus, the only reason for this perilous trip, perhaps the very last one he'd ever make. It made him feel very strange to think like that. Normally what you would call a positive rather than upbeat personality, he could rationalise any difficult situation coolly and analytically in order to make the best of limited time or resources.

Not that his resources could ever be described as limited. He had the power, if he chose to exercise it, to bring the furious wrath of hell and damnation upon a vast swathe of humanity. He could assume command of legions of battle-hardened warriors who would kill on his behalf without remorse, without compassion and who'd follow his instructions without deviation. His wealth ran into millions and he'd no idea how many businesses he now owned. Nor did he care. He had other people look after all that for him. This mission too, could have been dealt with by a faceless operative who would undoubtedly have eliminated this malignant threat with a surgical precision.

No, he had to do this one himself. The one thing he'd learned from almost three-quarters of a century on this rock could be summed up in one word. Family. The love towards and from your family had to be the most valuable and yet undervalued treasure in the entire panoply of human existence. As he thought back on the often momentous events in his life, he found that the moments that stood out, the moments when he'd really lived, had been when he'd done things for his family. He'd often let them down and they'd certainly had their share of sadness with the tragic early death of his wonderful wife who could never have been replaced. Yet he knew that they'd often drunk deep from that potent brew called love.

As he stepped out of the aircraft and felt the warm air pull at his light coat, he decided that without that feeling of love then a life is only half lived. Take away love and your world becomes a living tomb. Despite his vast wealth, he knew that none of it mattered as much as the love of his family. He didn't need anything else, not anymore. He'd learned to live far too late in life, he knew that now. He stood on the steps and tried to feel the presence of his son languishing close by in a Japanese prison cell. Tadashi shivered and felt sure he sensed another darker force at work. Love is all very well but what if that love becomes tainted by events and mutates into something savage and cancerous?

He thought again of Thaddeus incarcerated in a gaol cell. Of all the scenarios he'd imagined in connection with this situation that had been one he'd never examined as it would have been deemed unlikely in the extreme. But this had become an extreme situation in a very short time and despite the fact that he had accepted the possibility of his own demise he still felt angry that he had never considered that this might happen. His job had always been to fix problems and he'd fix this one too. Whatever happened to him personally in this unfolding piece of Japanese theatre had become irrelevant to Tadashi now. He knew his role; he'd learned his lines years before, painful words rehearsed a thousand times in his head even though he'd never anticipated having to deliver them.

It appeared his 'top-secret' memo had been lost in translation as Tadashi accepted a salute from a long line of US and Japanese military ranks, standing patiently in the dark of night for the rare opportunity to meet a true American hero. Tadashi briefly nodded and then shook hands with each of them before hurrying towards the nearest building to begin the next stage of his mission. As the enormous plane began to taxi noisily across the tarmac he could just be heard barking out questions to his personal aide who scurried to keep pace with his older but still sprightly boss.

Chapter 15

Ridge had the scent of blood in his nostrils. He'd spent the entire day trailing Kazuo after contacting Colm last night and relaying his most up to date intel. He'd convinced his far more experienced brother-in-law that there had to be something fishy about the guy and to his complete surprise Colm had agreed. In fact, he'd gone along with everything Ridge had said even to the point of allowing him to buy a throwaway mobile and for the two of them to communicate freely, Colm having done likewise over in Valparaiso, Chile where he'd been attending a two-day wine convention.

After the karate class, Ridge had followed Kazuo back to his main apartment. Thaddeus had informed him that as far as he was aware Kazuo normally lived alone. Although he'd said he knew he had two or three rental apartments and it must have been in one of those that the dead girl had been found in. Thad hadn't been too sure about Kazuo's personal life as he'd often seen the guy with glamorous young girls on his arm which he'd said wasn't uncommon when you were a co-owner of a modelling studio. Whether he'd been romantically involved with them Thad hadn't been sure and he'd said to Ridge that the only thing he could be certain about was that the guy wasn't gay.

Keeping someone under surveillance when you haven't a clue about the local transport system had proved awkward initially. But after his first panicked ticket-buying fiasco where he'd ended up vaulting a barrier in order to maintain visual contact, Ridge had relaxed when he saw that hiding in large crowds would always be easier than tailing someone down empty streets. It had only been later that night after standing in the street outside his apartment for three hours and he'd totally given up on the guy re-surfacing again that he'd been forced to hire an expensive taxi to get him home. Totally exhausted, he'd been so focussed on following Kazuo that he'd not taken in where he actually was in the sprawling chaos of the city.

Today, in daylight, he felt much more confident and he could now navigate the main transit routes without breaking into a sweat every five minutes. Plus he'd made what he considered to be a breakthrough. Operating on pure adrenaline, Ridge had spoken to Colm before crashing at two a.m. and then been back out the door of his hotel before 7 a.m. this morning. His work ethic had paid off when he saw Kazuo walking back towards the apartment with a thin plastic bag of everyday convenience items. The still sleepy Ridge hadn't spotted Kazuo at first and so had been standing far closer than he'd have liked but it had been this close call which had yielded a tiny piece of vital evidence. For Ridge had clearly seen through the stretched plastic of the bag a packet of what could only be women's sanitary products. He couldn't make out any branding and hadn't been quite close enough to tell whether there had been English text but nevertheless, he knew instinctively what the product had to be.

So, there must be a female staying in the apartment. Wheels and cogs had begun clicking in his head at that point as to whether it could be Thad's missing friend. Had she been the girl in the forest? He had a visit to the prison scheduled later and Ridge made a mental note to get as much information about the young model from his friend as he could. In the meantime, he stared up at the towering building and tried to work out just how he'd be able to gain access to the apartment. He'd normally attempt to bluff his way through awkward situations and he'd found in the past that this approach worked more often than not. He'd found that people were inherently trusting and decent in his opinion, despite some of his past experiences. He had an idea.

He glanced up at a large digital clock a hundred metres further along the street above the entrance to what appeared to be a large shopping mall. The morning was half over and Kazuo hadn't re-appeared yet. Didn't he ever go to work? Ridge surmised that the glamorous world of photography and modelling probably didn't really 'do' mornings. He didn't like the idea of abandoning his surveillance but so far it hadn't yielded very much and he knew he'd only be able to get away with it for so long. Besides, he needed to eat something or he wouldn't be any use to anyone. His idea wouldn't take long and he could be back on watch within five to ten minutes. If Kazuo had anything whatsoever to do with any missing girls then either this apartment or one of his rentals must be the key to the puzzle and Ridge had become sure it would be this one. Just as he tossed the idea around in his head, fate dealt him a fresh card. The door in front of him opened abruptly and Ridge was forced to turn into the doorway he'd been sheltering in, frantically pulling his Japanese baseball cap down over his face while pretending to light a cigarette. By the time he regained his composure, Kazuo had put a considerable distance between them. But as the late morning sun struggled to penetrate the metropolitan gloom, Ridge noticed with delight the reflection of sunlight bouncing off several pieces of flashy-looking camera equipment. At last Kazuo looked like he planned to do some work!

Ridge darted off in the opposite direction and headed into the brightly lit arcade. Panicking slightly at the vast array of technology that assaulted his weary eyes he tried to focus on exactly what he needed. Then he saw it – a bookshop. Praying they sold magazines, he ventured in and tried to navigate his way to them as fast as he could. The store would have swamped any Glasgow bookshop but thankfully he worked out which floor housed what he needed. His initial idea had been to buy some expensive fashion magazines but then his eye became drawn to a vast selection of brightly coloured martial arts publications. The garish display swam in front of his eyes and the overall effect was akin to someone having thrown up across the covers and Ridge swallowed hard to prevent the unhelpful addition of his own personal artistic contribution. Thinking that these magazines might work better than the fashion ones, he chose one at random not having a clue if he'd picked the right style of karate. Then he grabbed a handful of chocolate bars for good measure.

Back at the apartment main door, he watched carefully to see if the place got any deliveries or non-resident traffic. He could see that many of the buildings also contained offices, usually up to a certain level but with Kazuo's building it wasn't so easy to work it out. The lower half of the building was sheathed in jet black glass which offered no clue as to what existed within and Ridge guessed that the place wouldn't be cheap. A place where people liked to be anonymous. At last, he saw a delivery guy in a head-to-toe navy and red uniform complete with a retro-style bell-boy cap making a beeline for the apartment door. Ridge watched carefully as the man pressed a gloved finger onto a digital screen next to the main door. Up until that point, Ridge hadn't been able to work out how residents obtained access as he'd never noticed anyone fumbling with anything as mundane as a set of keys. He'd begun to worry that there might be some underground entrance, maybe from a car-park, where the majority of residents gained access from.

The answer hadn't been as cutting edge as he'd imagined. The building had a doorman. The glass must be one-way and when any bona-fide residents approached, he simply opened the door to allow them quick and easy access. Everyone else had to first press a button. Ridge lifted his cap and ran a hand nervously over his head, forgetting totally that he had no need to smooth down his hair as he didn't have any left. He crossed the busy road and fixed on his best smile.

Ridge pressed the button twice for good luck and after what seemed like forever, the door opened and he was met with a cold stare. The doorman had been doing his best to affect a look of stoic aloofness but Ridge couldn't help noticing the man's eyebrows were giving away the fact of his astonishment. There would be no point in trying to communicate conventionally so Ridge reverted to his customary cartoon-like method of talking to foreigners when he didn't know the language. He bowed theatrically and thrust out the magazine.

'Good morning! *Konichiwa*!

I am tourist from Scotland! Far, far away. Land of whisky!'

He bowed again for good effect then mimicked the tipping of a glass towards his mouth. The man looked quizzically at Ridge's pantomime act then he stared down at his own feet as if embarrassed, before snorting quietly and then composing himself once more. He made no attempt to engage in any form of dialogue with the crazy *gaijin*.

Ridge pressed on, warming to his task.

'*Sensei* Shimura! I get autograph!

Come all way from Scotland. Big fan!'

Ridge did a faux 'worship' type of action, waving his arms up and down and feeling distinctly like some extra from the old *Wayne's World* movie before moving on to perform what might possibly have been the very worst application of a martial arts punch Tokyo had ever seen. He jumped in shock as the man suddenly became animated for the first time and actually broke out into a huge smile. Somehow the message had got through! The doorman continued to bestow his relieved looking smile upon Ridge and unleashed a torrent of good-natured chatter but at the same time, the bewildered Scot felt his left elbow being gripped by a vice-like hand and he found himself being propelled out of the door and onto the street almost as if he'd been floating. Unfortunately, it couldn't have been the message Ridge had intended, he soon discovered. The man continued to talk away manically and he pushed Ridge along the pavement, all the time pointing to something in the distance and occasionally jabbing a stubby finger at the magazine before indicating that Ridge should keep walking. Despite his protestations that he didn't actually want to go for a walk but instead he really wanted to go upstairs, the man insisted Ridge should go in the direction suggested and so he threw in the towel and bowed in thanks before walking away a broken man and rubbing a very sore arm for his troubles.

But having been so close he wasn't going to be put off now. He grabbed a vending machine coffee and nursed his bruised elbow. The chocolate bars didn't last more than a few seconds longer and despite his rampant hunger, he decided they wouldn't win any taste awards. Right now even the tepid coffee had started to taste good. Back at the entrance to Kazuo's apartment block, he stood on the opposite side of the road where he'd wasted so many hours. But the chemical chocolate must have kicked in fast when a peach of an idea came to him. He didn't know why he hadn't thought of it before. The doorway he'd been hiding in didn't have nearly the same expensive cachet of Kazuo's building. But if he could gain access and get to a high enough vantage point, then perhaps he'd be able to see over the road into Kazuo's apartment. He'd never thought to ask Thad if he knew which floor it might be on and added this to his list for later that afternoon. He remembered seeing a nice camera shop earlier in the glitzy arcade and so he decided to even up his odds a little while wondering if he could maybe arrange to borrow some cash from his wealthy but incapacitated big friend. This trip had proved a tad more expensive than he and Orla had anticipated and he'd only been here a handful of days. But he sensed that something had changed and his instincts had never failed him yet. So after a sugar-fuelled dash along the road, he emerged from the shopping mall just a few minutes later, the proud owner of a pair of Nikon binoculars that cost more than the first car he ever bought.

Like with all good plans, it had been so simple. The first person who emerged from the building opposite seemed happy enough to allow Ridge to enter and so with a huge smile he dived in and searched for the elevator. He saw that the block was a mixture of commercial and residential but couldn't work out which was which. So in a moment of inspiration, he decided just to head for the top floor and then maybe he'd be able to get onto the roof and try out his new toy properly. As the elevator powered smoothly upwards, Ridge stared again in horror at his new hairstyle in the spotless mirrors and banged his head gently for not thinking of doing this several hours ago.

The top floor must have been a more exclusive residential apartment, he guessed it might possibly be a penthouse and Ridge could only find a tiny stairwell which took him onto the roof. This only allowed him to access what he estimated to be around half of the roof area with a high wall cutting it in half. However, this noisier public side suited him fine as it faced down onto the street he'd been on and afforded him a direct line of sight towards Kazuo's apartment building.

His binoculars took a bit of getting used to and he'd not factored in the time of day. Bright afternoon sunshine blinded him as there were no buildings higher than him at that point and the upshot meant that Kazuo's building had become heavily shaded. Even with the incredible magnification of his binoculars, the rooms on that side were shrouded in gloomy darkness. He realised with dismay that he'd only be able to see who might be there if they put on a light when they entered a room. He'd more or less decided just to have a quick play with the binoculars and then come back again the following morning when his eyes were drawn to the unmistakable wooden karate *makiwara* post on the roof opposite. He'd seen a few black belt students punching an identical one at the *Shimura-kai* karate school and as he felt his breath quickening he scanned the roof becoming more and more convinced that it had to be Kazuo's. He lived in the penthouse!

Ridge took some photos to send to Colm and he scrutinized the windows of the floor below but saw no signs of anyone being there. He had just been testing the incredible power of the lenses on the people walking along the busy street twenty floors below when Kazuo's face filled his vision and he nearly toppled over the low balcony in shock. He had come back so soon! Adrenaline pumped through his body as Ridge saw how risky his first plan had been. But he also knew this might be the best opportunity he'd ever get to work out which apartment was his. He tried to see if the doorman showed any signs of talking with Kazuo but it was impossible to tell and at the speed Kazuo had been walking in through the door Ridge reckoned it would have taken a brick wall to slow him down. He licked his lips in anticipation and watched the highest of the apartment floors, afraid even to blink.

There it is! A light flashed from the top floor, immediately underneath the penthouse level. Ridge focussed in on what appeared to be an open-plan living area and he thought he could see a man who looked about the same stature as Kazuo. Then he imagined he saw the man turning and speaking to someone but couldn't be sure. Just for a split-second, he thought he saw her. It was a flash of white skin more than anything else that first caught his eye. A long leg moving fast and a fluid material, perhaps silk he decided later and then as quick as it appeared it was gone. Nothing.

It reminded Ridge of the young Roe deer on the island about this time of year. Invisible amongst the rust-coloured bracken, they'd only give themselves away when they moved, betraying their position with a brief display of white rump as they scarpered into the trees.

He grabbed his phone and tried shooting a few seconds of video just in case the person reappeared but the distance meant that the picture quality became too indistinct and certainly no match for his new binoculars.

Still as a heron back on the Sorsay shoreline, he waited. It must have been twenty minutes later, with the light fading fast that the lights went off, and he guessed Kazuo must be on the move again. He ran for the stair calculating that he could get to the bottom just as fast. Breathing hard, he felt the hairs tingle on the back of his neck as he had the strong primeval feeling he might be closing in on his quarry. The elevator seemed painfully slow on the way down and he forced himself to calm down reasoning that he still had to see Thaddeus later and now he had a spectacular piece of good luck to report. He launched himself through the door just in time to see the back of Kazuo's head and he forced himself to hunch down to make himself smaller as he'd found himself doing all the time since he'd been in Tokyo. Then he began to follow the man.

Kazuo changed his route several times and Ridge began to worry that he'd been spotted and that Kazuo was simply leading him a merry dance. They travelled through the busy Shibuya and the even busier Shinjuku before heading further and further westwards. Ridge glanced at his watch and his heart sank as he knew he'd have to be thinking about turning back pretty soon or he'd never make it back to the city centre in time to visit Thad. Somehow he knew he should keep going and he pursued Kazuo doggedly through two more changes before the man took them back out into the semi-darkness of late afternoon and Ridge was forced to jump into a taxi and utter the immortal instruction, "Follow that cab!"

The taxi driver understood but that appeared to be the sum total of his understanding of English. Ridge gripped the seat so hard his fingers lost all feeling. Where were they going? After twenty minutes the traffic thinned out but so did the daylight and now he panicked that the driver would lose Kazuo completely and the entire journey would have been a waste of time. Just when Ridge had given up all hope the taxi swung hard into a lay-by and the man pointed excitedly up ahead. Ridge saw they were outside a US facility of some kind and hoped Kazuo wasn't fleeing the country. Did that mean the girl had been killed? Had he spooked him? Why were they at a US base? Did that mean Kazuo had somehow become involved with the Yanks? Was *that* the set-up?

So with all these thoughts fighting for space in his jangling head, Ridge paid the guy by credit card and tried to see where he'd gone. The place seemed massive and there was a security patrolled entrance which he knew he'd *never* be able to blag his way through. Fortunately he saw that Kazuo hadn't been processed into the base either which meant Ridge had time to back up a little and work out what to do next. He couldn't believe his luck when he found a reasonably high brick wall which he could just pull himself onto and then hide behind a conveniently placed gorse bush. He thanked the stars that he'd thought to purchase the binoculars as he scanned the entrance to the base. There he saw Kazuo alongside his car, pacing up and down and running his hands through his hair. He might still have been a relative stranger to Ridge but at the same time, you didn't have to be a psychologist to see the guy was as nervous as a long-tailed cat in a room full of rocking chairs.

Ridge took a minute to survey the rest of the base with his new toy and as far as he could see it looked more like a complex of office buildings rather than a base. He saw signs that made him think it might be a small airport but from where he stood he couldn't see the actual airstrip or any aircraft. He guessed he was only looking at a small portion of the place. As he scrutinised the area his mind raced with ideas about what Kazuo was up to. Maybe there was an employee of the base tied up with the murdered girl? It might be just a lowly technician or someone as ordinary as that. Maybe Kazuo had killed before and he might have used a contact at the base to smuggle bodies out of the country? Or had the girl's death been a hideous mistake and she had been due to be shipped out alive, to be trafficked and sold to the highest bidder? Kazuo certainly seemed to enjoy a lavish lifestyle and that penthouse couldn't be cheap.

He swung the powerful lenses back towards the entrance just in time to see Kazuo being ushered into a small glass-walled office adjacent to the guard's booth. He continued to pace around and by only moving his fingers subtly, Ridge found he could zero right in on what had to be a very agitated man. Fresh ideas crashed through his head. Maybe I'm barking up the wrong tree here entirely! Perhaps Kazuo is an innocent party in this, just as Thaddeus is? Ridge had experience of so much governmental duplicity that nothing could ever surprise him again. The other nagging feeling he began to have watching Kazuo wipe the sweat from his brow was that he might be turning himself in. But why come all the way out here? There could be no doubt in Ridge's mind that whatever was going on, Kazuo had every bit as much invested in this as Ridge did. He saw that Kazuo had, somewhat reluctantly, taken a seat at the prompting of a security officer, having previously declined the offer several times. The man left him and Ridge turned his efforts to following the security guy out of the entire barrier area and off into the relative darkness of the base.

Almost as soon as he'd disappeared he emerged again from under powerful sodium lights and this time he had a colleague alongside him. They appeared to be escorting a civilian, a much older man. Ridge strained his tired eyes but he couldn't see the guy's face. They must have been waiting just under cover of darkness, unseen.

Despite his obvious age, the way the man carried himself hinted at a military background and the way in which the other two were behaving made Ridge think the man must either be under arrest himself, or be someone with considerable authority. Thoughts of international shenanigans crept back into his head as he swept the binoculars up and down the scene. Dressed casually in that chinos-and-golf-jersey style that only Americans of a certain vintage can pull off, the man brought up a hand to salute the barrier guard and Ridge caught the gleam of a gold watch. This man had to be involved in Thad's imprisonment. Ridge felt his heart thumping as he watched Kazuo jump to his feet as would an errant schoolboy on the arrival of the headmaster into the detention class.

Ridge held his breath as he saw the older man being escorted in. From his vantage point, Ridge could only see the back of the man's head but he had a clear view of Kazuo. There was no handshake, saluting or any other sign that these men had any personal connection whatsoever. Was this strictly business, above all else? Ridge swallowed and continued to question what he was looking at. He fished in his pocket with one hand as he suddenly wanted someone else to be able to help him with this conundrum. He felt cold and tired and unusually powerless when he looked at this little man who seemed to engender so much fear or respect from others. He swapped the binoculars for his phone and flicked the screen to video. Not being able to see anything at all with the naked eye, Ridge tried to switch between the binoculars and the phone to see that he wasn't missing anything.

It seemed like Kazuo was doing most of the talking. Then Ridge saw him hand over a slip of folded paper which the other man instantly put in his trouser pocket, without giving it a second glance. Ridge suspected it had to be a cheque or some form of payment. So that's what this was all about! Kazuo must be paying his dues to this Mr Big, whoever he was. Then the older guy turned and left. Again Ridge noticed there hadn't been any friendly handshake or wave, it had been purely business. He almost fell off his little wall as he stretched too far to get a better vantage point to catch the guy on video as he strode back into the now sinister darkness. He hastily jumped down and peered around the side of his wall. Kazuo sped past a minute later and Ridge turned around to face what he knew would be a long journey home. He felt exhausted and very alone.

He'd only walked a few minutes before he began weighing up whether he needed to invest a second mortgage in the first taxi he found. As luck would have it, he saw one lined up a hundred metres ahead on the opposite side of the carriage-way. The sign on the roof had only Japanese writing on it but the colour red told Ridge it would be available. Decision made, he started to run. He'd never be able to retrace his route on public transport so he braced himself for the hefty taxi fare. Feeling guilty about the lateness of the hour, he wondered how his friend had been faring, now that he would be facing another night in prison after Ridge had apparently let him down. *I'll phone the Embassy from the cab*, had been his only thought as he stood on a central reservation waiting for his opportunity to dart across to the sanctuary of his taxi.

That was when his phone went off and he fished it out knowing by the bleep that it must be a text and wondering what the time must be back in Scotland. He didn't recognise the number, but that didn't matter. The text read-

CALL IMMEDIATELY – THADDEUS SUICIDE BID – HOSPITAL

Ridge stared at the screen in terror. Had his friend tried to take his own life? His head spun and he felt the strength ebb out of him. He thought he would throw up and fell to the ground hearing himself wail like a wounded animal. Then it became a guttural roar that rose up out of that dark place he'd not visited since his brother died on a lonely mountain.

He'd failed again.

But then it stopped, just as suddenly as it had begun. The heat left his face and he knew he wasn't going to be sick. This time he wouldn't let it happen. He'd fix this.

Ridge lifted his head and pulled himself to his feet. He saw two students looking over at him, obviously concerned for his safety and tried to give them a reassuring wave. His taxi had vanished. It would be a long walk after all, but to a different destination.

Chapter 16

The lights were off in his room, that much he understood, but something had awakened him, something untoward. Still groggy and nauseous from the drugs, Thad turned as carefully as he could, but still the room spun uncontrollably and he thought he might throw up yet again. He forced himself to open his eyes. The prison hospital glowed coldly through his glazed window and he turned, inch by inch, towards the other side of the room. The anaemic lights from the corridor hadn't penetrated that far, or maybe there lurked in here something more powerful than magnets and electricity. He had a visitor. An unofficial one, judging by the darkness outside.

His eyes clouded over for a brief moment and he blinked hard to see if there really was someone there, or maybe he had been hallucinating again. The last few hours had put him off experimenting with drugs again for a long while, that was for goddamn sure. The room seemed to be unusually quiet. He couldn't hear any sounds emanating from the machines hooked into his arms and the normal clattering and banging from the corridors had also mysteriously abated. Had he just got used to the place? Or more likely he hadn't woken up yet. He knew he needed sleep and so he allowed his head to sink back down into the cloud-like pillow and began to drift back off to sleep again.

'Can you hear me?'

Thad jumped. That whispered voice. It didn't come from inside his head, of that he was positive, or almost anyway. He strained his eyes. Still nothing. Forcing himself into a slightly raised position, he scanned the dark corner of the room again. There! Something moved.

'Who's that? What the fuck, man?'

The whisper replied. 'Quiet now or you'll wake the dead.'

Thad started up in horror. Is that it? Am I in the after-life? Not having been a major fan of mainstream religion, he'd never held much stock in the whole heaven and hell scenario. And in any case he'd always suspected that if it did, in fact, prove to be the case, he'd be far more likely to be downstairs. Now, this didn't feel like Hades to him. Not yet anyways.

'Am I dead?' Thad felt immediately foolish for saying that, but he had to know.

He heard a subdued laugh and then the voice came back through the blackness.

'No, you're not quite dead yet. Close.

Very close. That's why I am here. To prepare you.'

Thad stiffened in fear. *Holy fuck.* I'm being visited by the grim reaper himself. But in the back of his befuddled mind, he felt there was something he recognised about the expressionless voice. He couldn't think straight enough. He'd just go with the death thing for the time being.

The muted voice continued.

'Death is never far away, my friend.
But be assured, I will be watching over you.
Your suspicions are correct in many ways.
I am death.
I've been a bringer of death to many souls.
Time is short and I have work to do.
Be ready...'

*

Thaddeus awoke the next morning, tired and confused. His first instinct had been to glance quickly around the room and particularly over in the far corner. Now brightly lit and clinically clean, the room remained coldly efficient and he couldn't see how it could ever have been capable of harbouring evil spirits, or even the Angel of Death himself.

Chapter 17

It could be a lot worse, Ridge tried to reason with himself. At least Thaddeus had pulled through and there had been no question that he'd tried to end his own life. Back in the prison hospital again, he would be safer from now on, the Embassy having demanded assurances that he'd not be put in danger again. The embarrassed prison authorities had even granted the unusual concession of an armed Marine guard at his bedside. The ironic thing had been that the Embassy lawyers had been hopeful that Thad would have been getting bailed around about now. Colm hadn't seen anything coincidental about that, not one bit.

'It's bleedin' obvious Ridge,' Colm had said immediately.

'Whoever is behind the original frame-up, and even possibly the actual murder, is getting jumpy and couldn't afford to let Thaddeus out to investigate further. The police say they've received some fresh information that casts doubt on Thad's involvement and so someone tried to kill him first instead.'

Ridge had messaged Colm with the video he'd taken the night before. To begin with, Colm had been extremely brusque with him and more or less told him to get back on the plane home. Ridge got the feeling that he wished he'd gone over to Japan himself and that if he had done so then they wouldn't all be in this mess. Then Ridge had lost it for a moment and unloaded his frustration and worry at his brother-in-law in an outburst of rage which had probably been building up ever since the shadowy Irishman had shot his friend Zakia in cold blood right in front of his eyes.

'I know you think I'm a fucking amateur, Colm, and I don't want to know *half* of the evil things you've had to do over the years, but don't forget it was me who tracked this guy down and it's probably me who's put the wind up them too.'

'Yep! And nearly got yer best pal killed in the process. Listen up Ridge, I'm sorry to be so hard on you but it's only because I care about what happens to you. You're after being in an alien environment, totally alone and up against a probable murderer with a grudge of some kind. I don't want to be telling my wee sister that her eedjit husband has gone and got himself killed, now do I?'

Ridge could see the cold logic in his first statement and was genuinely moved by the emotion contained in the rest of it. But he wasn't going to back down.

'What about this Mr Big then? Should I go to the author-'

'There is no Mr Big-'

'But, I saw-' Ridge interrupted angrily, only to be cut off himself by a weary-sounding Colm, his voice plainly struggling to remain patient and calm.

'No!

The man you saw wasn't any Mr Big.

Well, not in the way you're after meaning! That man over at Yokota Air Base was Thad's dad. He's come over to take charge of this situation personally and I think he's more qualified than anyone, don't you?

So my advice would be to leave well alone. You've done a great job with yer reconnaissance work and I'm sure that'll be very useful, but my advice would be to come on home safe to my sister. Failing that, just restrict your activities to watching over Thad until he gets bailed and in the meantime stay safe and keep out of trouble.'

Chapter 18

Tadashi didn't sleep for long in the narrow military issue bed. He'd been tired enough for sure. But the combination of the poor quality of his furnishings and the tortured mind games twisting and turning like eels in his weary brain, meant that he had rolled out after only an hour. Looking out of his small window at the cheerless surroundings, he wondered how many military personnel had shared equally bleak nights in all the similarly anonymous compounds he had built around the world. It depressed him to think that men and women would have spent their last ever night on earth contemplating their fate from a window such as this. He sat brooding over his black coffee and mapped out exactly what had to be done next.

Meeting that monster face-to-face had been as painful and heartbreaking as he could have imagined, and it had taken all of his immense self-control to maintain his cool demeanour in front of the man. Of course he knew that this had been just a formality, the moving of the first piece in a menacing game of chess. The dark truth would emerge very soon and only then, when both players understood how the board had been constructed, would he know whether his perilous strategy had been successful. He had been used to getting what he wanted in business but far less fortunate elsewhere, and so here in Japan on this dark night he couldn't decide which way this contest would go.

But in a way, the encounter had helped him to separate out his own feelings of personal guilt about the past from his far more powerful instincts of preserving the family he had left. If he could safeguard the lives of Thaddeus and his two sisters, and bring balance to the scales of justice at the same time, then perhaps he could exonerate himself for his past misdeeds.

Tadashi checked his watch and calculated how much time he had left. Kazuo had unwittingly given him the exact location of their next meeting. The dark woods would be impenetrable to modern day technology, he was acutely aware of that. But the fool hadn't thought about the vast array of electronic weaponry Tadashi had at his disposal before he went anywhere near the Suicide Forest. He plotted the exact GPS coordinates of the entry point into the woods and then he'd had some tech geek input the directions Kazuo had furnished him with into a computer simulation which generated, footstep by footstep, the exact route and final bearings of the proposed rendezvous. He then had a satellite triangulation plotted and forwarded on to his one and only backup contingency.

He pondered on the wisdom of this minimalist operation. He could easily have cashed in even a miniscule portion of the vast wealth of debt owed to him by the US military machine officially and legally. They'd have a veritable army descend on the forest, razing it to the ground if necessary. But unofficially, he'd also got at his disposal an altogether different kind of weapon, one that didn't need to ask permission from Congress or even provide a reason. But he'd decided that he didn't want to take either route. His life experiences and particularly the events of the last few days had taught him that there would always be consequences in life. Action and reaction. This purely personal battle demanded a personal response, no matter the outcome.

But that didn't mean he intended to let this hideous little man dictate everything that would happen. Tadashi had personal debts to score in respect of Kazuo equally as valid as any his adversary had with him and he needed a guarantee of sorts that his personal wishes would be taken care of irrespective of his survival or not. He'd received a solemn promise from a phantom known around the world as 'The Piper.' So he knew his wishes would be respected. And if ever you wanted to truly curse an enemy, then all you had to do was to link his name to that shadowy sponsor of sorrow and it would be done.

He'd been informed about the so-called suicide attempt by his son. He'd known straightaway that it hadn't been genuine, but he also knew implicitly that if Kazuo had actually wanted to kill Thaddeus then he'd be dead. The drugs overdose presumably administered into Thad's prison food would have been precisely calculated to make his son seriously ill, but more importantly, to make sure that he understood the seriousness of the situation. The only reason for Thad's brush with death had been to force Tadashi's hand. It had worked. But it had breached the rules of the game as far as Tadashi was concerned and so he'd taken advice from his one-man team and they'd both agreed it would be entirely appropriate to engage the services of a couple of additional resources, old friends who would never show up on any passenger manifest, nor mention their involvement to anyone, upon pain of death.

He reviewed his plans and checked his watch for the thousandth time. The timing of the next few hours would be critical. He had bargained for the next meeting to be several hours later than Kazuo had initially requested, without giving any particular reasons or seeming to be particularly attached to the outcome of the discussion. Thaddeus would not be over the effects of his poisoning just yet, and he needed to be sure of his recovery before he could give Kazuo his full attention. Then there was the matter of his two daughters. He'd never been the father he'd intended to be to any of his children, and although he hadn't become estranged from his two girls in the way he had with Thaddeus, he'd also not developed with them that deep bond he now had with his son. He owed it to the girls to talk things through with them, possibly for the last time, and to tell them how much he loved them and how proud they had made him over the years.

By the time he'd completed those calls, the disparate elements of his plan would have aligned themselves in accordance with his wishes, his loyal yet terrifying avenger and a trinity of mischievous black magic.

Chapter 19

Ridge left the hotel early as had become his habit. He'd told Orla that Thaddeus had caught a stomach bug which had meant he'd been transferred to the prison hospital for a couple of days and that was why he'd not had a chance to speak to him. He also bent the truth a little when he'd assured her that things were going according to plan and that he fully expected Thad to be bailed within the next 24 hours and so he'd soon be back on the plane home, with or without their big pal. Orla hadn't sounded totally convinced by this and her questioning had been laser-focussed. It seemed that she'd had some kind of message yesterday, in an encrypted format that she'd not been able to fully decipher. Cursing Ridge and Colm for all their ridiculous schoolboy codes, she'd told Ridge she thought it might have been from one of their ex-Marine mercenary pals who'd saved their skins back in Central America. It had been the same three lunatics who'd also arranged emergency transport for Orla when she'd almost given birth to their first child Isla, whilst they were being attacked by ground to air missiles in Northern Pakistan.

Ridge had got her to painstakingly transcribe each and every word to him over the phone in case he got a chance to speak to Colm again, although he couldn't imagine what he would be able to do about anything over in Chile. He could at least tell his wife that he'd genuinely no idea why any of the 'Diamond Dogs,' as they had nicknamed them, would be contacting them after almost two years.

Travelling by taxi once again, having persuaded Orla to transfer additional funds into his account, Ridge headed back to the air base in direct contravention of the plan for the next few days that he'd agreed with his brother-in-law. He thought about the strange confluence of people and events in his life over the last week or so after such an extended period of peace since their first wee one had been born. He decided that it was completely understandable that Thad's dad should be over in Japan to help overturn the ridiculous charges levelled against his son. Tadashi Kamaka was a tour de force of a man and Ridge couldn't help feeling a little bit safer knowing he'd be meeting him soon. Although when he'd made his earlier call to the Yokota Air Base and asked to be put through to Tadashi, he'd been fobbed off with what he imagined was their stock answer to such telephone probing. They'd never heard of the gentleman and there had been no-one of that name anywhere near the base. In the end he'd just accepted that this must be part of their security system and so, on the second and third attempt, he'd insisted they took a note of his name, cell phone number and noted the fact that he was intending to visit this 'gentleman' in the next few hours.

He leant his head against the taxi window and stared out at the strange bustling city that he'd never had the time to get to know. He felt a dull pain arc up through his skull from his damaged shoulder, where a bullet had ripped through flesh and bone all those years ago, just after his first crazy encounter with the 'Dogs.' At that time he'd thought Orla to be dead and he'd been living a selfish and self-destructive existence on the other side of the world. Thaddeus had persuaded the three marines to risk their own lives in the most outrageous manner, just to help Ridge rescue a young friend. In doing so, they'd kicked over a hornet's nest of Central American thuggery and unleashed the vicious fury of one of the most dangerous men on the planet. Yet they had prevailed. But Ridge knew he and Orla would be looking over their shoulders for years to come.

And he felt like looking over his aching shoulder right now. Because sitting cocooned in that Tokyo taxi, it hit him like a punch to the jaw. At no time in his life had he ever been in communication with Thad, Thad's dad, Colm and the Diamond Dogs without some serious shit about to go down. He swallowed hard as the taxi approached the gates of the airbase. If that was the case, he thought, *I guess I'm right in the middle of it again.*

Because it had taken him so long to travel back into central Tokyo the previous night, added to his worry that he couldn't guarantee that Tadashi would agree to see him, despite their reasonably strong personal connection, he had indicated to the taxi driver to wait five minutes before heading away from the base. He'd only ever met Tadashi once before but it had been one of those situations where the normal boundaries and formalities were swept aside. For some reason every time he thought back to that time, he would hear the chop-chop-chop of helicopter rotor blades, despite the fact that they had met in a hotel suite in Washington DC.

He checked in with the Marine Private at the drop down barrier and used his real name for the first time in a very long time. The soldier checked his name on a manifest and asked again if his visit had been sanctioned by the military. Ridge laid it on a little thick about being former comrades and so forth. The man gave him such a withering stare that he found his words falling away and he decided just to keep quiet and let the fates decide. He was politely ushered into the same glass fronted kiosk that he'd watched Kazuo being taken into and he sat patiently staring at the floor. Each time a vehicle entered or left the base he found himself jumping up nervously, and it was only at that point he began to worry what the fuck he would do if Kazuo returned for a second appointment.

A frustratingly long hour later, with his transportation long gone once again, Ridge had reconciled himself to a long trudge back into the city. He must have missed Tadashi, he decided.

Surely the guy wouldn't have stiffed him like this after everything he and Thaddeus had been through? He saw a uniformed officer approaching and on a whim made up his mind to be as awkward as possible. He'd wasted half the day on this trip and he was tired and hungry. Why the hell should he bend over when the only reason for his visit was to try and help a friend in trouble?

The guy walked in and saluted him which wrong-footed Ridge immediately. Then he saw from the silver insignia that the man must have been a Captain, although Ridge suspected he might be even younger than he was. Over six feet tall with a spray on haircut and shoulders as wide as a refrigerator, the guy had US Marine tattooed all over him. Ridge instinctively tried to salute back which only made him feel even more awkward. And when the guy motioned for him to sit down, he gladly slumped into the plastic chair, all thoughts of macho posturing spent in the presence of so much superior grade testosterone. Then the officer smiled and Ridge had to shield his eyes from the glare of several thousand dollars worth of dental perfection. *Too much dude*, he found himself thinking and then he laughed inwardly as the guy whipped out a clipboard and pretended to be reading and taking notes. So far not a single word had been spoken and Ridge began to get a funny feeling about this guy. In the background he swore he could hear bagpipes playing and he wondered if there could be a Scottish battalion visiting the base. He coughed and prepared his throat for his very best Gerald Butler impersonation. But the guy beat him to the mark.

'Mr Walker, my name is Captain Nathan Reece. I'm sorry to have kept you waiting for such a long time and that your visit has proved fruitless. We have no records of any individual of that name on the base neither can we locate him in our visitor manifest for the last year.'

So far so fucking predictable, Ridge thought until the man did something weird. He glanced up pointedly at the security cameras, which Ridge hadn't even noticed, and then he flashed open his prone right hand just above his enormous square knee, like he'd just tried to flick something horrible off his fingers. Ridge could easily see what he'd done but he guessed the man's hand must have been hidden from the overhead camera. It was as if he was signalling the number five, but Ridge couldn't for the life of him work out why. So had the soldier positioned himself deliberately to put his back towards the cameras? Not expecting anything like this, Ridge couldn't hide his confusion and he gave the Captain a questioning shrug. He was met with an instant tick of annoyance and the Captain closed his eyes for at least a second before they snapped open as if he'd just had a minor electric shock. He again glanced down at his knee as he spoke slowly and theatrically.

'Therefore, sir, I respectfully advise you to make your way back to downtown Tokyo and I hope you enjoy the remainder of your vacation. We have the ability to arrange transport for you Mr Walker-'

Five finger hand flash...

'But in our experience, sir, we would advise you to engage a taxi on your own-'

Five finger hand flash yet again.

'-which will return you more speedily than if you had to wait for one of our preferred service companies to drive out from the city.

If that is acceptable, Ridge Walker, then I bid you good day.'

Ridge sat open-mouthed as the officer flashed his five finger thing once again before standing up and saluting. The motherfucker had called him *Ridge*. He'd almost whispered it right enough, but he'd definitely said it. This time Ridge could see something unmistakable in the man's eyes and if he'd been in another time and place, he might have thought the guy was giving him a 'come hither' look. Ridge grasped the fact that the Captain was somehow a friend and he pumped his hand a little too enthusiastically before being hurriedly ushered out.

Okay... Ridge watched the soldier march off into the shadows and wondered if he'd just imagined all of that. Just in case, he'd made up his mind he wouldn't be going anywhere for a full five minutes and he just hoped that he'd not mistaken the

134

theatrical message. He knew he couldn't stand right in front of the base and so he began walking away, but at a snail's pace. Assuming he would be signalled to re-approach the barrier once the allotted five minute period was up, he kept his eyes peeled and made to scoot back as fast as was humanly possible. Looking at his watch, he saw it was four minutes to the hour, so he'd pretty much decided that the Captain was going to let him in when there was a shift change. Maybe he'd a friend on duty or a favour to call. In any case, the guy must be acquainted with Tadashi personally to know his name was Ridge, and not Richard, as per the trusty clipboard.

He was just in the process of retying the laces of his trainers when there was a sudden commotion behind him. As he glanced up over his right shoulder he saw a car whizz past. Going at speed, the car had passed him before he had the chance to stand up and try and see who was in it. Cursing, he stood and wondered if he'd missed his chance. But even Usain Bolt wouldn't have been able to catch that ride. Ridge saw that the barrier hadn't come back down. Thinking this might be his chance to gain access to the base, he turned away from the disappearing car and started walking back as casually as possible. Then another anonymous American SUV came racing out of the base and this time the window was down and he saw the Captain at the wheel. The car slowed for a moment and the soldier nodded hard and yelled. 'Meet me just down there, but *run!*'

Glad he'd just tightened his laces, Ridge gulped some air and tore off down the road as fast as he could. A hundred metres ahead the black car idled and he ran across the road and jumped into the passenger side. He'd hardly got his second leg in when the car surged forward and he had to cling onto the grab hold, only barely managing to pull the door closed. 'Fuck!' he heard himself exclaim and the soldier laughed before taking a hand off the wheel and proffering it to Ridge.

Ridge jumped and just pointed to the road, strapping his seatbelt with lightning speed.

'I'm Nathan! Pleased to make your acquaintance Ridge Walker. I'm a friend of your friend Thaddeus! We're following Mr Kamaka because I have some serious reservations about what the fuck is going on here. You can get out if you like but not until we catch the lead car and then I'll drop you off in slower traffic. You wanna bail?'

It all made sense now. Only a gay man could be so 100% ridiculously perfect fucking beefcake. He was riding shotgun with one of Thad's conquests. Ridge laughed. It had to happen sometime.

'Fuck no! Let's do it Nathan, glad to have some company, to be honest!

Chapter 20

The busy traffic slowed their progress and allowed Ridge's racing pulse to calm down. Nathan had met Thad only recently and unsurprisingly he'd been approached to do a little modelling work. Ridge didn't have to wait too long for the inevitable question, and he saw that this guy had got it real bad.

'Hell no! We're just good buddies... from way back, over in San Fran.

Been through some scary times though and I'd give my life for the big guy.

That's why I'm here.'

Nathan had been beaming at him and Ridge saw him start to well up before he focussed his attention back on the road. They had maintained a casual distance behind Tadashi's car and it seemed likely the marine had done this sort of thing before.

'Yeah, we get a wide variety of stuff overseas,' Nathan read his mind. 'Most of it is uber-dull, but then every now and then it brightens up.' His smile lit up the cabin and Ridge didn't have to tax his brain too hard to work out what had brightened up this guy's world.

'Is Tadashi on his own?' Ridge ventured cautiously. Nathan nodded. 'Yeah! Unusually for a civilian, but lucky for us, or this tail would be a lot more complicated what with all our vehicles being this standard Ford SUV. Any colour as long as it's black, right?'

Nathan confirmed Ridge's suspicion that Thad's dad occupied a unique position for a non-service individual, which allowed him special privileges. But it had been this relaxed and off-the-radar situation that had spooked the big soldier.

'We have protocols for everything around here. Standard operating procedures are in place for a reason. To keep our personnel, and those under our duty of care, safe from danger. The problem with a maverick personality like Mr Kamaka and, I mean no disrespect by this, people like you Ridge, is that they can jeopardise their own safety and that of people around them.'

Ridge could offer no argument here and so nodded in silent acceptance.

'And I've read the files, Ridge. I know that Thaddeus had recently posted allegations about a Mister Shimura which were conveniently discredited. And I also know the two men met back at the base. My fear is that Mr Kamaka will do something reckless or illegal to further the case for his son and that this will hinder Thad's early release. Now I don't wanna see that happen for personal reasons as I'm sure you can imagine. But there's no way I can allow Mr Kamaka to do something stupid and end up in the jug, either. Not on my watch. You know what I'm saying?'

Again Ridge nodded, but stayed quiet. He could see that this guy could be useful but he'd not be the type to take any risks. Not the kind of guy he needed right now. Even with those shoulders. Ridge had worked out even with his limited knowledge of the terrain, that they'd been heading west and away from the main city, so he wondered where could they be going? He wished he'd done his homework on Kazuo; he didn't have any idea where he had come from, if he had family nearby or anything. Ridge glanced around him and gritted his teeth with frustration. Perhaps Nathan had been right? Protocols and mavericks in a nutshell.

'Okay, Nathan. Any idea where we're going? What do your protocols tell us?'

He saw that the guy had picked up on his sarcasm and so he couldn't be that bad.

'No friggin' idea my friend! Looks like we're headed out towards open space soon, which will make surveillance harder. That's Mount Fuji over that aways. You'll maybe get a chance to see it if we get a break in the weather.' Ridge smacked his forehead hard.

'Bloody hell! I know exactly where we're headed, Nathan.

To the forest, the Suicide Forest!'

Nathan stared across at Ridge, the doubt clear in his face.

'Aokigahara? No way man! I've heard of that place. Round here I think they call it The Sea of Trees? What the fuck would he be doing there? You sure?'

But Ridge just knew that must be where they were going and then as the black SUV took another turn towards the mountain area he became positive. He poured out his thoughts and ideas. 'I've been there myself! Just as a tourist... got completely and utterly fucking lost! I honestly thought I would be wandering around there for the rest of my life. Fucking horrible place, bodies and shit all over the place! But then, by pure chance, just as I'd found my way back, close to a car park, I saw him, the bastard... AND he had a young lassie with him, tall as fuck, could easily have been a model. Tadashi must be going there to meet him!'

The Marine Captain focussed on the car five vehicles in front and shook his head as if having an internal dispute with himself. 'I don't get it, Ridge. Why would Mr Kamaka want to go to a place like that? There's not even any goddamned cell reception! It's got to be the last place on earth you'd want to meet with someone.'

Ridge suddenly felt very frightened for Thaddeus.

'Nathan, something very fucked up is going on here. You know that Thad got poisoned, don't you? Maybe this Kazuo Shimura is a really bad fuck after all? Where better to do some evil shit, than a place that's off the grid and so scary that you'd have to be bat-shit crazy to go there? Tadashi won't be the one wanting to go there. My guess is he's being ordered to go and I don't like it one wee bit!'

Now they were inside the tourist park area of Mount Fuji, Ridge recognised some of the roads. If his hunch was correct then they'd be turning away to the left and down towards Aokigahara within minutes. The traffic slowed to barely walking pace and Nathan began prodding buttons on the impressive array of technology that enveloped the cockpit of the car.

'Ridge, you know that I can't go much further don't you.' The guy seemed genuinely abashed and he held up his free hand in an apologetic gesture. 'The SUV is chipped and we are expressly forbidden to go off the radar. I doubt if I'll get more than a few miles further. Seriously, I could lose my commission, what I'm doing here is already way too risky!'

Ridge couldn't believe what he was hearing.

'So? What you're saying is you can't even break a couple of stupid fucking regulations to help catch the guy who tried to poison your boyfriend! What are you? A fucking robot? I'd have been better off getting a taxi!'

Ridge yanked hard at the door handle despite the fact the car was still moving. It wouldn't budge. He slammed his hand against the glass in frustration. 'Let me the fuck out!'

'Wait!'

Nathan pulled Ridge roughly round and pointed a meaty finger in his face. The car rolled gently forwards and several tourists were glancing at each other and nodding towards them. 'Just calm down, okay? Let's just see where this'll lead us before we take any more hissy fits...'

Tadashi's car turned directly into the spooky forest road and towards the car park where Ridge remembered re-discovering civilisation. He looked over at the dingy cafe which had seemed as beautiful as the Taj Mahal just a few days before. Just then, a red light started flashing on the dashboard and Nathan pulled the car over. 'This is as far as I can go, Ridge,' Nathan said meekly. 'But I'll wait here for you, over there in that car park. I can give you four hours.'

Ridge could see there would be no point in arguing with the guy and in any case, he could be back in less than ten minutes if the last meeting between Tadashi and Kazuo had been anything to go on. Nevertheless, as he turned and allowed his eyes to probe the outer edges of the dark forest, he suddenly felt lonely and defenceless. Then he remembered the phone in his inside pocket. Without a moment's thought Ridge fumbled it out and placed it on the central unit of the big car.

'You might as well have this.

If I don't come back, for whatever reason, after your precious four hours is up, use this phone. Don't give it to anyone else.

There's only one number on it and you won't be able to speak to anyone directly. Just leave a clear message, saying exactly what the situation is.

142

Nothing else. No questions. Just my location, who I'm following and who you are.

Got it?'

Seeing the other man nod uncomprehendingly, Ridge patted Nathan on his oversized shoulder and got out without another word. Despite the slow moving vehicles he saw he'd have to move fast to catch back up. So with a backwards wave, he found himself back on his own again. *That was fucking short-lived.* Breaking into a slow jog, he growled and pulled his lightweight jacket tighter as the storm clouds gathered overhead.

Chapter 21

Kazuo checked his watch again and groaned. He's not coming! He paced the perimeter of the clearing, checking and re-checking his preparations were still in place and then every so often stopping still, listening. The forest would often get him like that, he should be used to it by now. It wraps you up in a suffocating blanket of silence, so much so that if you make the slightest bit of noise yourself, it drowns out everything else. You start to imagine you heard something or you think you almost heard something, and would have, if you'd not been making such a noise yourself. So you stand stock still like you've been frozen in time like some of the more ghoulish denizens of the forest. But nothing. You hear nothing. Then after a while, you begin to wonder what noise really sounds like, noise made by other souls, living souls. And so it begins. The madness.

The forest had been his only choice for this showdown. He'd been looking forward to it for years now. Revenge had been eating into him like a corrosive acid, burning his insides, and slowly but relentlessly reducing him from a rational human being to no more than a flesh and blood cage enclosing a demented monster. He'd not made any plans for what might ensue after today. He'd never expected his scheme to have worked so well up until now and apart from a minor hiccup with the playboy model, he couldn't have scripted it better.

It had to be the forest. The venue of his father's descent into madness and his living tomb. Kazuo stopped pacing for a moment and thought about whether he would continue to search for the body of his father after this day. He hoped that vengeance might slake his thirst for the macabre place. It may even cure him of his bloodthirsty madness but he feared he'd fallen too far now. What if his father was still alive? Maybe he'd wandered out of the forest, out of his mind and unable to communicate? It happened. Often people would rediscover their zest for life after a botched suicide attempt. But Kazuo knew he'd scrutinized all of those avenues no matter how unlikely they might have seemed at the time. He'd trawled the asylums, the old people's homes, VA hospitals and homeless shelters. But no-one had encountered a deaf man who'd lost his mind.

He knew he had to be the last person in the world to judge another. He'd lost his own sanity without the help of any atomic bombs. But the fallout from that awful day in August 1945 had destroyed him, as surely as if he'd been standing alongside his eleven-year-old father. It grated with Kazuo how the modern generations would gripe and moan about how life had become so tough and yet they'd allow themselves to become lazier and more culturally corrupt, generation after generation.

He tried hard to keep his personal life private, but sometimes it would come out and he'd tell someone about his father, Hiroshi. As a young boy, Hiroshi had been a musical prodigy by all accounts, including his own father, who himself had been an accomplished violinist and had pioneered classical music in Japan and set up one of the first violin factories. Forced to convert it into an aircraft parts factory during the war, Hiroshi's father had died in the burning ruins after a US bombing raid. The young Hiroshi had survived the attack, only to witness the horror of the Hiroshima bombing just a few weeks later. Badly wounded, he'd lost most of his left hand, and several fingers of the other hand, as he'd held up a burning roof timber and saved the lives of three tiny school friends. Recovering over the next year, the young boy had struggled to come to terms with the fact that not only would he be unable to play the violin, he'd never hear again.

Kazuo strained to hear any approaching sounds. Still nothing. He'd tried to imagine what it would have been like to lose his hearing. He'd not been blessed with musical genes, according to his mother, but he had often wondered if perhaps his father had encouraged him more then he might have blossomed into a fine musician. He still had his old violin somewhere, gathering dust and more of a memorial to his father than a musical instrument. He remembered seeing his father weep with the frustration of not being able to hear the young Kazuo massacring yet another masterpiece. Feeling the pain etched so clearly on his father's face, Kazuo soon lost interest and found his talents lay in the visual arts and in the punishing practice of karate. He'd grown up hating the Americans and even today he actively avoided doing business with them, much preferring the European style magazines and art houses. Of course, he had to employ them every now and then, when it suited his purposes. Even that over-confident Thaddeus le Grange, complete with his pretentious fake surname, had been recruited for a reason.

But that reason had not arrived in this elaborately staged mausoleum. Kazuo thought about what he'd do if Tadashi failed to show. His first instinct was to inflict pain on somebody, to dull the continual pain that lived in his head by watching another squirm in agony. He'd already killed a young girl earlier that day. Naive and uncomprehending until her last few minutes of life, he'd raped and strangled her only to boost his confidence for this meeting here in the forest. Why had he chosen her? No real reason apart from her being an American and having annoyed him at the dojo. Next would have to be the blonde girl, he decided, not because he felt done with her, but because she would be easiest and quickest. He could get another soon enough although that hadn't been part of his grand plan, as he'd promised she would be the last one. His dead father would have maybe understood the earlier murders. Vengeance for past misdeeds. But he'd never countenance any killing after Tadashi had made reparation.

Wait. That time, he swore he heard something. Kazuo sank down into a low stance, his legs wide apart, ready to move with speed and power in any direction. He listened again. The bells. At long last! His trip wire had worked. He imagined he could hear bird sounds high above him. Virtually impossible in these vast woods he knew, but all the same he felt uplifted by the notion. Light and airy notes that made him think of twinkling lanterns and the fragrance of cherry blossoms during the Kanda Matsuri festival his parents had enjoyed taking him to as a young boy. Kazuo glanced upwards, nervously. Directly above him, he could only see darkness, the trees arching into a protective canopy, destroying life below rather than fostering any. He'd chosen this makeshift clearing largely because it did actually have a small area of natural light which would be essential for his proposed plan. So even here in the darkness, he knew that above the trees there would be light and sunshine. Maybe that was the same as heaven, out of sight to the human eye, but still there nevertheless. He longed for that to be the case but deep in his heart, he understood that heaven would not welcome him. Instead, a warm wind fought its way through the clammy air like the last breath of a dying man and that's when he saw Tadashi.

Moving fast for an old man, Kazuo thought. He raised himself up, glancing around for others as he did so. Tadashi appeared to be on his own, as they'd agreed. Two men alone in a forest of ghosts. Kazuo nodded slowly. It was only then that he allowed his arms to come from behind his back, to reveal a long curved sword in his right hand. This traditional katana sword had been given to him by his father on his thirteenth birthday. Two years later his father had died alone in this forest and today his death would be avenged.

Chapter 22

Tadashi had taken longer than he'd expected to follow the directions. His knees hurt and the terrain had been treacherous, resulting in him falling frequently into the mossy limbs of trees long since perished. He didn't like to think what else might be mouldering under his feet and despite the peril of his proposed encounter, he actually felt relief as he first caught sight of the clearing.

He stood for a few moments foolishly thinking he was alone until his straining eyes saw the shadowy outline of a human head, just inches above the petrified bracken. His next mistake had been to arrogantly assume he'd arrived undetected and it had only been when his eyes had become accustomed to the darkness that he'd seen a pair of black eyes glinting with hatred. He bowed and forced himself to break the silence. 'Shimura.'

'Welcome Kamaka. Here, move closer where I can see you,' said the other man, his voice trembling with emotion. 'I have prepared comfortable seating for us, with refreshments if you so choose.'

Tadashi stepped cautiously forwards and saw that Kazuo had indeed spent what must have been a great deal of time and effort preparing for this encounter. He wondered what other delights might lie in store for him as he saw the sword for the first time, pointing to a low wooden bench adjacent to a small table. He sat heavily and prepared for the worst. Kazuo moved quickly and sat opposite him on a slightly more elevated bench which Tadashi presumed to be the seat of judgement. He watched as the man brought out a porcelain flask and slowly poured a rich coloured liquid into two small saucers. It had been many years since Tadashi had drunk the sweet rice wine and as he rubbed his sore shins he decided to allow his host to make the first move.

'Thank you for honouring the death of my father by your presence here. You have surprised me yet again, Kamaka.'

'I hadn't known of his death and for that, I apologize. I would have been honoured to attend his funeral as I had always considered him a friend.'

Kazuo jumped to his feet, snorting angrily.

'You lie! You were no friend to my father, you were a traitor to him and to Japan!'

Tadashi raised his hands in an attempt to placate the other man. He could see this hadn't got off to the best start, yet he had a feeling that progress could still be made out here in the Sea of Trees. The sky had darkened since his arrival and he didn't like the thought of making his way back to civilisation on his own. Kazuo glared at him and little flecks of spittle had gathered at the corners of his mouth, pursed in fury.

'You were no friend, Kamaka! You befriended him in order to betray him just as surely as the B52 bombers had done in 1945.'

Tadashi coughed quietly and then began speaking in the most conciliatory tone that he could manage.

'I have made many mistakes in my long life. I am humble enough to accept that. But you are mostly wrong in your judgement of me and, if you permit me, I'd like to give you my recollection of events. I presume that is one of the reasons you have brought me to this abominable place. May I proceed?'

Kazuo growled like a mountain lion and nodded imperceptibly.

Tadashi bowed again and continued to speak.

'Thank you. You were not even born when I met your father and mother, a delightful young couple and very much in love. I was sad to have left Japan before their wedding ceremony.'

'Yes! You left like a thief in the night did you not?'

'That's disingenuous Shimura, may I call you Kazuo?

Thank you. It is true. I left suddenly, but you must realise I owned a large conglomerate of businesses and I had effectively taken several months away from my duties, a situation which couldn't be allowed to continue. 1969 proved to be a pivotal year for me and you must understand that I was only twenty-eight years old in charge of my own airline business.'

'Once you'd got what you wanted you mean!'

'No, that's not true once again. I made a huge sacrifice because of my friendship with your parents, one that cost me a great deal of unhappiness.'

'You lie yet again! You stole my father's business! He'd lost his hearing, he only had one hand and then you stole his life's dream. You might as well have buried him under that concrete monstrosity you built.'

Tadashi growled. The man had gone too far and now it was his turn to stand up. But as he did so Kazuo swept the sword upwards and Tadashi found himself balancing precariously on a sharpened steel blade which pressed gently on his windpipe, just enough for him to know that his life could be over in an instant. Again he lifted his arms and his eyes examined the younger man carefully, before he felt the sword tip pull back and he was permitted to sink back heavily onto his seat.

His brain ached with the pain of what he wanted to say to this man. He felt the years of resentment bubbling to the surface, and he alone knew the fundamental wrong of it all. Kazuo had learnt a twisted version of history from a broken man and Tadashi knew he had it within him to change everything with just a few words. But he also knew that if he misread the situation, then he could die within seconds. Most of all he worried that if he were to perish here in this dark forest he'd be unable to protect his family from the messianic madness of this mistaken fool.

Some secrets were best left in the dark, whereas some will free your mind. Tadashi knew he had to work out what Kazuo would want to know most and then decide what he would do with his newly acquired knowledge. Knowledge is power so they say. In this case, would it become a powerful weapon of retribution?

There was only one way to find out.

Tadashi leant forward pushing up his sleeves and in the spirit of openness and trust, he took a gamble. He reached for the nearest saucer and took a tentative sip and then another larger one, emptying the contents down his throat. The *sake* tasted better than he'd anticipated and much more pleasant than he remembered. For the briefest of moments, Kazuo stared at him like the way you'd look at a poisoned man to see the first signs of his imminent death. Tadashi felt his heart race and it wasn't just the effect of the alcohol. Then to his relief, he saw Kazuo nod, before lifting up his own saucer and draining the entire contents in one smooth movement.

Tadashi took this as an omen. 'May I continue?'

Kazuo nodded silently and Tadashi nodded in return.

'You are quite correct. The building was a hideous mistake but in my defence, it had been built to the exact and identical specifications of most of my US construction projects of those times. It was an ugly period.

But I stole nothing.

I had owned the patents that your father required. My transistor companies had the equivalent knowledge to that possessed by your father. That was how we had originally met. He needed a great deal of seed capital to advance his quite brilliant ideas for the cochlear implant factories but my organisation had almost unlimited cash reserves at that time. I got paid by the US Government before I did any work for them. He couldn't compete with that. When I bought out his only remaining patent, I made sure to include generous allowances which I would imagine has allowed you to live a very comfortable life. You wouldn't have-'

'Comfortable but lacking in honour!'

Kazuo had risen to his feet again, banging his hands so hard that both the saucers had bounced off the wooden surface and onto the forest floor.

'You bribed him, Kamaka!

He never recovered from the betrayal of a man he considered a friend!

For many years he brooded about what you'd done. With every advance in the technology of hearing aids, he would tell me that he could have done it better if he hadn't been betrayed by the fake-Japanese traitor. I never knew who you were or if you had even lived beyond that time. Father never even told me your name but then I found a piece of paper with your name on it.

I searched online for you. Somehow you have managed to be almost non-existent online despite your many ventures. More crooked deals no doubt.

But then your vanity got the better of you!

I found the *T.Kamaka Research Center* at your famous Quantico training base!

Then I knew I would find you. I would kill you...'

Chapter 23

Ridge caught up with the man soon after they entered the cool darkness of the woods. What he'd imagined to be bad weather had proved to be fast moving swirling mists that he guessed must be a constant feature of the foothills of Mount Fuji and not unlike the cold mists on the mountains back home. Just as he'd begun to step reluctantly off the tarmac, he felt the fingers of warm sunshine run up the backs of his legs and across his shoulders. It just made the forest seem even colder by comparison and he found himself slowing down to savour the last few seconds. With any luck, he'd be back into the bright afternoon before long.

He had no idea where the man was headed and very soon the forest became the same alien and unwelcoming place it had been before. None of the surrounding features were remotely familiar and he didn't feel any happier to be back. But having someone a few hundred yards in front meant that he didn't feel like the last man on earth this time. It reminded him of his teenage cross-country running days. He'd push himself beyond the limits of normal people, wracked as he'd been by the pain of losing his older brother and blaming himself for his tragic death. He normally raced on his own after the chaos of the first half mile and he preferred running at his own speed, which usually meant most of his fellow competitors would be trailing in his wake as very few could live with his blistering pace. But even then, he'd like to have at least one or two to chase. The fox liked to have sight of the rabbit. The going always seemed easier if there was someone to follow and so he'd use that to get him through the tiresome middle sections of long races and then he'd sail past them, to coast to victory near the end.

Today, the challenge would be not going too fast and end up blowing his cover. Tadashi must be feebler than he'd thought as he seemed to be having considerable difficulty with the terrain, but Ridge put some of that down to his short stature and the emotional weight he'd be carrying through the trees. Still, he appeared to know where he was headed and Ridge wondered how the hell he could have got any GPS device to work.

It had only been a half hour or so when Tadashi stopped altogether and immediately Ridge felt concerned for the man. He'd never be able to face Thaddeus if he let something happen to his old man, and he kicked himself for not leaving himself some kind of breadcrumb trail for the route back. He needed to get closer. The ground was so soft and sponge-like there would be little danger of cracking a branch or anything like that. He'd be more likely to trip on a root branch and break his neck. Ridge squinted his eyes and tried to see why Tadashi had stopped. It seemed as if he'd been cast in stone. Ridge watched carefully but he couldn't see Tadashi move at all and despite the cool of the forest, he felt pinpricks of sweat break out across his face. He couldn't see Tadashi looking down or to the side. He just stood looking straight ahead, still as a statue. Ridge had begun to get really worried that Tadashi had had some kind of a breakdown. His own mind had started playing tricks with him, so much so that he was just on the brink of walking straight up to check he was still breathing, when he moved. Ridge blinked at first. But he'd disappeared! Moving far faster than before, Ridge tried to make up the distance and then he saw him again, more clearly now due to some natural light fighting its way through the gloom. Wait, what was that? Yes! There was another man there. Was it Kazuo? Ridge edged closer, inch by inch. He had a bad feeling about all of this.

There were just the two of them as far as he could see and Ridge calculated his odds of successfully overcoming the karate master. Not great, he decided, but at least he'd have Tadashi as backup. The meeting appeared amicable enough. But what was that? His heart sank as he saw Kazuo brandishing a Samurai sword, the blade absorbing any available light and glinting back at him maliciously. *Holy fuck.*

He had to get even closer. If it looked like kicking off, then he needed to be able to react faster and if that bastard had a sword, then it didn't look so good for old Tadashi. What the fuck was going on? As he crouched down and gently stepped through the undergrowth Ridge began to get a better handle on the situation. The two men were sitting face to face and appeared to be talking calmly. Good news. Ridge felt like kicking himself as he could easily have taken Kazuo out with a single shot from this range even with his less than perfect eyesight. Nathan had been packing a sidearm and there would have been a larger gun secreted somewhere on that SUV for sure. Why on earth hadn't he thought of that an hour ago?

Ridge knelt down and peered through the foliage carefully, keeping as much to the shadows as he could. There seemed to be a natural clearing of sorts, and it meant he could see more easily, but then he would also be more easily spotted if he wasn't careful. The two men were still totally out of earshot. He couldn't get a clear enough line of sight to work out what was going on. He tried to think like a soldier and scrutinized his immediate surroundings to figure out some kind of rough plan as to what he could do to improve his position. It was then that he heard the faint hum of a generator only a few feet in front of him. He guessed it would be the same type of portable AC unit of the kind he'd hired back on Sorsay, when he'd first begun the cottage renovations before the mains electricity had been established. But what would someone need a power unit for out here? Ridge tried to see if there were any cables nearby, but the forest floor literally crawled with tree roots and plant life. If he cast his eyes towards his own feet it was almost like when you stand for more than a moment on a beach, in that intoxicating few seconds between a wave crashing over your toes, and the undertow of sand pulling back underneath your feet. Keep still for a further second and then your toes will be invisible under the sand.

He glanced upwards more in frustration than anything else and then he saw them. They were so obvious once you'd seen them, thick black cables wrapped in heavy duty plastic tape and trailing up the trunk of a huge tree and then across the canopy to several large halogen lights. So, the bright light that bathed the clearing wasn't entirely natural and again he wondered what the point could be. The lights were probably the same sort of thing Kazuo would have aplenty in the studio, but even so, it must have taken him ages to lug all of this through the forest. It could only be the actions of a complete madman. Again Ridge questioned his own sanity for butting heads with the guy with zero back up. He checked his watch. He'd been in the forest for an hour which meant he could still get back to the car park and recruit Nathan if he really wanted to. Assuming he didn't get totally lost. First, he had to work out what the fuck this meeting was all about. An old pal's reunion or a conference of war?

Ridge saw that he might be able to get closer to the action by circling around to the other side of the clearing and it struck him that he'd be more safely hidden by the darker shadows all the way round. The generator didn't give off much noise, but in the cold silence of the forest, even a little noise pollution meant it was that much harder to hear anything else going on. If he couldn't see properly then at least he might be able to hear more clearly if he moved further round.

He was satisfied it had been a good plan of attack so he backed up slowly and turned away from the action to make his way safely around. But instead, he walked into the point of a Japanese sword. Ridge stared into the angry eyes of a man long past the boundaries of rational behaviour and he gulped carefully, feeling the blade scratch his throat as he did so.

'That's far enough! You are a stupid man to come here. There are enough lost souls in the Sea of Trees! You are just in time to watch one overdue arrival and the merciful release of another.'

Ridge ducked and swung his head away fast. 'You think?'

What happened next he couldn't be sure of, but he felt his right leg give way for no valid reason and then something hard hit his head sideways, and he fell downwards into the enveloping blackness of the forest floor.

Chapter 24

He could only have been out for a few seconds as Ridge found himself being roughly man-handled onto his front. As he fought to avoid being suffocated in the deep mulch of leaves and moss, he wriggled against the superior bulk of the other man who had succeeded in efficiently tying his wrists together behind his back. Ridge glowered at Kazuo as he staggered clumsily to his feet at the point of the curved sword. He guessed it wouldn't have been the first time he'd held someone captive like this. Kazuo prodded him to walk into the clearing, the blade never far from his throat.

'I repeat.

You are a stupid man. Because you did not think

First, you did not think I could see you follow me.

A *gaijin*!

You did not think that I would see through your pathetic attempts at surveillance and subterfuge. A baseball cap cannot disguise a *gaijin*.

It is there in the way you stand, the way you walk, the way you hold your head.'

Kazuo brought the sword up and to the right, before sweeping back down leftwards in a fast and powerful arc towards Ridge's head. Ridge closed his eyes and waited for his imminent demise. Again, it had come to this. Risking his life all over again in a needless argument, not of his making. A wave of adrenaline-fuelled regret washed over him and images of Orla and the children streamed through his anguished brain. Visions of his family, dressed in black, the islanders shaking their heads pityingly as if they'd always known no good would come from the younger Walker lad, any more than with his wayward brother.

He felt the wind caress his face accompanied by a gentle sound like the brief *crump* a bonfire would make, just as the petrol alights. Then nothing. He opened his eyes to be faced with the maniacal gleam of his tormentor.

'I am a samurai!' he roared as lumps of spittle gathered around his mouth.

'I have *zanshin,* therefore I am trained to be vigilant, to be ready! Did you not think I would have this meeting place secured from trespassers? Your western ignorance activated a trip wire fully ten minutes ago, yet you remained unaware of it.

You have no *zanshin!*'

Ridge blinked back his emotions and tried to exercise some of that awareness. Thankful that Kazuo had no plans to kill him at that point, he began to work out what to do next. It wasn't the first time Ridge had been in this sort of situation either. The crazy guy couldn't have any idea of what he'd done in the past, and he had to use that to his advantage. He saw Tadashi out the corner of his eye. He'd moved since Ridge had last seen him and he now knelt in the middle of the clearing, on a small square tatami mat. Tadashi didn't look at him and he sat tall with his back straight and his head held proudly. Ridge glanced back a second time and to him, it seemed like Tadashi must have been drugged, as he sat so still, he appeared to be in a trance. Then he turned his attentions back to the man holding a deadly weapon in his face. Time to play poker he decided. Not that he held a particularly strong hand, but that hadn't stopped him in the past and this guy had started to piss him off.

'Very fuckin' good pal, but yer not impressing me one bit with all your mumbo jumbo crap! You can prance about all day in yer fuckin' pyjamas if that's what floats yer boat, but if you want tae cut ma heid off, fuckin' go right ahead. Knock yourself out!'

Ridge cleared his throat and spat angrily at Kazuo's feet. Kazuo stepped back for a moment at this outrageous defiance. Ridge couldn't swear to it but he thought he saw a flash of fear in the man's eyes, before he recovered his poise.

'Ha! You think I want to give you *honourable* death?

No. I have other plans for you. I will let the forest decide.'

Kazuo turned abruptly and swung the sword again, this time in the general direction of the seemingly unmoved Tadashi, who continued to stare straight ahead. Ridge saw how angry this made

Kazuo and he guessed that earlier flash of steel had been a similar gesture of frustration.

'You! Do you know this ignorant *gaijin*?'

Tadashi didn't respond.

'Perhaps he is a lover of your playboy son?' Ridge winced as Kazuo swung the sword around to within an inch of his crotch. There had to be a way to get out of this. Ridge twisted the rough twine binding his wrists and to his surprise he found it to be tied far more loosely than he'd initially thought. It wouldn't be easy to work it enough to get a hand out while this monster was watching him, but it gave him something positive to focus on while Kazuo continued with his theatrical oratory. 'Well, you shall see the manner of his death before you travel to the same destination, my old enemy.'

Ridge tensed his shoulders and pulled harder at his wrists, trying hard to switch off his mental 'pain gates' as he used to call them when running. After his brother's death, he'd discovered an unusual ability to close down any sensation of pain, almost to the point of severe and permanent detriment to his body. He became the master of his corporeal self and it had been this skill that had made him a cross-country champion.

Kazuo grabbed Ridge and pulled him roughly over to the other side of the clearing, where he pushed him up onto a fallen tree trunk about the width of a narrow path. Balancing for a moment, Ridge wondered what the hell was going on. Then he noticed what Kazuo had just picked up from a pallet of equipment that he'd not seen before. It was a long stick with a slight hook at the end, like a shepherd's crook suitable for a basketball player. Kazuo held Ridge by the shoulder and using him as leverage, he reached high up into the trees above and yanked hard downwards, almost knocking Ridge over in the process. Ridge fought hard to keep his back away from Kazuo as a long rope fell down heavily across the pair of them. He saw the rope had a small loop tied at the end. A noose!

Tadashi coughed loudly and two pairs of eyes followed the sound. 'No!' he said loudly, but with no indication of panic or any other emotion whatsoever. 'I have never seen this boy before in my life,' he bellowed, the power of his conviction belying the untruth of the statement. Ridge gazed across at the old man with admiration but couldn't decide whether this fresh information would help or hinder his survival prospects. In any case, Kazuo didn't seem to have paid much heed, and next, he placed the noose around Ridge's neck and pulled it tight, just enough that he could stand straight and keep breathing. Ridge swallowed self-consciously as Kazuo made a great show of tying the rope off around a nearby tree. He prayed that this was still just an elaborate and overly dramatic scare tactic.

Kazuo then patted him on the shoulder as if waving off a friend, or congratulating a co-worker, before he turned away and began busying himself with equipment that Ridge couldn't see. Tadashi had gone quiet and a claustrophobic silence blanketed the unreal scene. Ridge fought hard to keep his balance as he tried to pull his hands from the twine. He'd thought he'd guessed the purpose of the unstable log had been just to make it all the harder to wriggle free, giving Kazuo time to get away. But as he watched Kazuo begin to set up more lights and other studio equipment, he felt the blood pump harder in his armpits as the true horror coursed through his body. He'd been completely wrong.

Kazuo hadn't wanted to delay his release. He had designed this specifically to prolong the agony of his death. Already his legs were beginning to shake due to the fact that he couldn't put all his weight down through his heels. It had taken a few minutes for Ridge to fully comprehend the nasty plan and he forced himself to take long deep breaths to calm his breathing and avoid the dreaded cramp which would end his life.

Chapter 25

Sweat pouring from every pore, Ridge found it harder to see what Kazuo was up to. His eyes were stinging with salt and he'd been surprised by the strength of the afternoon sunlight which blinded him all the more so, because he couldn't move an inch to avoid it. The regular trembling in his left leg had become uncontrollable and longer lasting each time. He knew that when the right leg went the same way, he would slip off the log and into oblivion. He'd given up on freeing his hands as it just added to his fatigue, and his only concern became balance and breathing. He'd had his eyes closed for minutes at a time so he could focus better, and each time he re-opened them, the 'studio' would be more complete. The huge film camera seemed to be pointed at where Tadashi sat and a horrible feeling overcame Ridge. Everyone had seen those macabre videos from Syria and Iraq and Ridge now accepted deep down that this would be his fate, along with Thad's dad. He thought constantly of his family back on Sorsay and hoped that they would never see his death. But then he'd shake even more and so had to try and blank out all feeling and think only of balance and control, breathing in and breathing out.

Ridge opened his eyes as he heard a commotion in front of him. The sun had moved westwards, and he could see a little better without having to alter his posture which he'd managed to stabilise satisfactorily for a few minutes. Kazuo addressed the camera and talked about the glorious Edo era of Japan and the subsequent ignominy of their surrender in 1945. He railed against those who had betrayed the ideals of Japan and Ridge saw him swing that sword towards Tadashi once again.

Then Kazuo placed his sword back into his belt and for a moment Ridge thought that maybe that would be it. The elaborate and shocking charade had ended. There would be no atrocities here today. Then he saw Kazuo stride over to Tadashi and bow before handing him a smaller shorter curved sword that had been sitting on a silk-covered table nearby.

Ridge stared in horror as he watched Thad's dad take the sword and unsheathe it, before placing the scabbard gently by his side. Kazuo had stepped back so as not to impinge the view of the camera and so Ridge also had a direct view of the scene. The last of the sunlight caressed Tadashi's impassive face as he held the sword in his hands. Then he looked up and directly forwards, his eyes like glistening circles of obsidian. He opened his mouth and his chest expanded as he began to speak loudly and clearly as if to a crowded theatre.

'Kazuo Shimura! I have something more to tell you!

I will divulge the ultimate truth, if you spare the life of the *gaijin*!'

Ridge held his breath as he saw Kazuo scratch his head and walk around in a tight circle, clearly not expecting this development and unsure as how to proceed. He then smoothed down his hair and walked slowly over to Tadashi, partially obscuring Ridge's view. He stood directly in front of Tadashi and bent stiffly from the waist. All Ridge could make out was that Tadashi was talking quietly and then, without any further warning, he heard Kazuo roar some indecipherable word and step backwards. Tadashi continued to kneel and he held the short sword reverently in his hands, with the sharp end pointing towards him. He smiled up at Kazuo and plunged the sword into his stomach. Kazuo took another step back and shouted again. It sounded like '*Eiyah*' which wasn't unlike the instinctive word all wee boys in Scotland would yell when they hurt themselves. Not believing what he was seeing, Ridge saw Tadashi slump over for a second, then he saw with horror that he was wrestling the sword deeper into his torso. He sat up straight again and looked up once more at Kazuo who then took his longer sword and swung it up and through the beams of light and back down into the black shadows. By this time Ridge had closed his eyes.

Chapter 26

Thad rearranged his pillows for the hundredth time because when you were stuck in a prison hospital these things became amongst the most important issues in your world. He'd finally come back down to earth from the cold sweats of the morphine withdrawal. The authorities were conducting a thorough investigation as to how someone had not only messed around with his food, but also injected a near-lethal dose of morphine into his saline bag. He didn't know which to be more relieved about, the fact that he hadn't lost his mind as he'd feared, or just that he was still alive albeit in the suspended animation of this hospital bed.

His arms shook with the effort of lifting the pillows and he laughed to himself as he recalled the last hour or so where he'd challenged the Marine guarding his room to a one-arm push-up competition. The guy had been close to a decade younger than him and Thad had been feeling vaguely flirtatious in his loose hospital gown. But either he'd lost his charms, or the guy had been standard issue straight, because he'd not made any impression whatsoever. But he had tried way too hard to beat the guy and now he was paying the price. There had been a serious reason for his sudden interest in physical jerks, when the doctor had told him he'd be transferred tomorrow to the regular cells. He'd received better news too that his bail might be imminent, But what concerned Thad more than even the position of his pillows, was that crucial few days between leaving the sanctuary of this hospital room and leaving the actual prison. Somebody out there had a grudge against him and they'd proven their superiority over the local security bods only too well.

Apart from the worry of being moved into the mainstream cells, Thad had begun to feel more optimistic about his immediate future. He guessed that Ridge had been to see him while he'd been wired to the moon and he missed his little Scottish pal. He'd made up his mind that once this ridiculous charade had played out, he'd wave a fond, but final farewell, to Tokyo and enjoy a few weeks recuperating on that famous Hebridean island Ridge kept harping on about. Thad never normally watched TV unless forcibly tied to a chair, but he'd become hooked on a Highland time-slip drama called Outlander over the previous twenty-four hours. And as he scrambled for the remote control with his good hand and settled himself down for the evening, he wondered if there would be *any* gay men on Sorsay.

Thad would never forget the next few minutes and they would forever remain a nightmarish blur of rushing, panicked bodies, flashing lights and the feeling that the walls were slowly and inexorably moving inwards to crush him and him alone.

He'd not settled on anything to watch and had almost drifted off into that pleasant sleep where you might be listening to a programme, but your eyes were closed, and you'd begun to assimilate parts of the programme into your half-dreams. The door had opened with a greater rapidity than normal, strong enough to cause the suspended-ceiling panels to rise angrily in unison. Thad jumped as his guard and another civilian, probably from the Embassy, rushed into his room and even in his stupor, he could see their eyes darting between each other and everywhere but at him.

Thad reacted without thinking, 'Whoa! What the fuck guys! Where's the fire?'

The guy in the suit, his face chalk white, held out his hands as if about to address a large crowd. He opened his mouth and his eyebrows rose as if they had advance warning of what was coming next, but then he just stood there. The soldier coughed theatrically and the suit stepped forwards a foot or so closer to Thad's bed. 'So... it's just that, I'm sorry to-'. The Marine elbowed him out of the way, clearing his throat loudly as he did so.

'It's your father, sir! Mr Kamaka. He's dead, sir'

The suit piped in, suddenly re-animated, 'In a tragic accident, he-'

'The hell it was! He's been murdered, sir!'

Thad stared at the two men as they jostled for position on the hospital floor and offered their conflicting versions of his Pop's death. He had no response for them. He forgot to breathe. He couldn't find any words of his own and then, at last, he took in a huge gulp of air and hauled himself up from his pillows. He had to find out if these guys were for real, or if the morphine still had a vicious last spasm left to fuck him over one last time.

'MOVE!'

Thad roared as he swung his arm towards the men and flicked the television over to the news channels. But there it was. *Breaking news... Leading US businessman believed dead after video sent to local Tokyo news station... Content of video too graphic to broadcast footage... American Embassy has confirmed the man's identity and next of kin being informed.*

'But? Pop was in Tokyo? But why didn't he... It's a mistake right?' Thad stared imploringly at the two men but saw straightaway there had been no mistake.

'I can confirm that Mr Kamaka had been a US Air Force guest since past Tuesday, sir. That much is fact.

We have a copy of the tape, sir, at present, it is being analysed by a team from the FBI, sir. It appears genuine and it shows your father being executed by-'

'Executed?'

'Yes, I'm sorry sir, we believe so.' The Marine studied his feet.

'But-'

'By sword,' the suit interjected. 'By Japanese sword.'

Thad stared at the men and then back to the news channel where the story still flashed along the bottom of the screen in capital letters. *Leading US businessman.* His dad had been murdered. By sword? Who could have done such a thing?

The realisation hit him like a train.

Chapter 27

The yawning Marine had earlier refused a shift change, and now as the hospital quietened down and medical staff melted away into the shadows, he'd begun to question his sanity. Of course, as soon as he'd heard about Thad's dad, he'd reported in about Tadashi's unofficial visit, from first, Kazuo Shimura, and then the unsuccessful attempt made by a certain Richard Walker. He'd alerted his superiors to the fact that the civilian had been apparently known to the Kamaka family and that the timescale was congruent with the events concerning the death of Mr Kamaka. He neglected to mention the car journey to the forest and at the time his reasons for doing so had seemed the right thing to do for his long-term career prospects. He'd risked his position by volunteering the information he'd given, but under the circumstances, he knew he couldn't have kept silent. He had been mildly concerned about where the tourist had gone, but at no point did he consider him to be more than an overly enthusiastic friend with too much time on his hands.

This initial worry about the safety of the foolish Scot had been mistranslated. Knowing that Ridge Walker had been such a good friend of Thaddeus, but being unable to furnish any more than vague reasons why he was privy to this knowledge, had been galling for him and suspicious to the authorities. As the Japanese had recently exonerated

Kazuo Shimura, there had been no possibility that they would view him as a potential murderer. With the harsh glare of international media pressure pushing the police to find some quick answers, the bizarre consequence of Nathan's testimony had been that Ridge had become Public Enemy Number One, with his passport photo now being flashed up on every news channel, along with increasingly graphic clips from the forest videos. Kamaka's body would hardly have been cold before lurid accounts of his many exploits around the world had begun to emerge, and not always being portrayed with the sympathy, or respect, the Americans would have preferred.

So, for a short while at least, the hospital had become a dark but still welcome sanctuary for his troubled mind, as he'd begun to weigh up his military responsibilities against his personal feelings. He knew he'd become too fond of the wild Thaddeus to be wholly analytical about the situation. Thankfully Thad had been heavily sedated and when Nathan had last checked into the room, he'd been out cold, with no change predicted for several hours at least. So at that point, he'd thought he still had a few hours to make up his mind on which side of the fence he stood.

He had instinctively known that something wasn't right about all of this, apart from the obvious fact that a US citizen had been potentially framed for a murder, then professionally poisoned, only to find out his own father had been killed in a barbaric and public manner. But as darkness began to shroud the city, Nathan found his mood had blackened and his judgement plagued by self-doubt. Had he unwittingly become an accomplice in the murder of one of America's most stalwart twentieth-century heroes? Why, for starters, had Ridge Walker been pretending to be a lawyer in order to gain access to Thad in prison? What had been so urgent that couldn't wait for the normal diplomatic protocols to kick in? And when the Scot's face flashed onto a screen there would be a different name to the one he'd introduced himself with only a few hours ago. Why would a tourist acquaintance of Thaddeus fly to Tokyo with a fake identity, just to visit him in prison, when any sane person would have expected him to be bailed within days?

What worried Nathan the most was what he'd say to Thaddeus when he awoke. He felt sickened to his core by his increasingly firm belief that the man he'd transported to the forest had been Mr Kamaka's killer. Had Thad been taken in all this time by his conniving friend? No, from what he'd heard of their exploits it didn't seem possible that Ridge Walker could have betrayed Thaddeus in such a callous and calculating way. So that meant the man he'd helped this afternoon had been a convincing actor and a ruthless assassin. So who or what was Ridge Walker?

Then there had been his latest orders, verbal and strictly off the record. Nathan closed his eyes and replayed the telephone call.

Listen, soldier. I don't wanna know why you happened to luck onto this case so fast but hell fire this is exactly the kinda stuff you hear whispered about Mr Kamaka in the Pentagon. The man was a goddammned national hero so I want you to embed yourself fully into this investigation and do whatever you have to so that the motherfucker that killed him is brought back to the US to face the full might of American justice.

I don't need to tell you how big of a deal this is. I got ex-Chief's of Staff, Sec Dev's and holy moly I even got former Presidents balling me on this tonight. Soldier, this is the kinda stuff that can make ya or it can break ya. I'm proud of what you did today Reece and we're all counting on a quick result. You hear what I'm saying?

Those words had ignited a fire of emotion deep inside him which reminded him of a similar feeling many years ago in small town Arkansas. Nathan had been given the credit for saving the chastity of a distraught fifth-grade cheerleader, when he'd stopped a high school jock in the process of undressing her in the boy's shower block. A subsequent search of the boy's home had revealed a hidden cache of female underwear and other personal items, stolen during the series of rapes and sexual assaults he'd eventually admitted to being responsible for over several years.

Unknown to almost anyone else on the planet had been the real reason Nathan had been able to catch the filthy brute in the act. Nathan had long worshipped the beautifully proportioned quarterback and he had been balancing precariously on a rusted corrugated steel bike shed roof, in order to catch a glimpse of his naked body. Even as he sat there, bathed in the aquamarine light of the hospital emergency lighting, he could still trace a finger along the jagged line the rusted metal had torn in his thigh in his haste to rescue the sobbing girl. His reward had been the adulation of his peers and the offer of a scholarship to the University of Arkansas and a place on their Marine-Officer Midshipman programme.

He'd worked twice as hard as any other cadet to make up for his deep-seated feelings of guilt, and in the process, he'd forged himself into an outstanding young Marine Corps Officer, to become proud of his achievements and to fully believe in his right to wear the uniform irrespective of his sexual orientation.

*

So it was with great difficulty that Nathan agreed to listen one more time to the enormous black man who crouched alongside him, immaculately manicured fingers wrapped around his left knee in a vice-grip. Nathan reckoned the guy must be at least 6'4. But somehow he hadn't even seen him until he'd just appeared out of nowhere, a face made from chiselled ebony, only inches from his own. Maybe it was the weird hospital lighting, but Nathan could have sworn the guy had had some work done to that face and his huge eyes were strangely alluring. For a split second, Nathan thought his past had come back to haunt him and this was some kind of poorly timed prank, until the guy started speaking and for the second time in as many hours, someone told him to listen carefully.

'Listen up, Captain Reece.

We ain't got time for conversation here. My name is Joe, Joey Barbarossa, but hey sugar you can call me Barbarella!

What you need to know is I'm Corps through and through and we got a top team nearby to extricate young Thaddeus here. Off the radar and we-'

'But surely that-'

Joe put the end of a long finger on Nathan's top lip and those huge eyes commanded silence.

'It's too dangerous here, lover boy.'

Nathan blushed and could have kicked himself for it.

'Even with you here, we can't guarantee Thad's safety and hell, we need you too. You owe it to us to help find that crazy Scotsman after you sold his ass as a motherfuckin' killer. Truth is, we be the bad-ass killers' around here, but we be mighty worried for Ridge Walker and time is not our friend tonight.

You with us?'

Nathan nodded. All questions thrown aside.

Chapter 28

Joey uncurled like a ballerina and started walking, holding all the time to Nathan's hand and the young Marine saw that he'd been about right. The guy was tall and even more built than himself, but he had a lightness of step that made him appear to float. He turned and spoke down into Nathan's ear quietly

'Okay, Captain. Your job right now is to wake Thad and bring him to the roof. The stairs have to be along there to the left of that door, correct? Cool. Okay, stick this in Thad's chest and the motherfucker will wake up real fast, that's for goddamned sure.'

Nathan stared at the small plastic adrenaline pen. He'd seen them in training of course, but never used one. He took it gently and listened.

'Now there's gonna be a lot of noise, okay? But you been in the field right?'

Nathan shook his head.

'No problem, amigo. The noise will be like nothing you ever heard, but don't panic none. We ain't in the 9/11 business here. That ain't our bag, no way. I set charges all the way up the building, just to create a diversion and let some of the prisoners below get a few hours of precious freedom. They might be motherfucking deaf, but they'll still be free on the outside for a while! The plan is nobody else gets hurt, okay?

The quicker we get Thaddeus on the roof, the less chance we might need to pop a cap in some Jap asses. We got a chopper to rendezvous in T plus 2 minutes so don't be shy in pushing that lazy fucker up those stairs, ya feel me?'

Nathan saw the big man glance at his watch, make a quick calculation, then smile at him, his teeth gleaming manically in the dark. He felt a push and heard a voice in his ear. 'Okay, Captain. It's go time!' Suddenly Joey had vanished and Nathan turned back towards Thad's room, the blood rushing through his ears as loud as a jet leaving an aircraft carrier.

He opened the door carefully before realising the stupidity of it. He had unwrapped the Epi-pen as he'd walked and the hospital lights came on automatically as he strode to the bed, hauling back the covers on the sleeping man. Luckily Thad had been sleeping on his back and Nathan first tried slapping him on the face a couple of times, just in case it might work, rather than use the dreaded pen. But he speedily dropped that course of action when the floor shook like an earthquake and then the first thunderous blast took out the windows. Thad lay unmoved. In a panic, Nathan curled the pen in his right hand and slammed his clenched fist into Thad's chest, jumping back in horror as his big friend leapt up with eyes like saucers and his good hand gripping the pen.

'Whoa! What the fuck!' Thad whispered, his dry throat barely functioning.

Nathan shouted. 'Come on! We've got to get out of here! Joey Barbarossa sent me! He grabbed the pen and pulled it out, dreading what would happen next. But Thad seemed to go into auto-pilot at hearing that name. He grabbed his gown and followed shakily out the door, still in his bare feet. The hospital rocked several more times before Nathan found the roof stairs and he got behind Thad and pushed him upwards. Suddenly he became aware of a much louder noise from the jet helicopter above them and he saw two pairs of long black arms reaching down to grab them both. The noise was incredible! Nathan could only give a thumbs up as the men embraced Thad before scooping him up and into the chopper. Nathan scrambled after them and within a minute, they had risen away from the smoke and chaos below into the black sky.

Chapter 29

'Sir! It's Captain Nathan Reece, sir.

Yes, sir! Copy that, sir, there sure is a hell of a noise going on around here!'

Nathan glanced around and couldn't help grinning at the still dazed Thaddeus and the other men, each pair of shining eyes confirming the success of the first phase of their mission. He couldn't be sure, and he felt that quite possibly he could still be dreaming all of this, but it looked like the intense gaze from each of the two tall black strangers in the cabin had been augmented by the application of eye shadow. Their eyes burned into him with the intensity of a big cat stalking a deer and so he shook himself hard to break away and convince his station chief that this was no hoax call.

'Sir, I followed your command, sir, and I did what I had to do to bring honour to the memory of an American hero, sir. Now I need you to send up every chopper on the base, sir. I am inbound with a precious cargo and I need a diversionary smokescreen before landing. Sir!'

Nathan swallowed hard and waited for the inevitable ear-bashing and the promise of imminent arrest.

'*Holy moly* son, that was you? At the *prison*?

You got Kamaka's boy? Is he-'

'Yes sir, sorry sir! The asset was under immediate threat sir, and I have a Special Ops team at my command, requesting your immediate hospitality sir!'

Nathan looked at the men, worried that he had overstepped the mark with his last comment, but all he saw was the nods and clenched jaws of men used to making tough decisions in rapidly changing situations. He glanced over at Thaddeus and felt an impetuous flush of redemption course through his veins.

'Well hell, come on in son! We'll send up every bird we got, and light up the sky for y'all.'

The chopper sounded like it was moving at warp speed and as he examined the interior of the machine, it looked different to the usual helicopter specification he'd seen since he arrived in the Pacific. The biggest of the men saw this and he inched closer. If Joey had been strong, then this guy was a brute. He introduced himself as Patrick, holding out a spade-like hand and Nathan guessed that he must be their leader.

'Nice work Nathan! You like the chopper, huh? We made a few modifications you might say. We been shot at too many times, so this fucker is-'

Patrick was interrupted by the pilot shouting something incomprehensible and Patrick replied before turning back to him.

'That's DJ up front there. He says we gotta refuel *muy pronto* so can you take care of that, my friend? We don't need to be on the ground for too long, okay. This mission ain't over yet by a long shot and the timing is critical. You in for the long haul, amigo?'

Nathan looked at him and then over at Thad who had become very animated and had been talking fast with Joey in the corner, their hands doing much of the work in the noisy confines of their steel box. Nathan saw Thad stop for a second and although he could see friend's eyes were wet with tears, his heart lurched as Thad gave him the biggest smile he had ever seen. He nodded back and shouted his reply to Patrick. 'It would be an honour and a privilege, sir!' Patrick laughed as he went to stand up.

'Hell you don't gotta call me sir. 'Pat' will do just fine and you should hear what the rest of them call me! Now let me speak to your station CO, will you? I gotta talk some serious turkey before we land.'

Joey helped Thaddeus wriggle into some black battle fatigues before the two men edged over to Nathan and each of them gave him a friendly shoulder punch as the engines roared for landing. He didn't see anyone making plans to exit the helicopter and the noise had risen to a crescendo. Pat had thrown his phone back over to him and the others were yelling in each other's ears. A couple of minutes later, the engines grew louder still and Nathan realised they'd only been idling up until then, as the chopper rose rapidly away from the base. It would be several days later before Nathan discovered that a paint store over on the far edge of the Yokota base had been deliberately blown up shortly after their take-off. The resulting graphic images went viral on the internet and succeeded in pushing the prison images off CNN, and most of the world's media, outside of Tokyo. Most people agreed that the hundred foot 'Jackson Pollock' multicoloured paint explosion, had been a significant artistic improvement on the original grey concrete. A Facebook site in support of further such military base enhancements had been set up within hours.

The other men had donned serious looking black helmets and after a quick thumbs up from Patrick, Nathan did the same. He'd no idea what was going on now, but he overheard that Patrick had requested a schematic of downtown Ginza District and Nathan offered to help here, as he appeared to be most familiar with the city. Thaddeus had his head on his knees after having anguished telephone calls with his two sisters and Joey had been on another internal comms device which Nathan had only just noticed popping out from the neck of his black flack jacket. Without thinking, Nathan nodded towards it and then to the cockpit, as if to ask if Joey could talk to the pilot with that device. Joey gave him the wickedest grin and spoke through the helmet comms. 'Hell no! We gotta an eye in the sky, our super-fly spy guy!'

Nathan hadn't a clue what any of that meant, but Thad immediately lifted his head and pulled off his helmet, talking at full speed with Joey. Nathan saw a furious look from Patrick and he quickly brought his eyes downwards to his feet, not ever wanting to be the root cause of this man's anger. Instead, he tried to see the PDA that Patrick had held up, and through Pat, he guided the pilot to an apartment building which had been highlighted on the screen. The men nodded towards each other and Thaddeus scrambled to his feet, pulling on a black bullet-proof vest and the same black-visored helmet the others had swapped with. Nathan made to get up but felt a heavy hand on his shoulder pushing him back down. 'You stay here' Patrick mouthed at him and so he watched as the three of them expertly exited the chopper and abseiled into the darkness.

Chapter 30

After only a second or two, the chopper rose up noisily and Thad only twigged he'd not been given a firearm when he landed on the spongy rubber of the apartment roof. Joey efficiently applied a small lump of plastic C4 to a tiny doorway and they all turned away. The door seemed to come off with the minimal amount of noise, but Thad wondered if maybe they were all still deaf from the chopper. He pushed to the front, knowing that his father's killer might be at the bottom of this short flight of stairs and in the certain knowledge that he had enough rage inside him to rip the man to pieces with his bare hands. Patrick had warned him off from killing Kazuo at this point, although Thad knew there would be little comeback from the 'Diamond Dogs' on this matter. He knew they loved Tadashi as much as he did, in their own unique way.

But the mission objective here, was solely to rescue Ridge. Thad had been consumed with worry for his friend. He felt numb about his father's death and even when telling his sister's, he'd felt the whole situation to be an unreal charade. But he knew that he'd be in pieces if Ridge had been killed on his behalf, after everything they'd been through. In the past, the boys had nicknamed Ridge, 'Mr Serendipity,' because of his uncanny good luck, but Thad hadn't missed the fact that no-one had been saying anything like that on tonight's trip.

Patrick nodded and they went in, slowly and in single file. Each of the tall men had to bend almost double to squeeze through the tiny descending stairwell. The apartment was in darkness and the men switched to night-vision, scanning the main living area then motioning each other to advance. Thad guessed the place was far smaller than the team had expected. They had the rest of the apartment searched in under sixty seconds, and the men soon found the cowering girl, draped in a sheet in the corner of the only bedroom. Pulling off his helmet and goggles, Thad swept Nea up into his arms and the two of them wept. Joey switched on the lights and Thad covered her modesty, as Nea hastily dressed and the men searched for any clues as to Ridge's whereabouts.

Thad could tell that Nea had been psychologically hurt from her radically altered behaviour, and the rest of the abuse had been obvious from the extensive bruising that he alone had seen. But she didn't know about any other girls, nor had she heard of a Scottish man called Ridge Walker. Patrick signalled that he wanted Thad to press her further which he felt reluctant to do, despite his worry about Ridge. Just then Joey spoke into his comms unit and the reply he got back made him jump. He looked at them all with wild eyes. 'We gotta go, immediately!'

*

Colm shut his phone and watched the man enter the main door of the apartment. That had been a close call. Vexed as he was, it would always amaze him how important timing could be with a thing like this. From Watergate to Benghazi, it all came down to good timing or bad luck. He knew that Joey wouldn't reveal any details of his call, just as he'd been instructed. The only mission now had to be the safe return of his eedjit brother-in-law. And Colm had been around the block enough times to know that if Thaddeus, or when it came down to it, even Patrick, had got wind of the fact that Kazuo had been about to enter the building, then neither he nor anyone else would have been able to prevent them killing the man. He didn't blame them either. As far as Colm was concerned, Kazuo Shimura was a dead man walking. That had been part of his promise. A promise he would make good on because he had failed so miserably in every other respect, on this most personal of matters. But he couldn't allow any more mistakes.

It had been his own mistake that he had been unable to get to Japan in time to prevent the death of his friend and mentor Tadashi. It had also been his mistake to rely on outdated technology that could be thwarted by something as basic and primitive as a densely populated area of trees in the lee of a mountain. But then again, he'd cultivated enough contacts to have had several satellites at his disposal and he could normally get his hands on virtually any type of missile, gun or bomb. Yet he still couldn't find Ridge Walker, lost, perhaps dead or injured, somewhere in or around the sprawling city of Tokyo. Colm stared upwards, interrogating the tall buildings and tried to picture what Ridge would have done, or where he had gone. The hotel had been easy to find, but Ridge hadn't left a single clue behind. Either he'd picked up a trick or two or he was having the same run of bad luck as the rest of them. He'd hoped the boys would have found him by now, but the very fact that he hadn't been at the apartment might mean he was still alive. Colm knew his sister would never forgive him for this. She owed a debt of gratitude to Tadashi, as did all of them, but in no way would she have traded his safety for the life of her precious husband.

Again he'd made a mistake here. Perhaps his own wife Juanita had been right when she'd sent him off with the warning that he might be getting too long in the tooth for this sort of thing. He'd often promised to 'retire,' and he genuinely wanted to walk away from his shadow life. But it wasn't as simple as that. Hiding in Chile had certainly helped, but he still couldn't see himself as an old man with a pipe and rocking chair. Even coming here to Japan had been a mistake and a fruitless one too. Every time he raised his head above the parapet, every time he used up a false ID, or pressed an old contact, he risked the possibility of being betrayed or just being unlucky. Colm wouldn't admit to believing in such things, but he of all people knew that one day everybody runs out of luck.

Tadashi himself had made his share of mistakes too. Normally one of the sharpest strategic thinkers Colm had ever met, Tadashi had taken his eye off the ball with this one. In Colm's vast experience with death, whether in the 'dishing out,' or the 'saving from,' departments, he found that when things became personal they also became dangerous. Tadashi had underestimated this killer and in turn, Colm had been complacent himself because of the formidable assets that he knew Tadashi controlled. Neither of them could have predicted this outcome thus far. Kazuo may have appeared as a deranged loser with one foot entrenched in the past, but he still contrived to use a locus of operations that precluded his enemy from using modern technology. A terrain that he'd spent weeks, if not months, exploring. Yet Colm allowed that Tadashi must have felt some degree of trepidation about this case, because he'd never before approached him with a personal promise in the event of his demise.

Today hadn't been the worst day. Thaddeus had been rescued and the first part of the promise had been kept. But Colm knew this had been the easiest part of the puzzle. Tadashi hadn't been entirely straight with him, and now, far too late, he knew why. If he had told him the truth from the start, Colm wouldn't have had to take a detour via Washington DC and so Tadashi would have still been alive. And they would all be drinking beer back in some anonymous ugly base he'd built back in the time that taste forgot.

Chapter 31

Ridge couldn't believe he could still be alive. He'd actually put himself into a state of suspended animation for the second half of the longest night of his life. Still balancing on his tiptoes, he had become adept at subtly altering his position to favour one leg or the other. He found that he could now tense his calf and ankle muscles in such a way that they would lock without cramping so often. But even if they did cramp, then he forced himself to not only endure, but embrace the pain, because it meant he could support himself for longer. *A cramped leg is a stable platform,* was a mantra he'd repeat over and over again. He had found talking to himself internally to be a good way to pass the time and he made himself do ridiculous spelling or memory tests. He'd gone right through the entire Bowie back catalogue and if he got stuck with a lyric, he would forbid himself to change leg as a punishment, and so it would go on.

It would be the little things that saved him, he was positive about that. What had the British been banging on about at the last Olympics? Marginal gains. Huge improvements brought about by countless insignificant little changes, which when aggregated together produced massive results. He hadn't paid a lot of attention back then, but now he'd become sold on the idea. He'd discovered that what he termed his 'bad' shoulder, had now become his best asset. The broken shoulder blade had grown back thicker and stronger as a result of his Central American adventure. Uglier for sure, but more able to bear the weight of his frame when he tilted his head at a certain angle.

Ridge learnt a lot about the workings of his body during the night. He found that if he bent his neck in a particular way, then the rope would be less likely to press on the main artery in his neck which soon made everything go silvery, and he'd know he was about to black out completely. Not only that, but when he did this, he could allow his neck to take slightly more weight. Initially, this hurt like hell, but then like his legs, he lost most of the sensation of pain and so he could effectively hang without passing out. He soon found out he had to keep his eyes shut because he discovered that he'd strained them by trying to 'see round corners,' which had proved impossible to avoid doing when his head was continually at a skewed angle. But this had proved far trickier than he could have imagined. To begin with, every time he attempted to close his eyes for more than a second, he'd lose his balance and nearly fall off the tiny area of the log that had kept him alive for those first hairy hours, before he'd become an expert at balancing with open eyes. Soon, however, he became a balance ninja, eyes open or shut, it made no difference. It felt like he'd been equipped with an internal gyroscope, holding his body in a fixed point in time and space.

He forced himself to stay positive and he'd made a long list of the things he would always be grateful for in life, and a plan to get around to all of the things that he'd never had the time to do. He wrote letters to his wife, each of his children, and to his mother. He vowed that if he survived that night he would never, ever, wear a neck-tie again in his life.

Desperate to stay alive, he even considered asking God to help him. He'd never been one for the Jesus and Mary brigade. His family's lapsed Protestantism had often been the cause of mild dispute between Orla and himself during their early courtship, before he discovered that a great deal of his beautiful wife's allegedly strongly held beliefs were just part of a deadly charade. But her devoutly Catholic parents were genuinely unhappy about the relationship, to begin with, and he'd had to work all of his charms to smooth over his complete lack of belief in a divine being other than David Bowie.

His life had been turned inside out since those idealistic days, and when he thought back over the last few years, he'd survived some ridiculously dangerous situations. Ridge shivered and not just because of the pervasive cold. Could someone up there have been looking after him after all? Maybe God was like an ever-patient parent who would always love his children despite their petulant outbursts and mocking defiance? He stood balancing precariously still and allowed the idea of an all-seeing divine being to see deep into his soul. And for a second or two, he imagined an invigorating breath of wind diffusing through his body like an early morning sea-breeze back on the island. He could have sworn he felt a renewed energy wash over him.

Then the little things started to align themselves in his favour. As the sunlight became warmer across his face he decided that given enough time, he would free his hands. The bindings had felt so much looser and because he'd lost all sensation of pain, he was convinced he would soon be free. He'd considered carefully about what he would do if he managed to get his hands out. He had imagined what most people would do and he'd previewed his own swift strangulation at this critical juncture. The most important thing had to be maintaining his balance. So he made himself promise that if he managed to free his hands he would do nothing for a full sixty seconds.

The forest had also taken pity on him. The temperature had dropped considerably during the night, but he hadn't frozen to death. It had been cold and damp, but this had helped him rather than hindered him. The rope that he hung from had definitely stretched during the night. Maybe it was due to the increased moisture in the air, but he knew he'd gained a few millimetres and that had made an incredible difference to his legs and ankles. It hadn't taken him long to work out that this moisture situation might not remain his friend once the sunlight became stronger. And more than anything, he knew despite all his pious positivity, he wouldn't be strong enough to survive a second night on the rope.

During the first few hours, Ridge had replayed every natural history programme, every adventure film and survival show he'd ever seen, in an attempt to extricate himself from the rope. It had seemed impossible initially. Then he'd hit on one possible way out, but he would have to wait until the next day. His wet hands had become looser and looser, but eventually fatigue got the better of him. So he concentrated instead, on perfecting his position, and unbelievably, he fell into a few hours of half-sleep, what he would later refer to as 'relaxed vigilance.'

But now the sun had moved above him and the warmth seemed to refresh his energy levels. He twisted and turned his hands, as he'd done for hours that night and almost immediately a hand became free. Forcing himself to stay calm, he pulled the rope off his other hand but didn't allow the thin rope to fall to the floor, as he would have done a week ago. It might be useful. Marginal Gains. Oddly enough, perhaps a rope might save his life. His heart started beating faster and immediately he felt dizzy and guessed his neck position must have altered. There was no way to prevent it. His arms had fallen loose behind his back and they were slowly rotating around to the front of his body into a more natural position. His shoulders had become so locked that he could no more influence the direction his arms were moving in, than he could control the inexorable movement of the sun. He tried to lift his hands but they wouldn't rise above a few inches, and in doing this he inadvertently allowed them to travel further around to the front. He still couldn't see them, but they didn't feel wet anymore, but instead seemed to be encrusted with mud or other forest debris. He wondered if he'd been crapped on by birds during the night and his tongue flicked out over his cracked lips in anticipation. He'd have eaten anything right then.

After a while, he'd been able to maintain his position while allowing his arms to come right around. Slowly he managed to lift them, inch by inch, up to his face. That's when he first appreciated how badly cut his wrists had become. The wetness he'd been feeling had been his own blood and he wondered how much he'd lost. Immediately he tried to work out if less blood gave him an advantage. Less weight, lower blood pressure, greater chance of fainting, more likely to cramp in other parts of his body. Assuming he could maintain his balance, it would be his arms now that would save him. He toyed with the idea of reaching up above his head and grasping the rope and simply pulling himself up and out of the noose. It was one of those ideas that might sound plausible when you read it in a book, but he knew he couldn't do it here, in the forest, for a thousand reasons.

The sun had become bakingly hot and despite the humidity, Ridge had stopped sweating completely. He analysed this new fact. Not an advantage he decided, and probably a portent of imminent doom, like the precursor to a heart attack. But it might be sunny enough for his desperate plan to work. It had been during the night when he'd been cursing the binoculars around his neck. While the strap had been protecting his neck a little from rope chafing, the weight of the binoculars had increased dramatically as the night progressed, and he'd dreamt about reaching down with his tongue and untying the strap, allowing them to fall to the ground. It was when he pictured the expensive lenses shattering on a rock, that his idea came to him. He had that stupid pair of reading glasses in his shirt pocket and he knew exactly what to do with them. Never would $5 have been better spent.

His right hand moved easier and so he slowly worked it up to his breast pocket and allowed it to hang there for a few minutes, like an impromptu sling. He couldn't believe just how wonderful an alteration in position could feel. Then he grabbed the plastic glasses and carefully brought them up to his mouth, allowing his arm to fall back and recover.

Next, he used his other hand to take the glasses and snap each leg off against his body, slowly and methodically, before inserting the body back into his mouth for another rest. This time he used his right hand to take the glasses, and by wrapping a bloodstained hand around the right-hand lens, he pushed the left lens into his chest, putting increasing pressure on the plastic bridge. He wanted the bridge to bend, but not break, and he had not the faintest idea how best to do this. But it was working! After ten minutes or so, he had the frame bent to ninety degrees. He held the plastic up to his face and allowed the light to pass through one lens. Still not enough. He swapped hands and tried again, feeling the plastic give slowly once again. Utterly exhausted by this point, he hooked the lenses back into his pocket and took a few minutes rest. His breathing had become erratic and he could feel his position had altered so he took some time to rearrange himself before the next phase of the operation.

He couldn't look properly at the forest floor underneath him, but only a few feet ahead. The clearing had become far drier than the majority of the shaded woods and this had given him hope that his plan might work. He would only get one shot at this, and if it didn't work he would probably be dead within a few hours. Despite the precarious position he was in, Ridge found it difficult to complete this final step. He had nothing to lose, yet he still had hope. If this failed, he would lose everything. Just then he felt the first warm caress of sunlight run down his back. The sun wouldn't be on him for much longer and he took this as an omen.

He fished out the bent lenses and dropped them in front of where he dangled. He waited patiently, knowing it could take a few hours. Back home on Sorsay, they had installed a fancy wood-burning stove and he remembered how difficult it could be to try and burn damp or unseasoned wood. To the inexperienced eye, it was impossible to tell the difference, until you spent a fruitless evening trying to coax life from a damp smouldering fire in a still cold, but unbearably smoke-filled room.

Chapter 32

He had gone into shutdown mode again, the efforts of freeing his hands and then manipulating the reading glasses, all the while maintaining his balance, having been too much. But the temptation had been there now. His hands had hung freely in front of him like bored teenagers with Mum and Dad out of town for the weekend. He couldn't stop himself, and for a couple of seconds or so, it was worth it. But then like almost all guilty pleasures, the instant gratification, the feeling of release, was swiftly replaced by anguished desolation. He didn't think it through like all the other stuff during the night. The combination of warm sunshine licentiously licking his face and the frustration of his failed fire-raising overpowered any remaining logic and so he was left godforsaken and doomed.

His arms had felt limber enough for him to get one hand above his head and to grasp the rope, just enough that when he pulled downwards, he could force the fingers of his right hand between his neck and the constricting rope. Then he let his right hand take all of his weight for the few seconds he needed to get his left hand in beside it and around the bottom of the noose.

For a brief merciful second or two, Ridge was able to haul hard on the rope and lift his neck off the rope entirely. So now he was hanging from his hands and he could move his head a minute distance from side to side inside the loop. Any fanciful idea about pulling his head out of the noose disappeared quicker than a New Year's resolution. He couldn't see it, but he knew the noose was far too tight for that. That would have been seconds before he understood his fatal mistake. His head now sat at a different angle and almost straight up and down, with his throat being compressed even further by his now-trapped knuckles. His elbows burned and he knew he couldn't have taken a hand back out of the noose for a million dollars. He closed his eyes and the world became a technicolour honeycomb, and this time he knew he was dying. His feet had begun to hurt more because his balance had been irrevocably lost and he felt waves of heat pulsing up his body. He couldn't fight it any longer and so he lifted his feet off his life-raft of a log and waited for the end to come. After everything he'd been through it had come to this, he would drown here in the Sea of Trees.

He'd been too busy thinking he was about to die, to notice the fact that his feet had felt suddenly cooler, but then warmer than ever. His nose didn't alert him either, blocked as it was with snot and dirt. It was his one functioning ear that told him to try and hold on a minute longer. Had he just heard a comforting voice? The crackling of the fire below him made him open his eyes and then he saw the smoke and the flames. The flames which threatened to consume him even before he suffocated to death!

Ridge pulled his body up as best he could, feeling like a worm on the end of a hook. Luckily the invisible forest wind had been blowing away from him, as the dry undergrowth had taken fast and the forest was becoming ablaze. He knew he had only seconds left before his legs fell back down and his feet would burn, just as surely as the rope burned his neck. He could hear voices too and he guessed his life must be over soon. The voices sounded angry and alien, and he twigged there was no chance he'd be going to heaven, despite his last-ditch conversion during the night. It would be the dark and diabolic realm of a different being for him. But the voices were getting louder all the time and they were shouting in Japanese! The next thing he felt was the burning leaves and moss singe his back, as he hit the ground with a thump. He floundered for a moment, thinking of the fires of hell, before angry voices pulled him to his feet. He squinted his eyes open to see a group of policemen, or soldiers, frantically trying to put out the flames and one man just staring at him as if he had, in fact, just stepped out of the mouth of hell. Then it all went dark.

The splash of water brought him round and when the soldier offered him his canteen, he grabbed it in his shaking hands and drank the entire contents. The cool water seemed to ignite fresh agonies and he winced as his injuries lined up for their first roll call. The forest felt colder all of a sudden as he sat amongst the smoke and he shivered violently. He felt queasy when he saw how bad his wrists were, and that he'd also be requiring a change of trousers pretty damn quick. But then hr felt his mouth stretch into a painful smile as a Japanese man swung a foil emergency survival blanket over his shoulders, his eyes unable to hide his astonishment at this half dead Westerner. Ridge thought this feeling must be how survivors of any tragedy must feel, pulled from the wreckage of a train wreck or a collapsed building. The only survivor of a plane crash, forced to live with that guilt for the rest of their lives. He still couldn't believe he'd made it. Had the crackle of flames been a miracle? It was only then that the images of Tadashi's death flooded into his head and he looked over to where a circle of men stood, their heads bowed and voices muted. Ridge leant forwards and added a fresh reason to change his trousers.

Chapter 33

The forest freaked them all out, Thad could tell. They'd dropped from the chopper only twenty minutes ago but already it seemed like hours. Maintaining radio silence in this place was like saying to an astronaut to remember and not take your helmet off. It was instinctive. But Patrick wasn't taking any more chances. Thad hadn't ever seen him this mad, and he'd known him most of his life. He knew how disciplined they all were. Despite the nail varnish, make-up and feather boas they were the best insertion, assassination, or extraction team on the planet and they never made mistakes. Sure they got injured and things rarely went to plan, but they were consummate professionals and these gigs were what they lived for. The Diamond Dogs worked together, trained together and partied together. They weren't encumbered by wives or children. They had no weaknesses apart from the odd over-priced off the shoulder sequinned dress or the latest fragmentation grenade.

Thad shivered, despite his bullet-proof vest. He still didn't feel 100% fit but there was no way anyone could stop him coming here to find his friend. Nathan had joined the team too, much against Colm's wishes, but again it had been non-negotiable. He was allowed partly to keep the Yanks on-side after their assistance the night before, but also because Thad had been adamant. Patrick had wanted to rip Nathan's head off a couple of hours ago, and probably would have if Thad hadn't been quick on his feet and quicker with his persuasion. He reminded Pat that Nathan hadn't slept for two days and there had been a lot of excitement during that time.

It had only been a few hours earlier that morning, that Nathan had remembered Ridge's phone, which had been left in the SUV. So the team now knew Ridge had been headed into the Aokigahara Forest. Nathan had been ashen-faced in the chopper. Thad had tried to make him feel better, saying that if they'd gone looking for Ridge last night then they wouldn't have been able to rescue either him, or Nea, and the two of them could be dead by now. The unsaid implication here, of course, was that they all presumed Ridge to be dead by now, and that this had turned into a body retrieval exercise rather than a rescue. And although the official word was still that they should capture, rather than kill Kazuo, Thaddeus guessed this would be yet another botched communication.

Colm too had messed up badly, and that had been another reason he'd allowed Nathan some grace. Thad had been told by a barely audible Colm, that his dad had patched satellite coordinates through to one of Colm's many secret cell phones telling him exactly where he would be meeting Kazuo. But Colm had been airborne at that point and the communication had got lost in the ether, only to ping his phone out of the blue just a few hours ago. It hadn't made any sense, until Nathan's revelation just after that. The team had been furious and barely a word had been spoken since they took off.

Thad turned to the left and right. Maintain visual contact at all times. This was no kinda place to go astray on your own. They'd not expected to be walking for this long, even allowing for the slow-going terrain. The smoke had alerted them before they'd arrived at the coordinates, and they were all experienced enough to know that something as unusual as this could not be co-incidental. So the chopper had ascended and then set them down slightly north of the location, so as not to have any smoke drifting towards them which might impair their vision. Thad stared up into the forest canopy. Not that the smoke would have much chance getting through this dense wood. But then he sniffed and he could smell it. He touched his broken hand to his nose, the filthy plaster cast still bright in the gloom. The others stopped and dropped. They must be close now.

He discovered that the others were slightly behind him to both sides, as if he was the lead aircraft in a fly past. Maybe his had been an easier terrain to cover but still, he should slow down to maintain formation. He looked ahead but couldn't see far. He guessed that they were probably the only living souls left in this dark and desolate place. Then he saw a flash of light! Or was it a reflection from something moving? Too big to be a bird, and there hadn't been much sign of wildlife so far, too depressing even for foxes. He strode forwards. There! He saw it again. Definitely a human, but what was it? He saw a brief flicker of light, then smoke. A man smoking? He pushed forward still, forgetting about his position. Could it be Ridge? The man vanished behind another damn tree trunk and then he got a half-second glimpse before he disappeared once again. Thad found himself breaking out into a run as he became convinced it was his friend. The muted crack of the rifle stopped him, just as the bullet ripped past his head and then another tore into his bad arm. Thad spun around in alarm, trying to find the faces of his comrades and he fell backwards as the comms crackled back into life.

'Man down. Contacts ahead two hundred feet and closing.'

Joey had been closest and his voice had remained calm, almost a whisper. Then Thad heard Patrick.

'Thad you okay to stay put? Repeat. You okay to stay put?'

Thad grunted in annoyance, more than pain, the bullet having gone right through his upper arm and he'd pressed his hand tight over the wound.

'Good. Okay, team. Stay down and do not engage. Repeat. Do not engage.

The bad news is we got serious company ahead. These guys are the highly trained 'Special Unit,' not your average-Joe cops.

Good news is they have a casualty, or a suspect, but seeing as the dude is puffing on a Marlboro, then I guess we is in luck for a change.

Hold on. Well hello! If it isn't Mister Serendipity himself. Holy shit, he's alive!'

Chapter 34

Ridge had been grateful for the cigarette, but what he really wanted was to get the fuck out of this depressing forest. There were six 'rescuers,' but Ridge got the feeling they weren't particularly interested in him. They'd spent the last ten minutes taking photographs of the scene and despite not being an expert scene of crime officer, he didn't think these photos were going to end up in any official files. He couldn't bear to go anywhere near the focus of most of their excitement and he had steeled himself for one of them to lift up Tadashi's dead body to pose for a selfie. It wouldn't take much for him to drop his guts again, if there was anything left.

When one of the men starting screaming at the others, then fired off a couple of shots, Ridge's first thought was that the guy had lost it. 'Don't blame you pal,' he muttered. 'This place'll drive you fucking bonkers.' He saw only trees and more trees. But out of sheer boredom and to satisfy his earlier painful frustration of not being able to use them while hanging around suffocating to death, he wiped the vomit off his binoculars and swung them up to his eyes. He had to shut the left one, which still hadn't straightened out yet, and so he peered one-eyed into the surrounding darkness. *Wow*, he thought, *these really are good, just a shame there's fuck all to see.*' He had just about exhausted his appetite for trees when a man appeared. A big olive-skinned man with his arm in a blood-stained plaster cast. Thaddeus! The little Japanese soldier seemed equally excited about this and brought up his rifle to fire off another volley, and so Ridge kicked the back of his legs and he fell forwards.

'That's my pal, you fucking twat!

Don't shoot!

Friends of mine! *Americans*!'

The soldiers had all picked up their weapons and Ridge could see Thad getting shot very easily here, so he moved as fast as he was able and danced in front of them, waving his foil blanket like some demented Christmas turkey making a last bid for freedom. The soldiers consulted as to whether they could shoot the suicide guy, as well as the insane guy charging towards them with one arm hanging off.

Ridge felt his foil sheet being torn out of his hands. And before he had time to react, a vortex of still smoking embers and ash spun around his face blinding him, and he heard the familiar sound of a helicopter shattering the silence of the forest.

As one of the men swung his gun upwards to fire off a silent round, Ridge saw him being barrelled into by a large black shape and the man tumbled into the darkness. Suddenly the soldiers were surrounded by men in black uniforms, all pointing assault rifles at their heads. Thaddeus shouted in make-do Japanese that they were not a threat to the men, and they were simply searching for one of their team who'd been missing. The apparent leader became extremely agitated and that was when Patrick punched him in the face, knocking him out cold. Three seconds later his team members followed suit, and so they quickly had a tidy heap of small soldiers amidst the hellish racket of the chopper and the whooping of Thaddeus and Joey.

They raced up the rope ladder with Ridge on Nathan's shoulders and Thaddeus being hauled up by Patrick, who immediately slid back down. 'Throw me a bag,' he called up to DJ on the comms. DJ gave Joey a nod and Joey knew what kind of bag he meant. He guessed who it might be for. He gestured to Ridge and shouted in his ear. 'We got bad news down there?' Ridge nodded and his face said it all. Joey disappeared out the helicopter to assist his chief.

Ridge knew he had seconds to tell his big friend. He pulled him into a big hug and tried to break it as gently as he could. He never wanted to see that look on Thaddeus's face again as long as he lived. They hugged for a moment longer, then it was all hands on deck as they carefully helped lift the body of Thad's dad into the cabin and gently laid him on the chopper floor. Ridge and Patrick shared a knowing look, and Ridge shook his head in answer to the unspoken question. He hadn't had the heart to tell Thad that his father had been decapitated.

Chapter 35

'Yes love, I promise.

No, it'll be fine, I'll book the tickets later, when I find a better connection. Yes just Thaddeus and me. No, I don't know where Colm is. Still in Chile for all I know.

No, let me, just in case. Yes, *today*. I'll get on it!

We'll both need to go to DC too, for the, you know. Will you tell mum for me? Great.'

Ridge hung up and breathed a sigh of relief. Partly so he could rest his still aching arms, but more so because he'd got through the call to Orla without either breaking down, or giving the game away about how close she'd been to attending a different funeral, a lot closer to home. He could have bought a flight ticket home easily enough, but Thad had suggested he hang back for a day or two so that he would have some moral support while he sorted out the paperwork concerning his dad. But also so that his neck would have a chance to calm down. The base medics at Yokota had given him some cream, but basically told him that he'd be badly scarred for life around the neck and on both wrists. So now Ridge waited to see how swiftly he could cultivate a beard.

He'd hoped to keep the sordid details safe from his wife, not because she was weak but because he didn't want her to be any more upset.

He'd be the first to admit Orla was stronger than him, but he didn't see the point of increasing the hurt caused by that little shit Kazuo. The Americans had made a huge fuss over the whole incident and demanded assurances, that this time, Kazuo would be arrested once they could find him. Bizarrely, both Ridge and Thaddeus were officially still wanted by the authorities, but Nathan had secured them safe passage within the base until Kazuo had been detained which they expected to be imminent.

The previous night had been difficult for all of them. Nea had left Tokyo within hours of Ridge's return, saying that she would never return to Japan. They could all see she'd been severely traumatised and needed the safety and security of her family. Ridge could have done with seeing more of his 'adopted family,' but the Dogs had only hung about for a few hours, as they knew they were attracting all the wrong kinds of attention and the base could only deny any knowledge about the 'top-secret' operation for so long. Ridge had the strongest feeling that they were expecting Colm to show up, and he had been secretly disappointed not to have seen him. It had been a bittersweet time for all of them, with their joy at Thaddeus and Ridge being safe, tempered with their collective sadness at the passing of one of their own, the lynchpin of their unofficial band of adventurers. Ridge hadn't really been able to talk to the guys for years, because the last time they'd plucked him from the jaws of death in a helicopter they'd also had to scarper pretty quick. So as was so often the case with friendships like those, they condensed a lot into a short space of time.

Ridge entertained the boys with stories and photographs of his wee children and they all agreed they'd rather go back to Afghanistan than have to deal with a baby in nappies. Ridge was shocked to see DJ had been piloting the chopper with his leg in plaster, from a recent misadventure. They all talked about their affection for Tadashi, 'the man who can,' and what plans they had for the future. As always Pat, Joey and DJ were vague about everything personal and evasive about the rest. Ridge told them about his cottage renovation plans and how much they'd love a restful week on his remote island home. They promised to do their 'Lady Marmalade' burlesque show one day, or DJ suggested maybe they would do an alternative Wizard of Oz. 'We'd call it somethin' like, 'there ain't no home like this motherfuckin' place,' whaddaya think Ridge?' Ridge said that would be just lovely, but could they please perform it in Gaelic.

Things were awkward enough and Ridge didn't want to rock the boat any more than he had, but he needed some answers and he'd vowed to himself that night in the forest that if he survived the rope, then he wouldn't ever shy away from challenges, difficulties, or opportunities ever again.

'So Patrick, you hear from Colm lately? I kinda thought he'd be showing up?'

Ridge would have had to have his eyes shut all over again not to have seen the tension between the three 'Dogs.' Each of them glanced at the other, as if to say, 'you first,' and he saw that Thaddeus had noticed too.

'Yeah, Ridge.' Patrick shuffled his feet like a big schoolboy when questioned by his teacher.

'I feel ya, bro. He was here in spirit, man, you hear what I'm saying?

He played his part, he played his part...'

Ridge knew something was going on that neither he nor Thad were privy to and with his resolve suddenly dissipating like the air from a punctured bike tyre, he decided to leave it like that. Sometimes it was better not knowing. He got the feeling that they all wanted to draw a line under this sorry affair and with Thaddeus grieving for his father, he felt it would be too painful for him to push it further. But that didn't mean he would drop it, not until he found the truth.

So he and Thaddeus waved the Dogs off in their helicopter and Ridge swore he could hear DJ singing *Somewhere Over The Rainbow* before the noise of the huge rotors drowned out everything else.

Then Nathan had turned up with a bottle of Jack Daniels as a peace offering, and so the three of them started with that then moved to Nathan's room where they drank some more and toasted the honour of Tadashi until they fell asleep in a heap on the floor.

*

Late the following morning, he'd just stumbled back to Nathan's quarters after calling Orla and grabbing a huge bottle of mineral water, remembering to knock loudly on the door, just in case. His stomach didn't feel strong enough for *that*. They were all availing themselves of the water when his door was banged even more loudly than Ridge's theatrical effort. Do they think we're *all* shagging, Ridge couldn't help thinking. He forgot that Nathan held a fairly high rank and so they all composed themselves before the aide was allowed in.

Morning Captain, sir!' The man saluted stiffly.

'Sir, the CO requests that Mr Kamaka's son calls the Embassy immediately, sir.

There's been another development. It's across all the networks again, sir!'

Ridge found the Embassy number on his phone and threw it over to Thad, while Nathan switched on the small television. He felt sick as they waited the two seconds for the TV to switch on. Had there been another girl found? Nathan flicked the remote and there it was! The top story once again. Breaking News! They all moved closer to the screen and listened carefully. Thad was now on to the

Embassy and the other two flitted between the incredible scenes on the TV and Thad's face, like they were watching a bizarre game of table tennis.

There was a man who they didn't recognize at first. Ridge saw who he was after a minute or so. Kazuo Shimura! The video quality was far poorer than with the horrible death of Tadashi, but even so, Ridge could see he was a broken man. Had he been beaten also? Ridge fervently hoped so. The man spoke Japanese and the film hadn't been subtitled for overseas viewers as yet, but bizarrely, the man also had several story boards in his hands, Bob Dylan style. The boards were all in Japanese script, but Nathan translated the bare bones of what Kazuo and the news guy appeared to be saying.

Kazuo had confessed to at least three murders, kidnapping and rape, and various other charges which Nathan couldn't translate fast enough. At the same time, Thaddeus relayed his call with the Embassy and it seemed he had been eliminated from their investigations and was a free man, as was Ridge. Tears ran down his face and Ridge reached over and squeezed his shoulder as they continued to watch the bizarre spectacle. Kazuo talked about honour and death and he said it was his time to pay for his crimes. He used a word that Nathan hadn't heard before, and they had to look it up in a Japanese dictionary. *The word was piper.* He had to pay the piper! Tears now came to Ridge and he felt goose bumps all over his body as Nathan repeated that phrase. He knew what that meant. He gave Thad a look and he hoped it hadn't been lost on him either.

Ridge stared in shock as Kazuo then said he would walk into the forest just as his own father had done and find his peace. They both leant in to watch him place the cards on the ground, then walk slowly and deliberately into the dark woods.

Thad handed back the cell phone and sat staring at the TV screen. Then he put his fist right through it.

'Liar!

How do we know he's going to kill himself?

He could be on a slow boat to China right now!'

Then he broke down in tears. Ridge saw that he probably needed to do this as he'd not really had a chance to let go and maybe now, with Kazuo dead, there could be what the Yanks called closure. Ridge left him nursing a bleeding hand and pretended to drag Nathan away for a bandage. 'Let's get some air eh?'

Ridge gave Nathan a potted history of their dealings with a shadowy character who appeared to be able to weave in and out of their lives with the same ease as he crossed borders, located villains and survived the deadliest of situations.

'And you know who this person is? Nathan gasped.

'Sort of...' Ridge replied, feeling slightly foolish about it all. Funny how it wasn't until you'd tried to explain something to a stranger, that you would begin to make sense of it yourself. Wasn't that a common thing with teachers? At times he'd been positive about who he'd thought was responsible for the legendary stories attributed to 'The Piper,' or 'The Phantom' as he'd also been called. But now here in Tokyo, he wasn't so sure anymore. Could 'The Piper' be one of the Diamond Dogs? Or had it been Tadashi all along? That made a lot more sense. But now Tadashi had been killed, so what did this latest development mean? Could there be a copycat? Or was it some kind of final homage? Who or what had encouraged Kazuo to take the honourable way out and lose himself in the Sea of Trees, just as his father had done before him? His head had begun to spin and Ridge thought he had the perfect antidote.

'Right then, Captain Reece.

We need a triangular bandage for one sore hand and another bottle from Mr Daniels for three sore heads!'

Chapter 36

It had been Orla in the end, who'd cut off Thad's plaster cast. She'd said it was a health hazard for the children and every time it got wet in the sea it had just become even filthier. The weather had been glorious for the three days they'd been back on Sorsay and Ridge wondered why he would ever want to leave again. He loved the place. They'd been outside the whole time, partly because it had been so beautiful and the cottage so very small, once you installed a Thad into it, but also to help keep some distance between himself and Orla. She had spotted his neck within five seconds of their arrival at the airport, and by the time they landed on the island, Orla had wheedled the entire saga out of Thad. Ridge had often told Thad that Orla had been trained by British secret services and now he knew it to be true.

So they climbed the only hill on the island and gazed down in wonder, as enormous waves crashed below in an eternal battle to topple the mighty stack of black rock known locally as McPhail's Anvil. Thad had looked sceptically at his friend, as Ridge pointed out the Witches Cave, three-quarters of the way up the treacherous cliff, where he and Orla had once lit a fire to warm their naked bodies.

Ridge had taken Thad kayaking and together they'd picked wild mussels off the rocks. Then he would watch his big friend racing through the surf, his mane of black hair, wet and bedraggled, like a demented spaniel and him just as happy as one too. It had been the best idea to bring Thad to the island. They didn't talk about Tokyo for a long time, each of them reluctant to re-open still sore wounds. This visit had been long overdue and Ridge knew it couldn't last more than a few more days and so it wouldn't be long before Thad climbed back onto his battle-horse and they'd only see each other every few years.

*

It had been obvious that leaving Tokyo had been difficult for Thad. Even at the airport he'd said to Ridge that he felt like he had betrayed his father, because they hadn't got a body to prove that Kazuo had actually died. It had taken all Ridge's powers of persuasion to stop Thad hiring a private militia and combing the forest inch by inch.

'Listen to yourself, amigo! You're going to end up as mad as that wee bastard, Kazuo, if you don't stop thinking like that! Let me tell you, when you go into that black wood to die, then you die. Period. You don't fucking well stroll back out of it, happy as fuck, a couple of days later. There's no happy ending for that place. They should cordon off the entire forest and not let *anyone* inside. If it was me, I'd burn the whole fucking place to the ground.

Christ knows how many fucking lives have been destroyed by those trees.'

Thad had listened quietly then he muttered, 'but you came back, my little friend. And of that I am grateful. Now let's get the hell out of Tokyo!'

On the plane, they'd both slept most of the journey, but Ridge had taken advantage of Thad's deep slumber to try and find out what had happened to Colm. He still had the throw-away cell phone which he'd left with Nathan and so he left a couple of messages and a handful of texts, each one angrier than the last. He knew Colm had been instrumental in planning the logistics of the Dogs' extraction mission. Those guys were normally impossible to get hold of and always busy in some god-forsaken hole, so to have brought them to Tokyo at short notice would have been no easy task, particularly with one of them sporting a broken leg.

But if he'd expected Colm to furnish him with some warm and fluffy sentiments about the bad guy getting what he deserved and the posse returning victorious, then he had been grossly mistaken. Colm had refused to return his calls and his abrupt texts avoided any mention of his part in the mission. And if anything, he seemed madder than ever when Ridge had prodded him about the likelihood of Kazuo escaping justice. In fact, Ridge had never received texts with the words, *leave well alone* and *forget it*, used so many times.

*

So that's just what he did. For the sake of his big friend, more than anything else, Ridge somehow managed to excise that painful visit to Japan from his mind. And for those first three days, it was almost like he had found his long-lost brother again. But that didn't mean the two of them floated around the island in a bubble of unexpurgated bliss. He knew Thad hadn't forgotten for a second what they'd just been through. But Ridge had other demons to vanquish. For some reason, he felt the death of his own father more acutely in those few days, than at any time before. He still hadn't worked through his feelings about the epiphany he'd experienced in the forest. He couldn't shake the feeling that it had been his dad's voice he'd heard, right at the end when he'd thought he was going to die. He'd looked at his own two children and projected forwards a couple of decades, imagining a world more dangerous than the one he'd run off to, feeling for the first time the pain and worry his quiet and sensible father must have felt after Gavin's death and then from his own wild behaviour.

They'd been swimming. It had been Thad's idea initially, before he found out how cold the fresh Atlantic water could be on Sorsay so early in the season. Ridge had gone along with it, seeing it more as a test of each other's manhood than a pleasurable vacation activity. The wind had picked up and the two men were shrieking like fisher-women as they chased each other through the ice-cold breakers. Ridge had never seen a man of ethnic diversity turn from honey brown to a morbid grey-blue before, and they had laughed like fools before sprinting back up the beach for the sanctuary of dry towels.

It was then that the bullet wounds, mixed with a myriad of assorted scars, became more obvious across Thad's shivering body. Ridge stared at Thad's fresh injuries and then he inspected his own ravaged shoulder, and his ugly, and oddly misshapen elbow. It hit him like a physical punch to the guts. He grabbed his friend in a bear hug, their towels falling to the sand and held him tight.

'Hey man! What's up? Can't it wait till' we get a room, dude!'

Thad laughed but Ridge could make out the concern in his voice and he let him go reluctantly, suddenly fired up with the seriousness of what he wanted to say.

'Christ Thad! Look at the state of us!

You look like you've fallen down from The Anvil over there!

We've got to stop doing this crazy shit before one of these bullet holes ends up in a more serious part of our anatomy.'

Thad pretended to look shocked while putting his hands over his genitals and pouting.

'I'm serious Thad! Listen, I've got a family to think about.

I hate to think what I put my old folks through over the last few years.

What if-'

Thad had stopped grinning. 'Shit! What the hell difference does it make now, amigo?

And you is lookin' at a motherfuckin' orphan here, anyways!'

Ridge stood and stared as Thaddeus grabbed his towel and stormed off down the beach, away from the cottage. He shouted half-heartedly, but the wind was against him. He could have kicked himself. *Fuck*, he cursed. He'd killed the vibe stone dead.

Chapter 37

Thad didn't stay away for long thankfully, but Orla had suggested they get the fire pit going. And so that night they cooked some gorgeous smoked fish and forced down some of Ridge's home-made bramble wine. A few of the younger locals joined them once it got dark, and Ridge suspected they'd been put up to it, not that anyone on Sorsay needed any excuses to have a convivial drink in good company. One of the lads had a pal from the mainland who'd brought an accordion with him, and before long they all had bright and shiny faces with even Thaddeus having a hilarious attempt at singing a sea shanty. The bramble wine tasted better with each new bottle, and by the time the last few embers were smoking in the increasingly cold light of dawn, they'd polished off the entire batch. *Job done*, Orla had whispered with quiet satisfaction, as Ridge crawled in beside her and fell into a stupor.

One of the grand schemes hatched during their impromptu party, was that Thad would go over to the mainland the next day and get himself fitted out for a kilt. After a great deal of alcohol-fuelled discussion, it was agreed that Thaddeus would adopt the Walker tartan, seeing as he was without one of his own. Ridge promised him that even the most thorough genealogy website would be unlikely to throw up a Highland sept connected to the name Kamaka. Thad arranged to meet the two lads with the accordion for the late morning boat, and so Ridge thought he should accompany him for the craic.

But the next day, the craic didn't feel so great, with little Isla bouncing on his queasy stomach and baby Alex bawling in his ear, as Orla changed his malodorous nappy. 'Never again.' He growled more to himself than anyone.

'Sure, is that you swearing off the evil drink? Again...?'

'No love, just the home-made variety.' Ridge groaned and handed back their eldest child.

Orla laughed. 'You'll get no argument from me on that score.

I was after using it for weed killer, so I was, so you spared me that wee job!

Still, at least you cheered up Thaddeus and we'll all be looking forward to seeing him in the kilt at long last!'

Thad was sitting at the big kitchen table with his head in his hands when Ridge came down. Ridge put his serious looking face down to the ill-effects of the bramble wine, until he began to speak.

'Buddy, I know you don't want to talk about it but I'm kinda pissed that your brother-in-law didn't show up over in Japan. I mean weren't he and my dad like part of a team? There's so much about Pop that I didn't know about and we had such a short time to get re-acquainted after all those wasted years.

Don't get me wrong, amigo! I sure do appreciate everything you, Colm and Orla did in bringing us back together. I guess that I would've felt a helluva lot worse if we all hadn't teamed up like that over in that Mexican shit-hole, and I really do cherish these last few years. We've had us some adventures haven't we?'

Ridge slammed the kettle down unintentionally.

'I'm sorry Thad. I really am. But I think you're *always* going to feel that you would have like to have spent more time, or had longer conversations, and asked more questions, when a parent dies. I knew my dad all my life. But even so, there's a ton of stuff that's come to mind even in this short a time.

But you can't turn back the clock, Thad.

You want a fry up?'

Thad stared sideways at the heap of sausages and bacon and shook his head.

'Honestly Thad. You don't know what you're missing!'

Thad grunted. 'Go ahead then, kill me a little more. What I am really missing is some answers, Ridge. An' I ain't giving up 'til I find me some.'

'I get that, pal, but I doubt that Colm will be able to shed any more light-'

'Don't lie to me, man!'

Thad slammed a massive hand down on the table and upstairs they heard baby Alex start to cry.

Ridge stood still with the heavy frying pan in his hand and briefly considered using it as a weapon. They both listened as all went quiet again and Ridge glared across at his big friend.

'Listen! Okay, I know what you mean. I've wondered about Colm and your dad and the guys too! A hundred times! But what's the point? Where will it get you?'

'It'll get me the truth. That's all I want. Truth and justice for my...'

Ridge heard the words fade away and he turned from the huge stove to see tears pouring down the big guy's face, unsure what to say to make him feel better. He decided just to be honest no matter how it sounded.

'I don't know that Colm deals in truth or justice, to be fair. A least, not the sort of justice that someone like me can properly understand. When he killed Zakia like that, I saw something in him that I never want to see again. It was like that time when we found out about Ed's wife. The look on his face scared the fuck out of me.

I don't think he's a normal human being, Thad. I think he's killed a lot of people, not just in the odd fire-fight like we both have, but in other ways. I'm not even sure what I mean, but to be honest, I don't want to know any more than that. His sister, my beautiful wife, only just escaped from that murky world with her life and there's no way I ever want to jeopardise my family again. Never. Do you understand me?'

'He's a soldier, Ridge. We need people like him, people who can give and take orders no matter how fucked up they might appear at the time.

Neither of us would be sitting here if it wasn't for him, right?'

Ridge swallowed. He rattled the pan in annoyance. Thaddeus was right. Colm had saved his life, more than twice. Suddenly he felt petty and selfish. He spun around, making a decision as he did so. Knowing instantly that he was being crazy, but at the same time sensing it to be the right thing, not the easy, but the right and just thing to do.

'Okay! Okay! What do you want me to do?'

Thad smiled for the first time that morning. 'Throw a coupla' more eggs in that skillet and then get me the go-codes for Colm. I'll contact him today when we're over on the mainland and Orla don't need to know a goddamn thing. You feel me?'

Chapter 38

Orla waved them off.

'Sure an' I want plenty photos, lads! Every new kilt, I want the pictures, okay?'

Ridge promised to faithfully record each and every 'outfit' for future blackmail purposes and he was glad to get away before his guilty feelings got the better of him and he told his wife they were going to be contacting her brother. He'd felt very clandestine, clutching one of his small rucksacks carefully concealing his iPad, telling Orla it was for transporting any tourist crap that Thaddeus would inevitably be purchasing, plus something special for that night's evening meal.

The two lads had turned up for the little ferry looking as right as rain and so losing Ridge a ten pound wager. The five-minute journey was a riotous recollection of the previous night with the ferryman's eyebrows set to permanent astonishment at the spectacle of the huge dark-skinned Yankee who had joked about finding himself a best quality new 'skirt.'

On the torturous car journey north to the nearest decent sized town, Ridge tried to dissuade his big friend from any thoughts of returning to Japan and instead regaled him with tales of Highland glory and treachery involving the local clans. Thaddeus was disappointed to learn that there wouldn't be a huge choice of Walker tartans, as most of them were not considered authentic and even the name wasn't one of the most respected names with 'walker' probably have come up from the north of England, where it was a term associated with cloth production. But Thad hadn't left his feelings of frustration and anger back on the island, and he vowed to scour the town until he found the tartan he wanted.

They spent the entire day shopping for a kilt and mostly inside a beautiful old building overlooking the harbour. It turned out there was only one suitable shop and it had sat there in a prominent position as long as Ridge could remember. The oak-panelled walls were disfigured by the obligatory stuffed stag heads and mounted antlers, but to Thad it was heaven. Of course, the staff quickly succumbed to his charms and before too long, he was surrounded by a constant huddle of assistants vying to be the one to tighten his kilt or rearrange his sporran. This meant Ridge could sit at the enormous old walnut-framed windows and set up the tablet to grind through the interminable protocols for contacting Colm. He made sure to snap the odd photo to keep up appearances and the sight of it all was genuinely hilarious, but at the same time, he found it difficult to switch between the two worlds. He also had a long family connection with this town and as Thad was becoming increasingly more camp with every passing minute, he didn't want to give anyone the impression he was Thad's lover.

Three times during the day, they took refuge in the peaceful sanctuary of a deserted coffee shop where they could talk without fear of being disturbed. By late afternoon, Ridge was becoming concerned.

'That's more than four hours, Thad. Even allowing for the time differences, he should have responded by now, shouldn't he? We're going to have to get the ferry soon and if we don't get through to him in the next few minutes, then we'll just have to come clean to Orla and keep the message sequence running when we get back.'

'Hell, I don't know, man. He could be out horse-riding or whatever the fuck they do afternoons over in South America! Why don't we mosey on back and see if my new best friends have finalised my order, then we'll man up and tell that amazing 'lassie' of yours what we've been up to?'

'Fine.' Ridge muttered, feeling glad to be heading back to the island and relieved not to have to deceive Orla any longer.

He hardly spoke all the way home. He had nipped away from the kilt shop to grab some red wine and a feast of Scottish fare for that night, when he'd bumped into an old school pal who he'd not seen for years. The guy was dressed in a funeral suit and when Ridge asked out of politeness who had died, he had been shocked to hear it was one of their classmates. 'Don the Prawn,' they called him, as he'd inherited the same old prawn boat his father had fished all his life. Dead at 32 from some undiagnosed congenital heart problem with zero warning.

Gripping the steering wheel an hour later, the white of his knuckles pushing up through his tanned skin, Ridge tried to reason with himself. Only grunting an occasional reply to an unheeding Thaddeus who was still higher than the sun after his successful kilt buying experience, he had to concentrate hard to prevent his right foot from flooring the accelerator. His brain raced faster still with the never considered possibility that something might actually have happened to Colm. For years now, Colm had been their protector, their shield of armour. Whether they approved of his methods or not, he had always been there for them when the chips were down. Until Japan.

But didn't he lead a perilous existence? Hadn't he been through horrible experiences, both mental and physical? Surely that would have a detrimental effect on your health? He wasn't a whole lot older than Ridge, but he must be pushing forty surely? The danger age.

The old car lurched faster over a blind summit as another chilling realisation hit him. Of course! It didn't need to be a dodgy ticker for Colm to be in trouble. From what Ridge had gleaned about his shadowy brother-in-law, there could be half the

Western world looking to settle a grudge with Colm. Why had Ridge just spent the last few months turning his tranquil wee cottage into a virtual bunker? So if he and Orla had felt justified in doing all of that, what the fuck must go through Colm's head when it hits the pillow each night? He felt a wave of shame wash over him as he thought perhaps he'd been acting very selfishly since baby Alex had been born. Living in their safe island bubble, he'd hardly given Colm, or even Thaddeus, a second thought until two weeks ago. True, he had been fulfilling his duties as a protective father and a good husband, he got that. But had he been a good friend?

Ridge glanced over at Thaddeus, who hadn't stopped gibbering about the history of his tartan and all of that nonsense since they left the town. The kilt shop hadn't been able to give him his kilt to take away there and then, much to his dismay. But they'd buttered him up no end with their lavish praise of his 'unusually strong and manly frame,' requiring a specialist tailoring service. Then there was the 'discerning choice' of the tartan he'd eventually gone with, being so rare and unexpected that they would have to commission it directly from the weaver himself. Ridge had been almost unable to contain himself on hearing the babble of nonsense he'd had to listen to, but he had to give them credit for a supremely efficient financial fleecing of his big friend. The staff even gifted Thad a fine looking set of whisky glasses engraved with the crest of his adopted clan. Ridge didn't have the heart to tell Thad that they used to sell stuff like that in the wee tourist 'gift shop' on Sorsay every summer, where there would always be a full-time job for one of the wee school kids, who'd sit pulling off the 'Made In China' stickers from the bottom of the plastic pipers and replace them with 'Made In Scotland.'

The pier was only a minute away and Ridge pulled over at the top of the hill, where you could just see the faint sparkle of lights on Sorsay towards the horizon. He frantically replayed the conversations of the last few hours, before the Dogs' left Japan, trying to dissect their words and the looks on their faces. Had something terrible happened to Colm and they had elected to keep it hidden? Did they decide that the death of Tadashi constituted enough pain for the time being?

Ridge looked Thad in the eye and he saw his big friend's mouth slowly wind down and then set in a grim line. 'What's up, dude? You look like you seen a ghost.'

'Thad. I want you to tell me the truth always, okay?

No matter how tough it might be and I promise to be the same with you.'

'Sure thing bro'. It ain't your fault you got a tiny pecker.'

'I'm serious, Thad. Do you think Colm's still alive?'

Chapter 39

Despite the slow but welcome lengthening of the days, night still devoured light with an unrelenting hunger and the biting wind that whipped off the sea seemed determined to make the most of it that evening.

Ridge had just checked the cooking and was setting the table back in the kitchen after they'd decided it was just too cold to eat outside. He'd read a bedtime story to young Isla, and baby Alex was fast asleep. Thad meantime, was still out on the patio wrapped in an expensive tartan scarf, explaining to a bemused Orla that if he'd had his new kilt on then he'd be as warm as a bug in a rug.

'It's all about the quality, girl.

When I git ma' Highland mojo outfit, I ain't ever gonna feel cold again, not even in this god-forsaken ice kingdom!'

'You think?' Orla leant up against the newly sanded larch door frame, her hands cradling a mug of coffee, having eschewed the dubious delights of the Laphroaig ten-year-old malt which her husband had picked up along with the traditional haggis and turnips for the celebration dinner. Ridge knew she'd suspected something was up and his own forced jollity hadn't fooled her for a second. They'd just had a long hug in the kitchen and he'd savoured the heat from her body, allowing it to flow through him, melting away for those precious seconds all his fears and doubts.

'Hell yeah!' Thad shouted into the house.

'Ridge, my man! Go git your old kilt so I can show Orla here exactly what I'm talking about! Come on girl, I'm freezing my whatsits out here. Let me show you that sample plaid I got, thick enough to stop a 9mm round, for sure.'

So they drank whisky and Thad ate traditional haggis, 'neeps and tatties,' for the first time, his red eyes bulging in horror at Ridge's description of the ingredients of the main dish. All the usual haggis jokes were wheeled out and despite the fact that Burn's Night was several months past, they even fished out a book of Robert Burns poetry and Ridge did a passable 'Address To The Haggis.' After the meal, Ridge showed Thad his own kilt, given to him by his father on his eighteenth birthday. The mood became more sombre at that stage and the two of them felt for Thad when he felt how much stronger was the weft and overall quality of the old hand-me-down kilt, compared to the modern sample swatch he'd been given.

'But listen, Thad. If your kilt had been made like this old thing, we would never be allowed to bring it over to DC next week, would we? It wouldn't pass the weight restriction. It's bad enough you bought the full hunting outfit, a sporran, shoes, socks and even that ridiculous hat! Who do you think you are, Samuel L Jackson?'

'Hey! He's the man, ain't he?

Can't believe they wouldn't let me have one of those knives, what do you call-'

'It's a sgian-dubh, Thad, and they always sell the plastic ones these days, but I'll get you a real one for your birthday, alright?'

Orla put a tray of coffees on the table and gave Ridge a pointed look.

'So boys? Why don't we have a nice sobering coffee, cut the bullshit and then you tell me what you were *really* up to this afternoon?'

Ridge slumped in his chair and lifted his hands weakly in a half-hearted defence.

'We were just trying to get hold of your-'

'Colm. You think? *No shit.* So what's he been up to now then?'

Ridge and Thad exchanged mournful glances.

'Well, that's just it, love. We haven't a clue where he is and he's not come back to us using the agreed protocols. I just checked a wee while ago after putting Isla to bed. Still nothing.'

Orla's eyes gleamed with that intense fiery green that usually meant she was about to get angry or passionate. In this case, Ridge suspected it might be a combination. But she had the look of a woman who thought she was on to something.

'So, have you eedjit's thought about phoning him?'

Ridge stared back at her.

'What? Calling him? He doesn't have a home phone like normal people, love,' he said.

Orla snorted in annoyance. 'Jeezo, Ridge. I bleedin' know that!

What about that wee cheap thing I found in your things from the trip? Is that not to do with him? Or is there something or maybe *someone* else you've forgotten to tell me?'

Ridge gulped and grabbed Thad's shoulder. He couldn't believe how he could have forgotten it. That stupid wee phone that had caused so much trouble already. He jumped up from the table and planted a huge kiss on Orla's forehead. 'You're a star, my love!'

Thad picked up his whisky glass and toasted the girl in front of him.

'To you, Orla! Beauty and brains, what a hell of a package!'

Orla was still blushing by the time Ridge bounded back into the kitchen and while he waited for it to come to life, Orla pulled out the iPad too. Normally a throwaway cell phone wouldn't have a snowball's chance in hell at getting reception out on an island like Sorsay, but Ridge had spent a small fortune on the unusual modifications to the cottage, including a powerful radio mast built surreptitiously into the chimney. The result was the only 4G reception in a fifty miles radius.

They checked the relevant Facebook groups, but apart from the fake auto-posts, nothing had been posted from Colm. Ridge looked at the two eager faces staring back at him and pressed the call button. They all knew how important this call might be. It rang and rang. At least it seemed to be working. But no answer. No answering service either. He put the phone onto speaker and tried again. Still nothing. Thad suggested texting just in case Colm could pick up texts but not phone calls. Ridge texted five words.

Where are you? Please call!

They waited a few minutes, none of them saying a word. Not one of them expressing the doubt and fear in their heart. Orla broke the torpor they were all falling into, by getting up and putting the kettle on again. She brought the whisky back to the table and Ridge saw she'd a glass for herself this time. He was her only brother after all. Ridge waited until the kettle had stopped singing and then he called a third time but by this point he'd given up any hope. They listened to the tinny speaker as one by one they each silently poured milk into their coffee. Then Colm answered.

'What?'

The three of them jumped to their feet, with Ridge's coffee mug spilling across the table. He grabbed the little phone, turning up the volume to max.

'Colm? Is that you?'

'Obviously.'

'Are you okay... where are you?

Thad's here, we've been trying to get you, you know on-'

'I'm fine, so I am, just not at home. You shouldn't-'

'We're sorry Colm, we're all just worried... after Tokyo, we-'

'Stop! That's enough so it is.

Listen, I'll pop over tomorrow, alright, keep an eye out will ye?'

'Tomorrow!' Ridge felt his voice go up several octaves and he saw Orla beaming as she made a grab for the phone. But the line had gone dead.

'Call him back!' she shrieked.

Thad reached over and took the phone gently from a stunned Ridge and slid it into his pocket. He glared at the two of them, not sharing in their excitement. 'I think he'd be real pissed if we did that, don't you think?' But nothing could contain Orla's delight as she bounced around the kitchen like an escaped firework.

'Tomorrow! Jeezo!

He must be awful close-by then?

Are we after spoiling his surprise d'ye think?

Ridge honey, where'll we put him? Isla'll have to come in with us so she will, or maybe we could put her up to her granny's, what do you think?

Tomorrow!'

Ridge could see there would be no point in trying to calm Orla down and he loved seeing her so happy. And if he was being honest, he would have been feeling pretty good about the news too, if it hadn't been for the dark cloud he'd seen cross Thad's face.

Chapter 40

Ridge rubbed his tired eyes. He doubted if Orla had slept more than an hour all night but he couldn't be annoyed at her. She had been singing happily from downstairs since before seven and despite his weariness, he sat up and gave a small thank you to the gods for making him listen to her advice about not removing the stopper from the Laphroaig as he'd wanted to. Thad had retired early, complaining about being poisoned with animal offal and bad coffee. But Ridge knew it had been something else troubling his guts and he somehow felt that he might be the root cause of it. It struck him during the night that there might be a little friction between the two men and he hoped there wouldn't be any awkward confrontation later.

He successfully persuaded Orla to take the children over to his mum for a few hours, just so as to give them all time to chat about what had happened in Japan and he promised they could do all the family stuff after that. They'd no idea when Colm would arrive and his normal style would have been to pitch up in the black of night, but that boat had sailed.

Then he filled Thad up with bacon rolls and dragged him out into the unsympathetic and windswept rain of a typical Scottish spring morning. His only intention had been to defuse any potential tension and to keep Thad's spirits high until the grand arrival. They still had arrangements to finalize for their trip to Washington DC and Orla had begged Ridge to talk Thad into staying on the island for the intervening period, so they could all travel over together. Ridge liked the idea but he knew Thad wasn't the kind of man to be corralled into doing anything he didn't want to.

'Hell, I ain't gonna cause trouble, amigo.

I just wanna know *exactly* how come the dude couldn't show up in Japan for my Pop, but he's miraculously available for a family reunion at the drop of a motherfuckin' hat.

You *do* hear where I'm coming from, right?'

They were walking slowly along a small stretch of steeply sloping slate beach at the bottom of the garden. In a few weeks time, the smooth stones would be baking in the sun by this time of the morning, sparkling silver with their winking eyes of 'fool's gold,' and the Walker family would all be sitting warming themselves despite the customary sea breeze. But today the slick black slates presented challenges and the two men had to watch carefully as they picked their way over the slippy terrain. Keeping his footing had been only part of the reason that Ridge's only reply had been a feeble nod down to his own feet. He found it difficult to argue with Thad's thinking. Why *was* Colm now so conveniently close by?

After a hundred yards they admitted defeat and turned back towards the cottage and just at that point Ridge felt his cell phone vibrate inside his rain jacket, giving him that split-second feeling as it always did, that he was going into cardiac arrest. Fumbling with his wet hands, he spoke without thinking, unwittingly giving away the fact that he was happy at the thought of seeing his brother-in-law again. 'That'll be Colm then!'

Thad had begun trudging faster up towards the cottage when Ridge instinctively grabbed his arm, even before the unexpected voice crackled in his ear. It was wee Seamus, the ferryman, a former school pal and the only person on the island to whom Ridge had told just the smallest details of their past troubles to. That was why the man had gone to the effort of calling on his cell phone, rather than just leaving a landline answering machine message. He was the only other person who had known that Ridge could even receive such calls on Sorsay.

'Hey Ricky, what's fresh? Listen, pal, I think I might've fucked up a wee bit, just the now. Orla's brother got here a couple of minutes ago and he'll be walking along the road to you the now, but then just after, this other rib comes steaming intae the pier, massive outboard on it, bigger even than the beast of a machine that dropped Orla's brother off.'

This time Ridge thumped Thaddeus and the two men stopped in their tracks.

'Go on...' Ridge tried to keep his voice flat and he scanned the area, not knowing what to look for.

'So these four guys, three of them dressed like they're off tae an 'Echo and the Bunnymen' gig, and the thing is, they seemed tae know yer man there. One of the guys, the one who was driving the boat, Irish lad like, friendly enough, asked me where about he'd been headed. Said they'd all been supposed to huv' arrived at the same time, and Orla's brother, what did he call-'

'Colm.'

'Aye, Colm, that's it. The guy said 'that daft bastard Colm' had promised to wait for them like, to help carry the drink and that and then they'd all arrive the 'gether like, for a surprise. So I didn't think at the time, and I told them where you are and that with the tide right in the now, they could beach the rib in front of the cottage nae problem and so they're heading round there the now. Did I say the wrong-'

'Fuck!' Ridge cut the call. He looked out to sea, but the entire island had been enveloped in a heavy blanket of grey mist and drizzle. The sound hit him first and despite it being so loud, he initially glanced upwards thinking it had been a helicopter such was the disorientating effect of the sea fog. A tiny voice inside of him said it had to be the 'Dog's' come back to save them once more. But instead he saw Thad's arm pointing seawards and he screamed too late as a black monster of a rib powered out of the murk and thundered onto the slate beach.

'Thad! RUN!'

The two of them ran as fast as they could, but before they reached halfway to the cottage, the sky had filled with the angry roar of gunfire. Any earlier doubts Ridge might have held as to the reason for the intrusion scattered as a shotgun blast smashed through his beautiful new chimney cowl and sent the pair of them scrambling up the beach like demented crabs. Thad had automatically gone into Marine mode and Ridge followed his zigzag pattern up the machair and across the road. Cursing that he'd not bought more established beech shrubs for his wee hedge, he vaulted it and sprinted up the garden and in through the door.

'Lock it Thad!' he screamed, as he hauled a heavy Indian blanket up from what had appeared to be a traditional slate floor. But underneath was a large metal case and Ridge stabbed at the electronic keypad before pulling up the hatch and reaching inside. He stared out the little front window but couldn't see the men, as his hand frantically groped for weapons. Thad locked the door and joined him by the window. He'd hardly said a word beyond his usual stock of expletives and Ridge forgot he'd not had the time to tell him about all the 'home improvements' they'd had done to the cottage. His big eyes grew even wider when Ridge lifted out a Heckler and Koch semi-automatic assault rifle, followed by a couple of magazines. Despite the danger they were in, he smiled and gave Ridge a reassuring shoulder punch. 'Holy fuck! We is gonna kick some ass!'

'There's plenty more where that came from.' Ridge spoke without taking his eyes off the window. All he could see still was grey mist.

'The windows are all bulletproof, Thad, and the walls are three feet thick so there's no fucking way they will get through that.

But I'm more worried about Colm, who's walking right into a fucking trap. It's obviously him they're after, so the fact that we're safely cooped up in here doesn't bother them one fuck... they'll kill Colm and fuck off back to wherever the fuck they came from and we'll all be none the wiser... and they'll probably not even bother with-'

'I wouldn't be too sure about that, amigo.' Thad slammed a magazine into his weapon and gestured towards the window. Ridge stared in abject horror as the black shapes of men in full-length greatcoats materialised out of the mist like the four horsemen of the apocalypse. The men walked slowly up on to the machair which formed a slightly raised strip of rough grass between the beach and the road. They stood in a line directly facing the cottage, less than a hundred yards away.

Ridge knew he'd been going into panic mode just then, but now it had all become clearer. He knew what he had to do.

'Jeezo Thad. They think Colm's in here, don't they?

They won't have any idea how long he'd take on foot and with all the mist, they wouldn't have seen us too well.'

Thad had read his mind.

'I know it.

We're gonna have to take these dudes on. Or else Colm's walkin' dead, an' I ain't finished with him yet either, not by a long shot.

These windows open, amigo? We got ourselves some motherfuckin' zombies to kill.'

The men stood motionless and despite his predicament, Ridge had to agree with the ferryman, in that they did look as if they'd stepped out of an 80's album cover, the sea mist wrapping around their legs in a credible facsimile of dry ice. They obviously weren't anticipating any likelihood of armed confrontation and he saw the guy in the middle look up at the sky for a moment.

Thad spoke quietly this time. 'What the fuck is they waiting for? Some kinda goddamn boy-band convention?'

But it was obvious to Ridge. 'They're looking to see if the mist is going to lift. See? Look the wind is clearing it there. I'm guessing we've got about sixty seconds.'

Just then a cold hand gripped his heart as he imagined what would happen if Orla just happened to stroll into this stand-off. He ducked under the window and reached back into the underground safe. To the left-hand side was what they called 'the button.' It opened up a secure communication channel which connected the cottage to Ridge's parent's house, even if the normal phone line was cut, or even if there was no broadband. Feeling sick at the thought of what it would do at the other end, he hit it hard. Orla's voice came over the safe's built-in loudspeaker. Ridge took a deep breath. *Thank God she'd been in.*

'Please tell me you boys are just messin' around over there. Has me brother got there yet and so you're-'

'No he's not here.' Ridge lied.

'But something's cropped up Orla and I'm deadly serious.

Do not leave Mum's until I call you back. Promise me?'

There was a split second of silence and Ridge knew the turmoil his wife would be going through during that time.

'But-'

'No buts, Orla.

Just like we said. *You and the kids*, remember?

Stay where you are. Call Seamus and tell him to keep the fuck away too.

I'll call you back.'

Ridge hit the button again, hating himself for doing so.

Thad was still trying to open the windows. He stopped and growled.

'Ridge, the motherfuckin' boy band's on the move. We gotta find a way to-'

'Here, see?' He showed Thad how to pop a little button on each side of the 'wooden' frame along the bottom of the window. When both were pressed simultaneously, the strip of composite material flipped back revealing a long thin strip of open window like a horizontal arrow slit. The space allowed them to see out and to shoot, but not even the skinniest wee mite would be able to gain access to the building. Ridge did the same on the left-hand window and took up position.

The four men now stood on the road, with nothing separating them from the cottage but a pathetic strip of young beech shrubs and a few metres of garden. But Ridge knew that had the hedge been more established, the attackers would have had the added advantage of still being invisible. Thad muttered. 'And so it begins, amigo.'

Ridge thanked the gods for the hundredth time that he had a friend like Thad. They watched in amazement as the men swung open their ridiculous black coats in unison, three of them revealing a double-barrelled sawn-off shotgun which they slowly brought up to shoulder height. The fourth guy had some kind of machine-pistol, smaller calibre, but likely to be more accurate. He stood directly in front of Ridge and it seemed obvious that he must be the leader. Ridge whispered, 'the guy on the left is mine.'

If Thad replied then his words were lost in the barrage of noise that engulfed the cottage. Volley after volley strafed the front of the cottage, rattling the front door and ricocheting off the windows. It took the men a few more seconds to realise that there might be something wrong with the picture. It was at that moment that Ridge fired. He hadn't been practising as much as they'd planned to do, but he'd chosen a high-velocity rifle from the stash of guns and he still caught the guy just below his head, possibly in the neck. Two shots. The man dropped to his knees and as the other three turned in complete shock and confusion, Thad fired off a burst of semi-automatic fire and the man on the far right spun round in that spasmodic break-dance of death that Ridge had seen too often.

Then everything seemed to happen at once. The remaining two men dropped to ground and scrabbled for any available cover of which there was very little, one going behind the bike shed on the left and the other sheltered behind the heavy wooden gate. The bike-shed guy pumped a couple of rounds into Orla's old car as he ran, and Ridge felt, then heard, the explosions as the car ignited. That's when he noticed a spray of fresh red blood in an arc across the window and he turned panicked to see Thad tearing a dishcloth in two, and attempting to tie it around his arm. 'I'm okay man! Just keep shooting. Sons of bitches got my sore arm too!'

Ridge turned back to see thick black smoke drifting past him, making it almost impossible to work out where the two guys were. Then he saw a black shadow appear out of the midst of the smoke and he'd just twisted his body around to fire off a shot, when he saw it was the unmistakable silhouette of his brother-in-law. Colm was pressed up hard against the cottage side of the bike shed and the guy was the opposite side. Ridge could see that Colm had a small side-arm, probably his beloved Browning 9mm. It was unlikely that the two intruders had seen Colm, but equally Ridge couldn't see how Colm would be able to make any headway with his bike-shed counterpart. Meanwhile, Thad had begun peppering the wooden gate with automatic fire and it wouldn't be long before the gate would be reduced to kindling, forcing the guy to make a tough decision.

Colm gave them a thumbs-up and Thad took this as a sign to intensify his attack. Just then a small ball flew up from behind the bike-shed and before Ridge worked out what he had seen, it hit the ground just in front of the cottage and exploded. Ridge felt the glass window flex inward slightly, like a slender plant swaying in the breeze, but other than that the grenade had caused no damage. Colm must have seen it coming as he'd turned away with his hands over his ears.

Ridge heard shouting between the two Irishmen and then each of them lobbed a grenade, one of them exploding on the roof and sending tiles smashing down onto the slate patio. He glanced up in horror, knowing the cowl had been blown off and that they would be defenceless against a grenade coming down the chimney. His mind raced with questions. The wood-burning stove was built from cast-iron, right? Would that make it strong enough to contain the blast force from a grenade? Thad had stopped firing and Ridge glanced over to see him still struggling to stem the blood flow. It was only then that Ridge spotted Thad had sustained an additional wound to his left hand. It looked messy and painful, but Ridge knew from experience that if Thad needed assistance he would ask for it. Thad was left-handed and if he couldn't shoot with his right hand then Ridge would have to take his weapon before the intruders guessed they had a window of opportunity which would leave Colm exposed.

Ridge peered through the smoke. The gate-guy had composed himself enough to start firing the occasional strategic shot, much as Ridge had been doing, but with far less effect. If the guy had known where Colm stood then it might be a wholly different outcome. Ridge wracked his brains to work out what to do next. They had reached a stalemate, with any move now being far too risky for any party to contemplate. They probably guessed Thad had been hurt, so if they had any field experience they would know to make their all-out strike sooner than later. They'd know the authorities were a long way away from Sorsay, but at the same time, it wouldn't be long before someone came along to see what all the noise and smoke was about. How long had the men been out there? Ridge had no idea how long they'd been under attack.

Ridge watched Colm edging towards the corner of the shed farthest from the guy behind the gate. It seemed as if he was planning the near-suicidal move of going around the shed. Surely he must have known that Thad couldn't give covering fire. It was crazy. Ridge knew he'd have to do something to distract the gate-guy. Thad had slumped over and Ridge guessed he'd been more injured than he'd let on. There wasn't a doctor for miles and if this situation didn't get resolved *muy pronto* his big friend was going to bleed to death on the floor of his cottage. He wasn't about to let that happen.

Grabbing the machine gun, Ridge sprayed the front garden, just narrowly missing his brother-in-law and then jumped up to the front door making an extra loud show of snapping open the deadbolts. Through the tiny porthole in the door, he could see Colm glaring at him as if he'd lost his senses. Then Ridge thought he saw a flicker of understanding cross his face. Ridge saw him edge further to the corner of the shed and so he made to open the door, feeling the shotgun blasts pound the steel plate. He slammed it shut and dived back to his window.

Colm had vanished and then he saw the gate-guy make a run for the far side of the cottage where the hedge had been first planted and so offering a little more protection. Ridge knew if the guy managed to make his way along it safely then he'd be at the cottage. Ridge had no idea if the back door had been locked or not. There was no time to check. All he could think of was his blood-drenched friend collapsed next to him and his out-numbered brother-in-law about to walk into a hail of gunfire. He had no choice. He pulled opened the door and charged out screaming his head off and wildly firing Thad's gun as he ran. The gate-guy crouched behind a raised bed and Ridge found himself in the open and unprotected. Colm came rushing around from the front of the shed and then all three men stood frozen for a second as a blinding flash of red light exploded all around them.

Unable to see or even think, Ridge dropped to the ground as above his head, the air exploded into a maelstrom of noise and gunfire. He'd no idea where it was coming from and he covered his head as he felt the air buzzing angrily above him as high-velocity rounds tore past.

He cautiously lifted his head to see the gate-guy spread-eagled close by, his legs and arms twisted in the unnatural pose of violent death. Further down the garden he saw Colm getting back to his feet and running his hand through his unruly hair. He'd turned to face the black outline of a man and a woman stepping gingerly out of a small aluminium Voe boat, which must have been driven out of the sea at one hell of a lick, as it now sat half-way across the road. Ridge shook his head and smiled broadly. He knew it was Orla, even before he saw her strap the sub-machine gun across her back and rush to hug her brother.

Chapter 41

'So you're owing me a new car now, is that it?'

Orla beamed at the pair of them as they all hugged each other. Colm laughed quietly.

'Sure that old thing, Sis? I'm after thinking he was doing you a favour!'

Ridge took Orla's face in his hands and kissed her long and hard. 'You've got to stop making a habit of this rescue thing you know. It's getting emasculating.' Then he remembered Thaddeus. 'Fuck.' Orla saw his face and knew instantly.

'It's Thaddeus. He's been shot at least twice.'

Ridge shouted over to an ashen-faced Seamus.

'Seamus, can you get hold of a car and bring Doc Hamilton over as soon as possible? Don't breathe a fucking word about *any* of this okay. He hurt himself in a boating accident, right? Don't worry! I'll sort it out when he gets here, I promise.

And we're going to need your help dumping these bodies at sea, so a wee bit of old chain might be a good idea too. Before you ask, no you can't have the rib, we'll need to torch that. But I don't see why you can't have that beast of an outboard for your troubles. Four hundred horses should more than make up for knocking a few bashes out the Voe boat, eh?'

Orla and Colm had run up to the house and Ridge dashed after them. Colm had patched up many a wounded soldier in his day and once they got Thad sitting up they were relieved to see he hadn't any life threatening injuries, assuming he didn't go into shock. A bullet had ricocheted into his left arm causing a lot of blood loss, but little tissue damage. Colm had pulled it out with tweezers after Orla had administered a judicious measure of the Laphroaig. The whisky was more for his hand injury which was very nasty looking. His left thumb hung on by no more than a few sinews. To make matters worse, Thad had groaned that they'd managed to hit the exact same bit of his hand as his karate injury a few weeks earlier. Orla had wrapped his hand in a tea-towel packed with ice. They all knew how sore it must have been because he hardly said a word. 'Oh Thaddeus, I never should have sawed that plaster off of you. You would've been fine if I'd left it.'

'Fuck that shit,' Thad spat through clenched teeth. 'I'd be dead if you hadn't girl, so don't you go getting upset about old Uncle Thaddeus. Ouch man! What the fuck?'

Colm tightened the bandage on Thad's arm with a theatrical flourish. 'There. Now Ridge go an' find this man a clean T-shirt quick as you can And Thad, don't let the doc take it back off you, like whatever okay?' He rubbed Thad's head for a moment. 'I'm really sorry about this, Thad. About a lot of things, to be honest.' He turned to Ridge, his game-face back on.

'Ridge how long do we have before the doctor arrives? I'm after thinking we'll dump the bodies in the bike shed until it's dark. Can you clean up some of the cartridge shells and wash some of that blood away. A bit of blood is understandable, but it's looking like a fucking abattoir in here. Orla love, can you play a hose over the car out there and sure we can pretend it was a drunken barbeque or something?'

Chapter 42

The next few hours were an exhausting pantomime of cleaning and hiding, and putting on a charade of holiday high spirits that had taken an accidental turn for the worst. They'd told the doctor that Thad had tripped up at the pier earlier and trapped his thumb between two boats, which was a relatively common injury among sea-faring folk, particularly where alcohol was involved. Thaddeus had become authentically inebriated by that point anyway, and with Ridge's mum having arrived with the two wee kids, the general atmosphere of pandemonium helped contribute to the fabrication of a plausible story. Orla had set a massive cold buffet on the kitchen table which had been ignored entirely and the Laphroaig bottle had been mysteriously emptied, along with enough wine to fill the quarry.

After the bemused doctor had left, Seamus took the black rib back to his pier and had the massive engine winched off the rib, before towing it back complete with some rusty chain and a drum of red diesel.

By then Colm had stripped the men of any ID, and their weapons had been appropriated into Ridge's secret armoury. Under cover of darkness, they dragged the four bodies out to the rib and Colm and Seamus towed it way out beyond the treacherous whirlpool, where they set it on fire and watched until it sank.

It wasn't until eleven o'clock, with grandparent and kids in bed, that the four of them were able to sit looking out at the fire pit burning gently on the rear patio and collectively take a deep breath and let it all go.

Ridge eased a shotgun cartridge cautiously out from under his arse and tossed it onto the handmade wooden coffee table and they all sniggered like naughty teenagers. He decided to take advantage of a lightening of the collective mood and broached a delicate subject, before too much more alcohol was consumed.

'So Colm, I'm sorry to have called you like that yesterday, but to be honest, we were all a little worried for you.'

'For me? You think? Was it not more a case of-'

'You can just stop right there!'

Orla's eyes flashed emerald fire across the room and each of the three men slunk lower in their seats. But her finger pointed accusingly at only one of them. Despite the potential fireworks ahead, Ridge couldn't help feeling proud of his wife and secretly a little relieved that she had taken the lead, rather than Thaddeus who might have been more likely to go postal with Colm.

'It was *me* who talked them into it, Colm.

Jeezo! You're my only brother. We all thought you might be dead, so we did! An' with you not helping out, over there in Japan, well we all-'

270

Now it was Colm's turn to raise his voice, something he rarely did. 'Do ye' know that for sure Sis? Are ye after wanting me to be fuckin' advertising me presence wherever I go, like some attention-starved teenager?

Jaysus! It's about time the three of you woke up to the real world out there, a world I have to-'

'Okay, Colm! That's enough!' This time it had been Ridge who'd sat forward angrily, as he heard Orla begin to sob into his shoulder. 'There's no need to be like that!'

'Ye think?' Colm spat back furiously.

They all jumped as Thad slammed his massive right paw onto the table and roared.

'Whoa, dudes! Let's just calm this the fuck down. This is all my fault!'

Colm sprang to his feet as if someone had stung him with one of farmer Finlay's cattle prods. Ridge blinked, waiting for the battle to recommence. Agile as a cat, Colm moved towards the patio and gently, conspiratorially, slid the glass doors shut, all the while his eyes scanning the others with an animal intensity. It could have been unnerving, even frightening, yet Ridge felt strangely comforted, as if enveloped in the protective aura of a powerful almost patriarchal force. The leader of the pack, the alpha male. Colm hadn't uttered a word to them, but Ridge knew they were all equally entranced by this performance and a crackle of electricity crossed the room, cutting through the last remaining eddies of fire smoke.

'No Thaddeus, you're wrong. It's *my* fault, so it is.

All of it.

An' I'm sorry, Orla, for giving it to you like that, you didn't deserve it, lass.'

Colm sat heavily next to his sister and pulled her in close while fixing the other two with that haunted look that always terrified Ridge half to death.

'But it's to you both that I owe the biggest apology.

I've let you down, so I have. More than that, Thaddeus, I let down an old friend and messed up on my promise, and I *never* break a promise.'

It was impossible not to hear the acrid regret in his voice and in the momentary silence, Ridge sensed that his brother-in-law had come to some kind of fundamental decision, a colossal shift in the tectonic plates of his shadowy world. He glanced over to Thad and saw he'd felt it also. For a few seconds, no-one spoke and the silence was deafening. Then Colm raised his hand as if pointing to the heavens.

'And I'll make you a *new* promise, here tonight. The people that came here, to despoil this island sanctuary you've created, they will be the last of their kind to do so.

Orla, you wanted to know how come I was so close-by? Well, you might not realise it, but over the water there, in that shite-hole Belfast, it's all kickin' off again, so it is. There's been a whole spate of tit-for-tat murders and it's after gettin' desperate, innocent lives being destroyed every day, just like the old days.

So believe it or not, Sis, but the fuckin' Brits had the bare-faced cheek to ask me to help them sort it.

Aye!

The very same ones who hunted me like an animal just a few years back, were beggin' me to pull them out the shite!'

Orla sat up in horror. 'But you said you'd finished with-'

'Aye! And I have! This time they just wanted *my expertise*. Imagine that! All legal and legit. But there's never anythin' straightforward about that place, or any of the players.

Obviously, I'm after ruffling a few feathers over there, people who can't let bygones be bygones and who want to dredge up the murky past, people who still talk about *The Phantom...*'

Colm stopped talking and looked around the room with a theatrical air, as if he thought he'd just delivered the final denouement in a whodunnit. But instead, he just saw nodding heads as if a predictable plot twist had only now been confirmed at long last.

'So...' Colm ventured onwards with a half-smile, 'when some complete eedjits called me on an unsecured line, while I was after being in one of the most heavily bugged areas of the planet, it was hardly surprising that the call was intercepted.' He glared at the three others, each of them suddenly interested in the intricacies of the grained oak table.

Thad stood up this time. 'So I'm guessing they followed you straight here?'

'Yeah, Thad. I doubt they had any notion where the hell I was headed, or even if they would have had enough time to tell anyone else either even if they had known. They'd have been a local hit squad. They were only after me and I'll bet they had expected me just to be nipping a few miles along the coast. They probably shit themselves when I crossed the Irish Sea, but by that time they would have committed themselves and they might not have had enough fuel to turn back, so that was that.

I led them straight to you, just like the Pied Piper.'

Ridge saw Colm hesitate for a second and then a rueful smile spread across his face, as he thought about what he'd just said. But a second was all the time that Thad needed.

'Yeah, okay dude. I totally get that part. We fucked up.

But right now I got bigger fish to fry, you feel me?'

He stood facing down the three others on the sofa but his anger was only directed at one man.

'Where was you at when my Pop and the Dogs were in Japan trying to save my ass?'

'Sit down Thaddeus, will ye? You're after givin' me a sore neck lookin' up at you like that.' Colm sighed and gestured to the seat opposite him. 'This is not a short story, nor is it going to be an easy one for you to hear. Are you sure you're ready to hear it?'

Thad nodded meekly and did as he was instructed

'So you all know that Tadashi and I had a 'business relationship,' right? He'd called on me to help American interests for years in places like Panama, Liberia and with our good friends the drugs cartels. So when I previously said that I'd just stumbled upon one of his websites back in the day, just after all that fun stuff in Central America, you've probably guessed that I wasn't being completely upfront about-'

'You mean that you were lying.' Thad might be willing to listen but he hadn't lost any of his pent-up frustration.

'Yes! And I was protecting both myself, your father and *you*, Thad. Something I had been doing successfully for some considerable time an' all. But Tadashi couldn't accept the fact that my eedjit runaway brother-in-law getting himself involved with his estranged son, was simply a bizarre coincidence. So, I lied to you at his direct request Thad, you'll just have to deal with that. There's a lot of things you don't know about your dad.'

Thad growled but Ridge could see he'd taken on board what Colm had been saying and so he shot him a supportive smile which his big friend accepted with a nod.

'When you got yourself arrested in Tokyo, I was still in Chile, quietly working my vineyard with Juanita. I'd had no contact with your dad for a long time, Thaddeus. I am officially retired and difficult though it is, I'm trying to keep it that way.

So once I found out, then I was playing catch-up just like everyone else.'

'So you're saying you didn't know my Pop was in-'

'Listen Thad! Your dad went to some considerable lengths to conceal his presence in Japan. He didn't want anyone to know and if you know him like you pretend to-'

Thad roared and leapt across the table and if it hadn't been Orla who got in between him and Colm, then the considerably heavier American would have flattened him.

Colm's normally pale face had reddened dramatically. 'Steady Thad! Will you just sit down and fucking well *listen* to what I am after trying to tell you, if you'd only give me a chance. Jeezo!

But that was a cheap shot and I apologize, but please stay in your chair, or so help me I'm out of here, so I am!

The only reason your dad had kept his trip under the radar, was to protect you and your two sisters. Don't you see that?'

Ridge saw Orla prod her brother, looking confident in her re-established standing, having just prevented Colm from getting a well-deserved thrashing.

'Hold on, I don't see that Colm. What do you mean?'

Colm let out a deep breath.

'Okay, Sis. Let's just say at this point that the whole Thad frame-up looks like a personal grudge against Tadashi, right? One in which the loony Kazuo is more than happy to involve our man Thaddeus here? So what would be the point of involving the two girls or even Ridge here any further and possibly putting them in danger? Are you getting this?'

They all nodded and settled deeper into their seats.

'I didn't even know where Tadashi had gone until he called me! By that time I had flown to DC, expecting him to be there. It's nearly eleven thousand miles for me to fly to Tokyo and so seeing as I couldn't get hold of Tadashi by the normal channels, I thought I'd make a start and meet him in

Washington, where it's a wee bit quicker. At that point, I had imagined us flying from DC together.'

'What did my Pop say to you, Colm?' Ridge thought Thad sounded like a wee boy all of a sudden.

'He said he had a very serious problem in Japan and it was the root cause of your own particular predicament, Thad. He said you might actually be safer in prison than free in Tokyo, but that was before the poisoning incident. Obviously, I immediately volunteered myself and any of my resources but he point blank refused at that time. He allowed me to contact Patrick and the boys, but forbade any of us coming to Japan for fear of escalating the situation and endangering Thaddeus. When I tried to find out more about what was troubling him, he said it was strictly personal and just another ghost from his chequered past come back to haunt him. He tried to convince me he had it all under control, but I could tell he-'

'So did Pop know this dude already?'

'He did. But I had no clue at that time. I did some digging in DC, spoke to your older sister Tiffany and eventually put the jigsaw pieces together. From what I'd gleaned, I knew my only course of action was to get to Tokyo as soon as possible and I jumped on the next flight, with 'The Dogs' planning to arrive soon after, once they'd assembled their usual toys.'

'Then you *did* go to Tokyo then?' Thad's face was a contorted question mark.

'Of course I did! But I just wasn't quick enough, Thad.'

'How come we never saw you?'

'Ah, but you did my friend! We had a nice quiet wee chat in the hospital, after you'd been poisoned, but you obviously have no recollection of any-'

'Holy shit!' Thad slapped his palm against his forehead as if suddenly remembering something important.

'I *do* remember, man! But I thought it had all been just a bad dream. I thought you were the motherfuckin' angel of death come to take me away!'

Colm laughed quietly.

'Fair play to you, I've been called worse than that so I have! To be honest, I wasn't sure how compos mentis you were. My main worry was you getting over excited and trying to leave the prison hospital before we were ready for you. I might've over-played the extent of your injuries a tad, but I'd just installed a team of crack Marines outside your room and there was no way you'd have been any safer out in the open.'

Ridge coughed and cleared his throat to speak. 'That would be Nathan?'

Colm smiled and nodded.

'So what went wrong Colm?' Ridge felt a hot wave of anger and claustrophobic panic course up his back and he clawed at his neck, as raw and bruised on the outside as he felt on the inside. 'You were there in Tokyo after all and so were the Dogs. So how did that wee prick manage to get away with what he did to Thad's dad? I mean, who the fuck is he anyway? Just some perverted wee bastard, right? You guys are the best in the world, for fuck's sake, I don't understand how he-'

'Ridge stop! Don't beat yourself up.

Kazuo was an extremely dangerous sociopath who had the time and intelligence to devise a plan which was supremely clever. He was an accomplished serial killer, to whom the authorities even now are chalking up murder after murder.

You and Nea are probably the only two people on the planet who survived being imprisoned by him.'

Thad stood up again, his eyes filling with tears and his throat croaking with raw fury.

'Yeah man, we fuckin' get it, okay! The motherfucker's a freakin' genius. So how come we ain't checking he's actually dead? That's why we gotta go back there and trawl that evil forest until we find his rotting bones.'

'Sit down Thad, please.' Colm raised his hand and pointed to the chair opposite which Thad ignored and remained standing, his strong back erect and proud, almost as if on a parade ground. Colm shook his head, looking to Ridge like a disappointed parent having to rebuke a wayward son. But then he glared up at Thad, took a huge breath and clasped his hands together loudly. 'You would never find him, Thad. Look what those woods did to Kazuo. It's a fool's errand, I promise.'

'The hell it is! You're good at making promises Colm. What the fuck did you promise my Pop anyways, not that it did him much good?'

'SIT DOWN NOW!'

The words ricocheted wildly across the slate floor and bounced off the smooth glass of the patio doors to assault their ears a second time. Ridge gulped as Thaddeus fell into his chair, as if he had been a marionette which had just had its strings cut. Colm had that black-eyed look which somehow made Ridge feel as if they were in a gothic horror story.

Then the monster spoke.

'I kept my promise!

Now I have to live with that for the rest of my life...'

Chapter 43

Ridge glanced at his watch. He'd no idea that they'd been talking for so long and so he stood up to break the sombre atmosphere and make some fresh coffee. The first flickers of light were peeking out over the flat horizon, but Ridge didn't feel like it would be much of a day. By the time he'd brought back a tray of drinks and some island shortbread, the sky had turned the colour of cold porridge. No-one spoke and Orla looked ready for bed. Ridge placed the tray carefully down between the serried ranks of long-empty wine goblets and finger-marked whisky tumblers. Despite his anxiety, he looked out beyond his reflection in the glass door and thought the sky seemed particularly weird. Normally it would be a rich mix of colours and textures, at times angry and more often beautiful and untamed. But this morning he decided that if he had been presented with a photograph of the scene in front of him, with the sky a smooth and unchanging grey, like dead flesh, he would have said it was a fake. Like it had been photoshopped. Badly. He decided it wasn't a good omen.

'I kept my promise...' Colm repeated his mantra quietly for the hundredth time that night, while the others had settled and even Thaddeus seemed prepared to listen to what Colm had to say.

'Okay Colm. Go on, man. I wanna hear the rest.

You keep sayin' you kept your promise, but my Pop got wasted by that sick dude an' so I don't get what your meaning is.'

Colm fixed him with a stare that would have stopped a charging bull.

'You think you want to know, Thad, but you don't really want to be hearing what's after coming next, honestly you don't.'

A deep growl rumbled from Thad's direction and Ridge knew he had to do something quick.

'Colm! I think we *all* need to know the truth here, however difficult it might be. We've all been through a lot and I can't see how you're going to make things any worse by-'

'Alright then. But don't say I didn't warn yous all.

The main promise I made to your father, Thaddeus, and I have to say, made under extreme duress in difficult circumstances was this. I had to stay out of the Japan situation no matter what, with only one major proviso being that if you or your sisters became endangered, then all bets were off.

He only cared about your safety, lad. I pleaded with him, but he insisted that his predicament was intensely personal and he was the only person on the planet who could fix it.'

Thad leant forward and groaned, his powerful frame rocking slowly back and forth.

'But Colm, man, he was my Pop! You guys should have been there for him! You bend the rules every day don't cha'?'

'I did bend the rules. I was there, but just not in time to stop what happened. I have done exactly what he had asked of me. I saved your life and rescued this eedjit here too. You have-'

'Ridge rescued himself this time, man...! *Mister fuckin' Serendipity* strikes again.

He near saved my dad too more than any-'

'No Thad!'

Ridge could tell that Colm was trying hard to control his anger but the frustration had begun to bubble through again and there was coldness in his voice now.

'That just isn't true, my friend. Your man here did an amazing job of surviving the night in that forest for sure. But he'd not have lasted out the day if we'd not got to him before Kazuo found out he was still alive. He'd contacts in the police and I doubt Ridge would have even made it back to Tokyo.

But I still owe you an apology, Thaddeus, because I never planned it to work out this way. I was fully prepared to 'bend the rules' as you say, to keep Tadashi alive. That man had been more of a father figure to me than my own dad. Sorry Orla... but it's the truth so it is.'

Orla nodded mutely, her green eyes admonishing him and willing him to continue.

'Your Pop was an amazing man, Thad, and it was inconceivable that he could have been taken down like that. We had the technology, the manpower and the will to destroy Kazuo and raze that forest to the ground if necessary.'

Thad wailed in anguish. 'So why didn't you man?'

'I was just too late.

My mistake, my only mistake and the worst decision I have ever made, was to agree to keep away and to fly to DC instead of Tokyo. Your father would be alive today, if I had taken the other flight. But I would never have found out the truth about why this psychopathic serial killer and rapist had his hooks into your dad, and we may possibly have saved your Pop but then you would have been dead for sure.

By the time your father sent me the co-ordinates of his meeting place in the forest it-'

'You knew where he was at?'

'I thought I did. Let me finish will ye?

As I said before, your da' was a clever guy. He used some clever tech to plot exactly where in that black wood that he would be meeting Kazuo. He told me he felt relaxed after his first face-to-face with the guy and that he was confident that he could iron out the difficulty. I was in mid-flight by then, not happy, and I confessed as much to Tadashi. He laughed and said just to keep you safe, Thad, and not to worry. He said he'd send me the location details.

If I didn't hear back from him after the meeting then, by all means, I could send in the Dogs and whatever it took to save his son.'

'So what in the hell happened?'

'What happened Thad, was that I already knew the truth about Tadashi and I didn't share his confidence. But I did feel that with big Patrick and a chopper full of toys, that we could easily extricate the old man even if he didn't want us to.

The problem was the woods.

Kazuo had chosen the woods very carefully, mostly for personal reasons, but also because they were impenetrable to modern technology. That's why it took so long to find you, Ridge, even though you still don't believe me that I got a dentist to fit you with a tracker back when you and Orla were having your 'domestic difficulties!'

Ridge found he'd begun to examine the inside of his mouth with his little finger. He saw Colm glare at him and so he stopped and let him continue.

'So firstly the clock was against us and then I found that the tracking tech was no use in the forest. We had a rough idea of where Tadashi and Kazuo might be but as you can probably imagine with that sort of terrain, a miss is as good as a mile.

Perhaps unwittingly, Kazuo had chosen the best place in the world to meet your dad, Thaddeus. But he'd had a long time to plan this, so he had. In fact there had been no particular timescale for his plan. He'd been fermenting his poisonous ideas for most of his adult life and it was only when you blundered into his modelling studio, that his evil thoughts coalesced into action.'

'Me! What the fuck have-'

'Everything!

Please don't be after taking this the wrong way.

I'm so sorry to say this Thad, but you were the catalyst and there was nothing you could have done to prevent it from happening. Kazuo had a pathological hatred for all Americans and more than that, he'd planned to kill your dad anyway. All you did was give shape and a time imperative to his scheming.'

Thaddeus had buried his head in his hands and Ridge could have sworn his big pal was sobbing. He slid off his chair so as not to disturb Orla who had dropped off to sleep and crouched down beside Thad, feeling equally helpless and confused about what had happened. He turned to Colm who'd turned a ghostly white in the anaemic light of the early morning.

'But Colm, I just don't get why that wee tosser would have it in for Thad's dad? Was it something to do with his military work? Did you not say they'd never even met before all of this?'

'They'd never met Ridge and yeah, you've hit the nail on the head.'

Thad lifted his head and slurred through his long damp mane. 'No way, man... his work? This is all because of some goddamned business deal?'

'Not exactly Thad. Now, are you sure you want to hear this?'

Thad nodded uncomprehendingly.

'Okay, but you'd better sit up then for I'm only after sayin' this the once.

You know yer da' was a big shot at an early age, what with his military base construction business and then later with his Vietnam airlift hero stuff an' all that, right?

Well in the late '60's Tadashi was building bases all over the Pacific. He'd taken an apartment in Tokyo as much for some personal space as much as business convenience. There he met a Japanese man called Hiroshi and soon became friends with him and his young fiancée Akiko.

Yer man Hiroshi seems to have been an amazing character and he and your dad became inseparable for a while, despite severe communication issues. He'd been almost completely deafened by the blast from the atomic bomb at Hiroshima. Then he'd also lost most of his fingers into the bargain holding up a burning oak beam that threatened to wipe out several of his schoolmates. It was Akiko who translated between them, what do you call it again? Signing, that's it.'

Thad rubbed his reddened eyes as if seeing through them for the first time.

'Wow that's freaky! I remember being with him back in DC, not so long ago, just after Pakistan, I think. We were in one of those long shiny corridors, you know, the ones you never think are gonna end. We were headed for lunch and I was in a hurry. Real hungry, you feel me?

Then I saw Pop wasn't alongside me and when I turned around, there he was with this young intern and a couple of other guys. I couldn't understand why Pop was spending such an unusual amount of time with them and then I saw she was signing for the guys, and my dad was nodding away. I never asked about it.'

Colm coughed and cleared his throat impatiently.

'So anyways, his own parents had been some of the very first Japanese to embrace classical music before the war and they'd built a violin factory near Hiroshima. During the war, they'd been forced to convert their factory to building aircraft and the young Hiroshi had lost both his parents in a fire after one of the nightly American bombing raids.

Are you starting to get the picture yet?'

They all nodded, transfixed, including a re-awakened Orla whose face was rapt attention.

'Now Tadashi was dripping in cash at this point, and had just bought the beginnings of his airline empire. Hiroshi was some kind of genius inventor and had apparently got plans for some kind of revolutionary hearing aid invention, a prototype for the cochlear implant that was soon to become the industry standard worldwide.

From what I can gather Thad, your dad had arranged to give Hiroshi the seed capital to build his cochlear implant factory. Hiroshi had the patents and all that, and anything else he needed got taken care of by Tadashi.'

Orla spoke for the first time in hours. 'So what's this got to do with any of us?'

Colm cleared his throat again and glared at his sister.

'I'm just after gettin' to that bit if you'd only give me a chance!

From what I learnt in DC and from Tokyo newspapers back then, it seems that Tadashi suddenly had second thoughts about the whole project. He bought out Hiroshi and flattened the ground where the factory was to be and the Yanks built another base there instead.'

'So this is all because my Pop ratted out some Jap over a business deal?'

'Yes and no, Thaddeus. There's a wee bit more to this story, so there is.

Hiroshi died in the mid-eighties and I found the news stories easily enough.

He went missing in the Aokigahara Forest and according to local gossip he had lost his mind due to being unable to hear music and in particular when his son Kazuo was learning the violin!'

Suddenly Ridge could see how it all made sense now.

'The forest!

That's why Kazuo chose that evil place, because it had claimed his own father!'

'Yes Ridge, the forest had personal significance to Kazuo and apparently he'd spent a considerable time searching for Hiroshi but they never did find his body.'

Ridge shivered. 'Not bloody surprising.'

'So I was right then, the dude blamed my Pop for everything and all of this shit is the result. But how the hell did he find out about any of it, he wasn't even born back then?'

'Right enough there Thaddeus. From what I can gather, yer man Kazuo didn't have a clue who Tadashi was, only that it was some half-Japanese, half-American businessman, until he found some paperwork with your dad's name on it after Hiroshi vanished.

Now, like the rest of us here in this cottage, Tadashi had employed a great deal of subterfuge to keep his personal details under the radar, so it was a long time before Kazuo made the connection. But eventually he traced him after some philanthropic gesture to do with that stupid training building at Quantico. Even your dad couldn't keep that under wraps. You'd have no doubt been there yourself Thad, when you were prancing around in the Marines.'

Thad shook his head in utter disbelief.

'Holy shit. So Pop got wasted 'cause of the *T. Kamaka Research Center*?'

Colm nodded. 'That's when it started to get personal, Thad.'

Ridge scratched his stubbly chin for a moment.

'So, if you found out all of this before you came to Japan, couldn't someone have taken out Kazuo long before he went to the forest?

Or couldn't me and the Dog's have done something... before you even got there?'

Colm looked at his brother-in-law unsmilingly. 'I can see why you'd think that, Ridge, to be honest, I thought one of you would have come to that conclusion before now.

It's true.

Patrick could've sent a rocket up his ass and all would have been well. Except we had explicit orders from Tadashi not to take out Kazuo, unless he was a direct threat to Thaddeus.'

'But why?' Thad let his head fall backwards in despair and roared up to the cottage roof, his sandpaper throat stretched and sounding as sore as his broken heart. 'Why would he care what happened to the evil fucker?'

'Because Thad, Kazuo was your brother.'

Chapter 44

'My brother? No...!'

Thad had slipped to his knees and he rested his huge head on the wooden table and wept. Ridge and Orla both moved onto the floor, wrapping their arms around him as they felt his massive back pulse in a tortured tempo of despair.

Only Colm remained sitting upright and pale in the early morning light. It wasn't the first time he'd had to pass on devastating news to someone recently bereaved. But he hadn't had to do it for a while and either he was out of practice, or he'd become soft in his semi-retirement. His short time with Juanita had been the most treasured period of his life and he longed to return to her and their sun-drenched Chilean vineyard. Maybe being in love had opened up doors to his heart that had been irrevocably locked fast for too long. There might be truth in all that nonsense about the dark and the light, one being necessary so as to be able to appreciate the other. Perhaps the fact of Thad being both a friend and a comrade at arms made it more painful, he didn't know for sure. He'd dreaded having this conversation and the worst of it was he didn't think things would be getting any better right about know.

He'd made a promise. Not an easy one, but then that's why Tadashi had been so adamant that it had to be adhered to. Selfish really, Colm decided as he watched his three closest friends in the world crumble in front of his eyes. It had been a mark of his utmost respect for the man that, of course, Colm had accepted his challenge and fulfilled it to the best of his ability. While it hadn't turned out exactly as he'd planned or wished for, he doubted any other man alive could have achieved the final result that he had painfully wrought from such a tragic situation.

Like always with the nature of his work, he would never be able to tell another living soul exactly what he'd done to discharge his duty to Tadashi, to execute his promise. But he'd made a fundamental decision just at that moment. Whether it was the right decision or not remained to be seen, and Colm hoped it wouldn't come back to haunt him like things had a habit of doing. He looked at his watch, then took a deep breath and exhaled loudly, hoping to attract some attention. This never-ending night had some mileage left in her yet.

'I'm sorry, Thaddeus, to be the one whose after having to tell you all this, truly I am.'

Thad lifted his head instantly picking up the change in Colm's tone of voice. The others moved aside a little to give him more space. Ridge watched him shake his head like one of the farm collies after a jump in the quarry and then felt the inevitable wet outcome as he wiped his big friend's tears off his own face.

'Tell me, man, just go ahead and tell me everything.'

'There's not a lot more to tell really,' Colm tried to reassure his friend as he nodded towards his sister to affirm her unspoken assertion that a fresh brew of her finest coffee would be in order.

'As usual with any events of the past, the truth gets written by those that remain standing on the field of battle, and in this case Kazuo had nobody else to inform him of what really happened and so his own warped account became his only reality.'

Thad growled impatiently again and Ridge could sense further eruptions if Colm didn't stop prevaricating. He decided to help things along. 'So Colm, how did all this happen then and how do you know so much?'

'I have spoken to Kazuo's mother, Akiko. She's living in an old people's home to the north of Tokyo. He sends her money every month, but apart from that she hasn't had any contact from her son in years and was very happy to talk to me about everything.

In fact I couldn't get her to stop talking. She had been very fond of your father, Thaddeus.'

'So they had, like an affair then?'

'Yes, but not in the modern sense. Akiko had been an intrinsic part of the friendship between the two men. Every sentence spoken by either of them had flowed through her. She loved her husband more than anything else, but as the two men had bonded so too had she become enveloped in their relationship.

It's fair to say that Hiroshi was a talented but flawed personality. His horrific injuries had skewed his judgement of the world and Akiko told me he often treated her poorly in the presence of Tadashi. He would be referred to today as a genius, but he was also a cold man not given to protestations of love, whereas your dad was younger, more impetuous and bursting with energy and dynamism.

It was he who fell in love and he asked her to come away with him. They only had intimate relations a few times, but as so often happens, that was enough for her to become pregnant. Tadashi immediately proposed, but she turned him down flat and married Hiroshi fairly sharpish after that.'

'So Pop was a spurned lover who took revenge by fucking over his friend. Is that really what happened?'

They could all feel the wretchedness in Thad's voice and the shared horror that the man they'd all admired so much could have been so petty and vindictive.

'No Thad, it's a little more complicated than that. Akiko told me a lot but she didn't have the full picture and it was in DC that I got the truth of the matter.'

'Did Akiko hate my Pop then?'

'Not for a second. She seemed to still have only the warmest feelings for him and not once in our conversation did she ever say anything bad about him. In many ways I think she regretted not running away with him, although she remained loyal to Hiroshi at all times.'

'So what really happened, man? It's killin' me...'

'Well, Tadashi didn't hang around for long, to be sure. But Akiko says that he left because she ordered him to, not because he left her in the lurch.

On the business side, it gets really interesting. Kazuo blamed Tadashi for stealing his father's scientific inventions and patents but in actual fact, it didn't happen like that at all.'

'Go on Colm, we're all ears so we are.' Orla had brought back the warm drinks which they all happily cradled in their hands.

'Tadashi was minted by then anyway. He had a ruthless reputation in his early days, but by then he didn't need to stitch up anyone, particularly in an unconnected industry and a friend.

So, when he learned that Akiko would be having his child and that the child's legal father was hell-bent on opening his factory, he had to act.'

Ridge and Thad glanced at each other and spoke with one voice, 'what do you mean?'

'Once he'd returned to the States, Tadashi found out that the Yanks were streets ahead with their own more advanced cochlear implant plans and they'd even started production of a rough prototype. Hiroshi's patents would have been worthless within a short time and his factory would have become obsolete, almost as soon as it had been built.

So what Tadashi did was protect Hiroshi and more importantly his unborn child, by ensuring they would be financially well-off for the rest of their days. The land originally set out for the factory was bought by the US military, at a hugely inflated price, just like the patents. I checked and the base that Tadashi built was only operational for a few years and it's now a semi-conductor factory for the car industry.'

Thad sighed and Ridge could see his huge eyes welling up. 'So my Pop just built that base there as a smokescreen for helping out his soon-to-be-born child?'

Colm nodded. 'Yep!'

'Did Akiko know that?' Orla asked.

'Sure she did, Sis.

An' yer man Hiroshi must've known that he'd won a watch financially, although Akiko swears he never knew anything about him not being the father. I'm not quite so sure myself, neither I am. By all accounts, he became a bitter and twisted man, long before he walked off into the forest when Kazuo was just a teenager.

It was just after that when Kazuo discovered a cache of documents that his father had hidden including some personal diaries. Akiko hadn't been aware of them and said to me that the grieving Kazuo had spent weeks deciphering the crudely written papers. He soon worked out that his mum had been involved with another man and when confronted, Akiko told him as much, but he never knew it had been Tadashi or even that Hiroshi hadn't been his biological father.'

Thad placed his coffee mug gently on the table and fixed his stare directly at Colm.

'So did my Pop have any contact with Kazuo or Akiko?'

'No Thad. Your dad was forbidden to contact them and he never saw Kazuo ever, nor did he ever get to speak to Akiko after he left Japan. Not when Tadashi paid out all that cash or even after Hiroshi went missing in the Suicide Forest.

Akiko had been adamant.

To be honest, Thaddeus, if anyone should have felt bitter and aggrieved, then it should have been your dad, not that lunatic Kazuo. He was the one who'd been rejected by the woman he loved and shut out of her life and of his child, whom he would never see.'

Orla sighed and wiped the tears from her face. 'But instead he responded only with goodwill and love. Your dad was some guy, Thaddeus, you should be rightly proud so you should.'

'I am!' Thad thumped the table. 'But where did it get him? The only time he gets to see his son, the ungrateful motherfucker kills him. And how the hell do we know if Kazuo's actually dead or not?

I'm tellin' you Colm, we gotta go back to that forest and hunt the son-of-a-bitch down!

We should go now before-'

Colm raised a commanding hand and a dagger of lightning reflected off the French windows. They all silently counted the number of seconds before the ground shook. They didn't have to wait long. The thunder rumbled across the sea and they knew the weather had turned as black as the mood in the room. Dogs barked in the distance and Colm felt the air grow instantly colder as if someone behind him had swept open the glass doors. He pressed his advantage, inwardly thanking Mother Nature's theatrical assistance.

'No Thad! I'm not going back there, ever.

And neither are you if you've got any sense left in that thick head of yours.'

Their three exhausted faces stared up at him and Colm knew there would be no fight left in them that night. He stood up and reached out a friendly hand to no-one in particular. 'Now look, it's getting bloody late or early whatever, and we all need to get some sleep. You've had a lot to take in and so let's sleep on it okay? Orla can you help Thaddeus here to his room and then point me to a comfy place to fall down love?'

*

In the end, only one face continued to look out across the choppy waters. Colm knew he had still more treacherous seas to navigate before he could ever sleep easy again. He'd just made a fresh promise to protect those he loved, but this time there would be no ambiguity about his response. The Phantom had been disturbed from his moody slumber, deep down amongst the murky depths of one of the darkest periods of modern history. Colm vowed he'd not rest until he allowed the monster to drag the unfortunate souls of those who had dared to provoke his wrath, all the way back down into the unrelenting blackness.

He held up a glass of blood red wine, inspecting it for a moment, curious how the knife edge horizon cut through the crimson liquid like an open wound. He felt the savage pain of that wound tear him in half, as he planned what had to be done to keep his family safe. For a split second, it became too much for him and he spun round and hurled the goblet against the rough stone wall above the hearth. The glass exploded into a thousand pieces, as if all life had been extinguished from a thousand worlds and his ruthless eyes became as empty and menacing as a starless night. Before the last fragment of shattered glass had landed on the stone floor, he had gone.

Chapter 45

The man clocked the surprised look on the security guard's face and struggled to suppress a rueful grin. But he couldn't really blame them for looking askance at him. They'd not seen him in this early in the morning very often and never on a weekend. Not even back in the bad old days when there'd be trouble on a daily basis. What was the phrase they used nowadays? Oh yeah. 24/7. He'd have to get used to lots of annoying American phrases soon enough. But he'd manage.

     He'd been up a hell of a lot earlier than even the guard could have imagined. He glanced around and now he was finally on his own, he allowed his face to relax into an unalloyed vision of complete happiness. A man truly happy in his work? Not quite. He punched his wall-mounted keypad to gain access to the secure area as he'd done too many times before, but for the very first time saw a beaming face reflected in the two-way mirrored glass window of his office. He still found it hard to believe only a couple of hours earlier he'd seen his sweaty features bouncing off another window. He'd stared for a long time at the screen of his laptop, as it showed him irrefutable proof the guy had been the genuine article. There in front of his eyes had been his bank account displaying a fresh deposit of one million Euros. After savouring the sight for some considerable time, he transferred the funds to an overseas account he'd not used for many years and closed the device with a satisfying click.

Now all he had to do was switch a couple of evidence bags, replace them with the ones he'd hidden in his briefcase and that would be it. He'd take the redundancy package they'd been haranguing him with for years and slam his notice letter on their desk first thing Monday morning. If it all went to plan, he and the wife would be sunning themselves in their very own Palm Springs condo within a month.

Chapter 46

The afternoon sunlight struggled to push its way through the billowing clouds as the late tide brought with it fresher winds and the promise of a brighter evening and perhaps even a trademark west coast sunset.

Ridge hauled on some clothes and made his way through to find the others. The cottage felt cold and not just because Orla had decided not to stay the night, anxious to be with her babies. Ridge vaguely remembered her muttering that she'd bring them back for tea-time, if he could remember to fire up the old range cooker beforehand. Then he detected the cause of the chill, a patio door not quite closed. It wasn't like Orla to do that and Ridge immediately felt the pin-pricks of anxiety criss-cross his body and he felt himself sink down into a crouch. It had only been a day since the peace and quiet of the cottage had been shattered by vengeful men with angry guns.

He peered out, but couldn't see anything amiss. He could still smell the acrid smoke from the burnt-out remains of Orla's car so he attempted to close the door, finding it stuck with what looked like tiny pieces of glass. Now alarm bells were clanging inside his tender skull and he turned back indoors to find Colm and Thaddeus. Curled up together perhaps? Not a chance. He found Thad on the floor beside Isla's bed, wrapped up in a fetching fluorescent pink blanket snoring his head off. Ridge kicked him hard.

'Sshh! Wake up, Thad! Come on, something's not right.'

Thaddeus dragged his huge frame up into an almost vertical plane and stumbled after his friend, muttering under his breath as he went. They soon ascertained that they were the only two people in the cottage. Ridge decided that Colm must have gone for a breath of fresh air and so the pair of them decamped to the kitchen, where Ridge ferreted about for some more food to frighten his pal with. Thad was naturally quiet after the earlier revelations and so Ridge stuck the big TV on mute, handed Thad a vacuum cleaner for the mysterious glass and allowed him to come back to life in his own good time.

For a few minutes, they busied themselves with their respective tasks. Ridge saw from the breaking news bulletins that Colm had been right enough about things 'kicking off,' as he'd prosaically termed the upsurge in violence over in Northern Ireland. Apparently a co-ordinated series of simultaneous car bombs had gone off throughout Belfast and the north. The casualties had all been people suspected to have had paramilitary connections and so the concern factor seemed to border on the 'who-gives-a-fuck' threshold, although there was possibly one ex-soldier involved. The BBC hardly gave the story more than twenty seconds.

The cardiac-inducing all-day breakfast was bubbling away in the pan and they each had a mug of black coffee savouring two of the best aromas known to mankind. Coffee and bacon. Ridge heard his phone ping and absent-mindedly glanced at the message. It looked odd and he was about to delete it without opening it but then thought at least it would occupy a minute or two of the painful silence between him and Thad before they sat down to the hot breakfast.

He couldn't have known that the bacon and eggs would grow cold and stale that day and only ever be destined to become tomorrow's lunch for MacGregor's pigs.

'Thad could you nip through and grab my laptop, it's just charging up next to the TV in the lounge? Watch all that glass, will you? Cheers amigo. Ma hands are greasy as fuck, but I've just received a weird file on my phone and I want to open it up on a bigger screen.'

Thad loped over and gave it to Ridge who had washed most of the fat off his hands. He opened up the screen and waited for his messages to download.

'What the fuck?' Thad stared at the phone and scratched his chin.

'Looks like an encrypted file Ridge, but if it is I don't reckon there's anything stopping us from opening it. It'll be a virus man, delete the mother and let's eat!'

'Aye no problem, just give me a wee minute will you? Go ahead and turn the heat off and stick some of that bread in the toaster while I open this up. I recognise something about the properties of this file type, seen it before somewhere. I think it could be something to do with Colm.'

The two of them sat at the breakfast bar and watched the little circle on the screen go round and round. He cursed the broadband speed, painfully slow at times, despite his extensive technological modifications. Looking back at that moment, Ridge remembers thinking it had been kind of nice doing something mundane and normal for a change.

Then the file opened. It was a video. On a private server and ready to play. Ridge swallowed and pressed the button.

Thad clocked it first. 'Whoa, motherfucker!'

Ridge heard Thad speak, but he found himself unable to formulate a response. The video was the one they'd seen before on Japanese national television, the one of Kazuo making his confession for the murders. Thad instinctively reached forward a huge paw to switch it off, far more interested in his food than watching the man who'd killed his father. But Ridge brushed his hand aside. 'Dude? This guy can wait can't he?' Thad growled.

But Ridge felt that something was different about this piece of film. The picture quality was a lot crisper and the colour more accurate to life rather than the sepia tone of the one they'd watched a hundred times in Japan. He guessed this was the raw file. The source file.

Thad was angry. But Ridge remained adamant that they should watch the video.

'Look Thad! This is the original file!'

'So what! Some asshole's playing tricks, sending us this tape we've seen a thousand times.

I don't *ever* want to see it again, you got that? If you-'

Ridge thumped him hard in the chest.

'Shut the fuck up and listen, will you!

This file is over five minutes longer than the one we've all seen.

It's not the same one. Now watch!'

So the pair of them watched the man they'd heard so much about the previous night. They saw his tears and only this time they could see far more clearly the extent of his facial injuries. There was no doubt that he'd received a severe beating before he'd made his confession.

'Look! See?'

Thad saw that Ridge had been right. It was a completely different version of the same video. This time Kazuo still held up his Dylan-style story boards, but someone had gone to the effort of having his words subtitled in English. They read his apologies to the victims' families and then they saw clearly him saying he now had to pay the price for his misdeeds. There it was in black and white on the screen. It said he must *Pay the Piper*.

Kazuo turned and began to walk away from the camera which was where the original film ended. Ridge pointed excitedly to the timer underneath, which still had several minutes left. He grabbed Thad. 'See!' Thad nodded, his eyes wide with apprehension. What were they about to see and why had it been sent to them? The two of them gripped each other like scared schoolboys watching their first illicit horror film. Kazuo continued to walk deeper into the forest and the light became darker until they couldn't see a single thing. Then the screen went blank.

'What?' Ridge screamed. He couldn't believe that that could be it. He turned away to kick something hard when this time it was Thad who hit Ridge hard in the guts.

'Whoa dude!'

Ridge turned back to see the screen was a white background with a few words only in capital letters.

'THE PIPER'S PROMISE'

The video flickered and then the picture reappeared, clearer and brighter than ever before. But now Ridge didn't want to see any more. He felt the bile rise in his throat and his eyes had filled with tears as if trying to shield him from the horror of what was to come next.

He knew instantly where Kazuo had taken them to. It was a place that he would never ever forget. A place where every leaf, blade of grass and even the faintest echo of birdsong would be forever etched into his consciousness. It was a place he would be forever running from in the bleak darkness of night. They were at the very spot where Tadashi died and he himself had only narrowly avoided being strangled.

The film quality was still only at the standard of a smartphone, but someone had gone to the trouble of bringing back studio lights and all of the equipment which the authorities had presumably taken out of the forest after Ridge had been rescued. The phone had been set up on a low tripod and it pointed directly at the man kneeling on a tatami mat at the centre of the clearing.

But he bore no resemblance to the other man who'd knelt there. Unlike his father, Kazuo babbled like a madman and even with no knowledge of Japanese, it was obvious he was begging for his life. He had none of the dignity of the other man. His back didn't seem able to hold him upright and he rocked back and forth, shaking his head and banging his hands on the mat. A bare arm appeared from under the camera lens and presented Kazuo with a short Japanese sword. Kazuo glanced up at the camera and Ridge could see for the first time the utter wretchedness in his face. His eyes opened wide and he studied the sword in his hands before throwing it into the trees like a petulant child.

The video appeared to stop for a moment and both Ridge and Thad found themselves craning forward to see how much time was left on the film. They both examined each other's frightened face. Twelve seconds.

The film came back on again and this time they saw that Kazuo had sat a little more composed and upright and he faced the camera with his head up. Tears still poured down his face with his nose and chin completely plastered with snot. He hadn't stopped talking, but now the sound was so faint it had become almost inaudible. A shadow moved across the screen and the two men sitting in the cottage kitchen saw something bright, flash straight out from under the camera. Suddenly Kazuo stopped talking and his head separated from his body, as the white light swung away and into the darkness. Kazuo's head wobbled for a moment, before falling to the left and they watched in horror as it rolled across the tatami mat, leaving a red slick trailing behind.

The film had been cleverly enough made so very few people would ever be able to tell who had sliced off the head of that horrible monster. But Ridge Walker knew. He'd noticed that just for a tiny second only, above the bare arm and shoulder of the person wielding the curved Japanese sword, the viewer could catch a glimpse of the side of a head. No features were visible apart from a brief flicker of hair. Bright red hair.

Chapter 47

The two of them sat horrified for a long time. Thad insisted on rewinding the last bit again and again. Ridge understood why. They had to be sure Kazuo was dead. Thad had fist-pumped the air for the first few times, but then the tears had started rolling down his face. Soon after that, he'd begun to wail and for the last twenty minutes Ridge had held his big friend as he'd sobbed into his shoulder. Then he made Thad promise not to tell Orla or any other living soul that he knew beyond all reasonable doubt who'd dispatched Thad's half-brother.

'Don't you ever call him that again, you hear?' Thad had said flatly. 'The motherfucker ain't no relative of mine, no way.'

They were still sitting in front of the laptop, long after it had gone into sleep mode, discussing how to behave towards Colm when he eventually appeared back from his island wanderings. Thad had felt bad for his earlier misgivings and bore Colm no ill will now that they knew the truth. Ridge was pleased his big pal would be able to move on with his life now that there would be no more nasty surprises. But a haunting dread had washed over him and he couldn't stop thinking about little Zakia, the tiny round bullet hole in the centre of her forehead, as he'd cradled her lifeless body.

Then the phone rang and the pair of them jumped. For Ridge, the real world of the here and now was a welcome interruption and he sloughed off his sofa companion and stumbled over to grab the handset. He saw there had been a missed call only an hour or so ago. He guessed it must have been when the vacuum cleaner had been on and he recognised the number as being from Orla's folks. He'd leave the message for Orla to play back when she returned. The caller ID told him it was his mum's number ringing now and he swallowed briefly and fixed on his best telephone smile. No more surprises, he told himself silently, no more surprises.

'Mum? Oh Orla love... how's the wee ones? I bet they-'

Shit. He could tell in a second she'd been crying. Had Colm been up there all this time and they'd argued? Sometimes the two of them could be very cruel to each other in a way he couldn't remember being with his brother Gavin.

'Have you seen the news on TV? The awful bombings over by?'

'Sort of love. We've had the sound down but I saw there'd been something going on just like Colm had been talking about last night. Is he there with you the now? We've made a huge fry-up and had been waiting for-

Orla? What's the matter, love?'

'Ridge he's not after coming back this time. Me Mam just rang...'

THE END

If you enjoyed The Piper's Promise, then make an author happy by <u>leaving me a review</u>

ALSO BY ALEX BRECK

The Ridge Walker Adventure Series

He Who Pays The Piper
The Piper's Lament
The Loss Report
No Place To Hide

The Lachlan Maclean Thriller Series

The Devil You Know
The Devil Inside

www.alexbreckbooks.com